Midsummer Dreams

Midsummer Dreams

Alison May

Where heroes are like chocolate – irresistible!

Published 2016 by Choc Lit Limited
Penrose House, Crawley Drive, Camberley, Surrey GU15 2AB, UK
www.choc-lit.com

A CIP catalogue record for this book is available
from the British Library

ISBN 978-1-78189-278-7

Printed and bound by CPI Group (UK) Ltd, Croydon, CR0 4YY

To Helen, with thanks for letting me borrow your name.
I hope this Helen lives up to your awesomeness.

Acknowledgements

Huge thanks, first of all, to my lovely editor and everyone at Choc Lit, and particularly to the tasting panel readers (Jo C, Heather W, Betty, Linda S, Liz, Jane, Caroline and Maggie) who took the time to consider and comment on *Midsummer Dreams*. I can barely believe that we're onto my fourth book already. Time really does fly when you're having a good time.

Actually writing a book can be a terribly solitary endeavour. There's an awful lot of sitting at home on your own trying to remember when you last washed your hair. So huge thanks to the people who lure me out into the world and effectively force me to maintain some basic personal hygiene, so family and friends across the board – thanks. Extra special thanks to my writing buddies at Pen Club, the ADC novelists and the RNA Birmingham & Marcher groups. You get me out of the house and then you inspire me to get back to the writing hovel and crack on with the book.

On this particular novel I'm not sure I'd even have got started without an hour at a dining table somewhere in Devon with the inestimable Julie Cohen. She is wise and forthright and kind enough not to actually bang her head against the table when she realises that the novel you're discussing doesn't yet have a plot.

And finally, as always, thank you EngineerBoy for many many different things.

Part One

Winter

Chapter One

Emily
January

I'm alone again. I'm walking along the road, towards the bridge. At first there are people all around me, laughing and talking. People I know. My dad and Dominic. It's busy and light and bright and safe. But then everything changes, like it always changes. The people stop talking and start pointing and whispering. Pointing at me. I spin around and around looking for a friendly face, but there's nobody I know any more.

I spin faster and faster and the faces mix and blur, before they disappear entirely, and there's only one face left. Mum. I lean towards her but she steps away, walking onto the bridge, high above the river and fields below. Whatever I try, I can't reach her. I can never reach her. I force myself to run towards the bridge, to get there before anything happens.

I'm too late. I'm always too late. And now I'm completely alone. My heart beats faster and faster, and I want to run. I want to run to my mum and beg her to take care of me, but I can't move. I'm pinned to this spot, always alone.

I open my eyes. The sheet's wrapped around my legs, like I've been trying to kick it away, and I'm covered in a layer of cold, horrible sweat. I force myself to breathe slowly, dragging the air into my lungs. I've only had the dream twice this week, the two nights I haven't stayed at Dom's. I glance at the clock. Ten to six. It could be worse. I screamed myself awake at three in the morning last night.

I sit up, pulling myself to the top of the bed so I can feel the solidity of the headboard against my back. It's cold. The central heating hasn't come on yet, and my skin starts to goosebump in the January air. I draw the duvet up around my shoulders.

I've lived in this house my whole life, but when I'm alone the place feels too empty. Things that should be familiar make me nervous. The cupboard, where I found my Christmas presents hidden when I was six, is a murky corner where unknown dangers lurk in the dark. I catch myself pushing doors all the way open when I come into the room, to squash whatever I imagine is hiding behind them.

My mouth is dry, and I need the toilet. In my head, I count the number of paces from here to the door and then along the hall to the bathroom. I think I'll wait until it gets light.

I stick an arm out into the cold and find my phone on the bedside table. One new email. It's from Dad. The feeling of connection calms me a little. What's the latest from Verona going to be? So far all his messages have been about interesting sessions at the conference he's attending. Ten days of presentations and discussions about the parallels and differences between the Renaissance and the Enlightenment periods in southern Europe. It's what passes for fun if you're a history professor, apparently. I've not heard from him for three or four days; maybe he's finally having a holiday.

Emily,
Hope you're well. I'm having a wonderful time.
Could you do me a favour and send the attached around to everyone in this list? Sorry to ask, but I don't have all their addresses and we're about to run out of the time we've paid for in the internet café.

I have a big surprise for you when I get back.
Lots of love,
Dad.

Then there's a list of people. I open the attachment. It's
a party invitation for the day after he comes home, and
somebody has had rather too much fun with the clipart. Not
my dad's style. Thinking about it, having a party isn't my
dad's style either. The surprise is intriguing though. I love
presents. I lie back on the bed and try to relax. Something
niggles. I open the message again. 'We're about to run out of
the time we've paid for.' We? Who on earth is 'we'?

Chapter Two

Helen
Three Days Later

Helen closed her eyes. In her imagination she could see him, feel him, almost taste him as he leaned towards her. She savoured every detail, each one so familiar from a million replays of this one perfect moment. The crisp cotton of his plain blue shirt; the breadth of his shoulders; the hint of stubble on his normally clean-shaven jaw; the bright electric blue of his eyes. Her skin flushed hot with the anticipation of …

'Helen!'

Her eyes flew open. The kettle in front of her was boiling, sending wisps of steam towards her face. Two mugs, with teabags already sitting in place. She looked around. Emily was standing in the doorway. 'You were miles away. What were you thinking about?'

Helen turned back to face the kettle. 'Nothing much. Just a daydream.' She poured the water with a shaking hand, and told herself to be calm. Emily wasn't a mind reader. She didn't know who Helen was thinking about. She handed the less chipped of the two mugs to her friend, and watched as Emily topped it up with three spoons of sugar.

They carried their tea upstairs into the spare bedroom. This was the point of Emily's visit. She was here to help repaint the bedroom before Helen's new lodger arrived. Emily sat down cross-legged on the floor. Her decorating clothes were straight out of the pages of a magazine interior design feature. The pristine denim dungarees were apparently brand new for the occasion. Her blonde hair was twisted under a bandana, with a few wisps hanging down around her ears. Helen's shapeless jogging bottoms, paint-stained 'Historians can always find a date' T-shirt and unwashed ponytail were no competition in the decorating style-stakes. Helen took a sip of her tea, before setting her mug down and using a screwdriver to prise open the can of paint.

Emily looked around. 'This is a really nice room. It's a shame you have to have a lodger. It would be great as an office.' Her eyes lit up. 'Or a nursery.'

Helen bristled. 'A nursery for whom?'

Emily shrugged. 'For children one day.'

Helen shook her head. 'Given that I'm single and have no intention of having a baby, I thought a lodger made more sense.' She stirred the paint in the can. 'Anyway I need the money.'

Her friend didn't answer. Emily lived with her father in the house she'd grown up in, and worked as his assistant. It wasn't nice to be nosey, so Helen had never asked, but she suspected that Emily wasn't overburdened with mundane issues like having to pay rent.

Helen tipped some paint into a roller tray and stood up. Emily was being kind; it wasn't a particularly nice room. It was small and pokey and the windows had clearly been fitted by trained chimps so there was a permanent draught from under the frame. That wouldn't be hidden with a fresh coat of paint. There was also a worrying brown mark slowly extending across part of the ceiling. That could be hidden, at least until it seeped through again.

The stepladder was borrowed from a neighbour, which meant Helen wasn't in a position to complain about its slightly wobbly nature. She balanced her paint tray at the top and climbed up. Emily stayed sitting with her tea on the floor. Helen resisted the urge to flick paint at her head. 'You could start on one of the other walls.'

Emily glanced absently around the room. She took another sip of tea. 'I'm so glad you asked me over today. I couldn't stand it at home.'

Helen had already heard the bare bones of the story, told with rapid fire anxiety and breathless indignation, the second Emily had come through the door. 'Tell me again. Where did he find her?'

Emily shook her head. 'I don't even want to think about it. It's horrifying. My dad and ...' she spluttered out of words. 'My dad and a cocktail waitress. It's disgusting. He goes away for two weeks and comes back with a cocktail waitress.'

It did sound out of character. Emily's father was Helen's boss. He was a comfortable, slightly tweedy, slightly distracted sort of a man. A doting father. A perfectly innocuous boss. Not a man you could easily picture having a steamy holiday romance, let alone bringing that romance back with him and moving her in to the family home. Helen's inner academic tutted. She was making an assumption. Of course Professor Midsomer might see himself as more than simply someone's father and someone's boss.

'It's horrible. My dad doesn't need girlfriends.'

Helen paused. She understood Emily's squeamishness at the idea of her father having a romantic life. Helen's own mum was a single parent, and Helen had clear memories of being mortified as a teenager when she discovered that her mum had been going out on dates. She tried a new tack. 'Well you're grown up. Maybe he was lonely now you don't need him so much.'

Emily found a paintbrush and started wafting paint around. Helen winced. Perhaps she could put a wardrobe against that wall to hide Emily's efforts. Of course she couldn't. A wardrobe would cost money. Emily pouted. 'I do still need him though. And it's my house. He can't just move someone into my house.'

Helen didn't point out that it was very much Professor Midsomer's house and, as such, he could move in whoever he damn well pleased.

'And you haven't met her. She's mad. Apparently she took him to a crystal healing centre while they were in Italy. Crystal healing?'

Helen stifled a smile. Emily was dead against crystal healing, but was a serial follower of the fashionable diet of the week, so long as the diets never required foregoing the mountains of sugar she laced her tea and coffee with, and the chocolate bar Helen knew she scoffed at her desk part way through most afternoons. To Helen's mind, crystal healing and fad diets were just different flavours of snake oil. She watched Emily jabbing her paintbrush at the wall. It was too much. Helen clambered down her ladder, grabbed a second roller tray and roller and handed them to her friend. 'This is better for walls. Just don't put too much paint on the roller.'

Emily shrugged. 'I've never done decorating before. Dad usually gets somebody in. Why aren't you getting somebody in?'

Helen shook her head. She was an hourly paid lecturer. That meant she had no permanent contract with the university, and an income that fluctuated between nothing and very little, depending on how many students signed up for the modules she taught. Her pre-credit crunch bank hadn't seen the pittance she earned as any barrier to providing her with a mortgage. Helen was finding it a growing barrier to paying the mortgage back. 'Because somebodies cost money. You don't know what you're doing, but I can pay you in tea.'

She watched Emily paint for a second. The roller seemed to be helping. 'Maybe you need to relax a bit about the cocktail waitress. If it's a holiday romance, it'll burn out on its own soon enough.'

Emily's face tensed a little bit, but she didn't respond.

Helen continued. 'Anyway, you probably won't be living there much longer. You were talking about moving in with Dominic, weren't you?' She fought to keep her tone light, as if she was interested casually, not in an obsessively-in-love way at all.

'That's not the point.'

'Right.' Helen climbed back up her ladder. She didn't care. Dominic could move in with whoever he chose. They were friends. She was friends with Emily. She was friends with Emily's boyfriend. It was all very straightforward.

'He's a bit distracted at the moment anyway.'

'With his dad?' Dominic's dad had been in and out of hospital for months. High blood pressure, a suspected mini-stroke, heart palpitations, chest pain; it was a catalogue of the consequences of a lifetime of sausage, bacon and a fried slice, but no less worrying for its predictability.

Emily stopped painting. 'I wish you could come to the party tomorrow. I need the moral support.'

'Isn't Dominic going?'

'If he gets back in time. You could come too.'

Helen shook her head. 'I'm not invited, and anyway, Alex is moving in tomorrow.'

Emily pouted, as she usually did when she didn't get her own way. 'You really think it'll peter out?'

Helen paused. 'What?'

'Dad and the cocktail whore.' The anxiety in Emily's voice didn't match the vigour of the language.

Helen nodded. 'I'm sure it will.'

Chapter Three

Emily

'We're so pleased for you.' The woman is clasping my dad's hand. She's doing the sympathetic head tilt that I've had most of my life to get used to. 'We worried that you might not find anyone after ...' Her voice tails off. There's no need to finish. She means after my mum, but nobody ever mentions her. They just tilt their heads and let the unsaid words hang there in the silence.

The doorbell rings. I yell that I'll get it and make my escape. The party is suffocating. I'm handing out nibbles and smiling politely, but all the time I'm wondering why nobody else is horrified. It's like the emperor's new clothes. Everyone must be thinking that this is crazy, but nobody wants to deal with the social awkwardness of being the one to point it out.

I open the door. Finally a friendly face. Dom. Professor Dominic Collins. I put my arms around his neck and kiss him quickly on the lips. He keeps his arms around my waist.

'How's your dad?'

He sighs. 'Still in hospital, but out of immediate danger, they say.'

'It's his heart again?'

Dom nods. 'And he's still refusing to talk about surgery. According to him it's a fuss about nothing.' He smiles at me. 'Sorry. Anyway I'm here. What's tonight in aid of?'

I haven't told Dom the story of the cocktail whore. I started to on the phone last night, but he was on his mobile at his mum's house and I could hear her in the background muttering about him frying his brain with that infernal gizmo.

He takes his coat off and hangs it in the hallway. He's wearing the traditional pre-middle aged academic uniform of trousers and shirt, but no tie or jacket. It's a look that implies that he is really wearing a jacket, but he's just taken it off at the moment. Dom's tall. He used to row when he was younger. He's still got big broad shoulders under his plain clothes. I like that. It makes him feel solid. He turns back to me. 'So?'

I try to form the words, but my brain has moved through anger and seems to be trying denial. In the end I shake my head. 'You'll see. Come on.'

He follows me into the kitchen, and I find him a beer, and pour another glass of wine for myself. 'We'd better go through.'

Dom arrived late, so the soiree is already in full swing. The living room is full of Dad's friends, most of them current or former colleagues, standing in huddles and chit-chatting like the sky hasn't just fallen in. They don't understand. To them he's just the boss, but to me, he's Dad. It's me and him. It's always been me and him, ever since Mum ... I slam the door that's twitching open in my head hard shut ... ever since Mum went away.

My dad's doing the rounds shaking hands, engaging in small talk, making introductions. I watch him for a second before I turn my attention to Her. Tania Highpole. Dad's surprise from Verona. She's tanned. I have no idea what the weather is like in Verona in January, but I'm telling myself it's fake. Her hair's a sort of golden blonde, which can't be natural either. She might have been a real blonde once, but not any more. I'm not even sure how old she is. Younger than Dad, but I bet she's nowhere near as young as she'd like everyone to think.

Dominic leans forward. 'Who's the woman with your dad?'

I still can't say it. If I say it, it will be as if I'm accepting that she's here and that all the stuff she said last night, while she was sitting in our kitchen, drinking our coffee, is actually happening.

Dad glances over and catches sight of Dom. Dad approves terribly of Dom, although I've never really been out with anyone he disapproved of. They're coming over. Dad shakes Dom by the hand. 'Thank you for coming. Let me introduce you.'

She's already waiting at his side, arm linked through Dad's, like he belongs to her now.

'Dominic. I'd like you to meet Tania. My fiancée.'

Dom splutters his drink. 'Your?'

Dad laughs. She smiles. Everyone's so bloody happy. Dad's stroking her arm. I don't want to see that, but I can't look away. 'My fiancée.'

She holds her free hand out to display the diamond that's weighing down her ring finger.

'Right. Well congratulations.' I wrap my arm through Dom's. We can all play the perfect couple game. Dom rallies from the shock enough to make a sentence. He's doing better than me. 'So, er, how did you get together?'

She giggles. 'Well, I was working as a waitress in a cocktail bar.'

Dom laughs. I dig my fingers into his arm. 'Really?'

'Oh yes. That much is true.' Another giggle. 'Sadly that isn't where we met. Actually we met because I got fired from the cocktail bar. Theo found me crying on the pavement outside.'

'A real-life damsel in distress,' my dad chips in.

'I was! Anyway, I was sitting on the kerb, in a foreign country, crying my little eyes out, when this voice asked whether I was feeling subjugated by the patriarchy?'

'What?'

Dad shrugs. 'I'd just come out of a two hour seminar on radical feminism and the redefining of historical paradigms from a female perspective.'

'You'd just come out of a bar.'

He nods. 'But the seminar straight before that.'

'And after that, I don't think you saw much of the conference, did you?'

Dad's gazing at her. It turns my stomach. 'Love at first sight. I wouldn't have believed it was possible, but …'

My fingers tense around Dom's arm. I look at Tania. 'And you dropped everything and came back to England with Dad!'

She nods. 'Pretty much.'

Something about that doesn't add up. People have commitments. Families. Homes. Normal people have ties that take more than a few days to undo.

Dom glances at me and shakes his head. 'I'm sorry. This was at the conference? You met in Verona? You were only out there for two weeks.'

Finally, somebody's going to say something beyond platitudes about how happy they seem.

'I know. We met eight days ago.'

'Wow. Erm … wow. Well, congratulations.' Dom shakes Dad's hand again and leans forward to kiss her cheek. I let go of his arm. I'm not going to be supportive of all the good wishes and cheek kissing.

'Excuse me.' I walk away. The kitchen is as good a place to hide as any. Another glass of wine. That's what I need. With a bit of luck it'll help me sleep tonight as well.

'Are you okay?'

Dom's followed me into the kitchen. We've been dating for nearly a year. We have a routine. I stay at his house three times a week; that's most Fridays and Saturdays and one night during the week. At work we maintain a friendly distance. I think Dom still feels weird about dating his boss's daughter. A year. Can you be 'just dating' for more than a year? Somewhere in the background there's a clock ticking on our relationship. I take a sip from my wine. Right now it's not my own relationship that's my main concern.

I point back towards the living room, towards the smiling, loved-up craziness. 'It's a phase.'

'I'm not sure sixty year old men have phases.'

'Well this is one.' Another sip. 'It's a mid-life crisis or something.'

'Maybe.'

'What do you mean "maybe"? People who are acting rationally do not come home from holiday with a cocktail waitress in tow. He doesn't know anything about her. He can't marry her.'

Dom leans against the wall. 'Well, it's not really up to us, is it?'

Logically he's right, but logic isn't helping me at the moment. 'She's not right for him.'

'Tania?' He shrugs. 'I'm sure she'll be fine when you get to know her.'

I shake my head. I have no intention of getting to know her. If I have anything to do with it, she won't be here long enough anyway.

Chapter Four

Alex

'So that's the bathroom.' Helen Hart, Alex's childhood friend and now grown-up landlady, pointed at the shower head. 'It goes down to a freezing trickle if there's a tap on anywhere else, so if you want guaranteed hot water let me know you're getting in the shower.' She stepped back into the hallway. 'So that's it really. My room's through there. I think you've seen everything else.'

Alex nodded. 'Thanks for this. Everything went a bit tits up at my last place.' He paused. 'A bit tits up' was something of an understatement. What had actually happened was that his housemate had found Alex in bed with the housemate's girlfriend, and started throwing Alex's stuff out of an upstairs windows. It had seemed like a good time to move on.

'That's okay. I needed someone after Susie went.'

Alex remembered Susie. 'Why did she move out?'

'Got a job in Exeter. Post-doctoral research fellow in eighteenth-century domestic history.'

Alex raised an eyebrow. 'Sounds right up your street. You didn't go for it?'

'I didn't want to move away.' Helen paused. 'So do you need any help unpacking?'

Alex nodded and let Helen follow him into his new bedroom. He looked around. One suitcase of clothes. One box of books. A laptop, and two plastic crates of miscellaneous crap. It wasn't much to show for twenty-seven years on the planet, but it fit into the back of his prehistoric Renault Clio, and he believed in travelling light –

no commitments, nothing to anchor him down, no hassles, no fuss. He hauled one of the crates onto the second-hand bed, and rummaged through it. 'There was something I wanted to show you.'

He found the crumpled photograph he was looking for and handed it to Helen. Two children, standing on the beach at Weston-Super-Mare, both clutching buckets, both stripped down to their pants. Alex guessed he must have been about six, which would have made Helen eight or nine.

'Oh my god! Where did you find this?'

'My mum sent it, when I told her we'd sorted out you renting me a room.' Alex paused. 'Are you sure your mum didn't bully you into this?' Alex and Helen's mothers had been best friends since childhood, and were now both godparents to the other's child. Alex could imagine his Auntie Paula being quite forceful in her opinion that Helen should help out her poor, homeless not-quite cousin.

'I'm sure.' Helen knelt down next to the box of books on the floor. 'You want these on the shelf?'

The shelf, plus the bed and a rickety hanging rail formed the full complement of Alex's furniture. He looked around. Clothes on the rail. Books on the shelf. It wasn't as if he had a wide range of other options. He nodded and watched Helen for a second as she started to unpack his stuff. She held up a book. 'Do you own any books that aren't to do with your PhD?'

Alex shrugged. 'I don't like reading.'

He watched Helen splutter. 'What? How can you not like reading?'

'I prefer looking at the pictures.' It was true. It was also, Alex admitted to himself, true that it was something he took great pleasure in telling serious, arty, academic type girls just to outrage them.

'But, how can you be doing a PhD? It's all reading.'

Alex laughed and picked up one of the texts in front of her. 'I'm doing tenth-century peasantry. Seriously, there's like hardly any written record and exactly four major text books. Why do you think I picked it?'

Helen looked at him. 'Well, I guessed there weren't very many people wanting to do it, so it was easier to get funding.'

'Yeah. Yeah. That too.' He chucked the book back over to Helen to stick on the shelf. 'Anyway I'm teaching now. I'm gonna be rich.'

Helen sighed the world-weary sigh of the long-standing hourly paid lecturer. 'How many modules are you teaching?'

'One.' He shrugged. 'Maybe one and a half.'

'Samson's modules?'

Alex nodded. Professor Samson had been his PhD supervisor for the last five years of a research project that had been supposed to last for three. They'd got along well. Professor Samson had adopted a pleasantly laissez-faire approach to monitoring Alex's progress, and, in return, Alex had adopted an equally laissez-faire approach to actually making progress. But now, rather inconsiderately, Professor Samson had gone and died. On the downside, this had left Alex with a new supervisor who seemed quite adamant that this was his last year of student-life. On the upside, he'd got an hourly-paid lecturing job covering the prematurely-departed professor's classes for the rest of the year. Every cloud and all that. 'Did you hear how he ...?' Alex's voice tailed off.

Helen nodded. 'Yeah. With the orange and the duct tape. He didn't look the sort.'

Alex flicked an eyebrow skywards. 'There's a sort?'

'Definitely.' Helen shot a look in Alex's direction. 'Like you. If you were found tied to the bedposts in the Norwich Travelodge nobody would bat an eyelid.'

That was the sort of comment a person probably ought

to take offence at. Alex shrugged. 'Do you think they'll advertise his job?'

Helen looked at him. 'You want a permanent job?' She crawled across the room and put her hand on his brow. 'Are you feeling all right pet?'

'Ha. Ha. I meant for you. I mean they're not going to hire another medievalist are they? The modules they already do are way undersubscribed. They'll want something trendy like all that gender stuff you're into.'

'We'll see.' Helen carried on unpacking the box. She held up a notepad. 'What's this?'

'PhD notes.'

Helen flicked it open. 'It's mostly doodles.'

Alex grabbed the pad from her and turned a few pages. It was true. His library sessions tended to be more doodling than researching. He held the pad open. 'But look. These pages are doodles of tenth-century peasants.'

He was secretly quite proud of Anglo and Saxon, as he'd named the bearded peasant and his equally bearded wife, who cropped up in doodle after doodle. They added a certain personality to his notes.

His landlady shook her head. 'Oh – are you around tomorrow evening?'

Alex shrugged. 'Guess so.'

'I've got some people coming round for dinner. You're welcome too if you're in.'

People coming round for dinner? At his previous address, the most formal thing anyone ever came round for was a drink. Sometimes there would be crisps, if they were really setting out to impress. Alex's own cooking skill level had stalled somewhere around breakfast cereal. 'Who's coming?'

'You might know them. Dominic. Professor Collins. He's a senior lecturer.'

Alex nodded. Everyone even vaguely associated with the

department of history at least knew of Dominic Collins. Collins was a Tudor historian, and the Tudors were the rock stars of English history. They were all beheadings and adultery and witchcraft and feuds with other rulers. That made the Tudor historians the golden boys of any history department, especially in a department where academic riches were spread as thinly as they were at the former teacher training college currently labouring under the rather unprestigious title of the University of the South Midlands.

'And his girlfriend. Emily.'

Alex paused. 'Midsomer's brat?' Emily Midsomer was departmental secretary and PA to the head of department. She was also, by utter coincidence the head of department's much beloved only child. Alex had never actually met her, but the received gossip-based wisdom strongly suggested that she hadn't got her job through innate brilliance and organisational skill.

'She's not a brat. We're friends.'

'Sorry.' Alex grinned. 'I'm sure she's very nice.'

'So you'll be here for dinner.'

Alex nodded. 'I'll be here.'

Chapter Five

Emily

'And if you could take the first exit at the roundabout, and then pull over and stop at the side of the road when it is safe and legal to do so.'

I do as I'm instructed, slowing down as I approach the roundabout, checking my mirrors and indicating, before I turn left. There are double yellow lines and then a pedestrian crossing, so I wait until I'm safely past both of those before I'm back to looking in those mirrors, and parking at the side of the road.

'That's great Emily. If you could turn the engine off.'

I do as I'm told, but I'm slightly confused about why we're stopping. I've paid for another twenty minutes of lesson and we're supposed to be practising bay parking. This is nowhere near a car park. Tony, my latest driving instructor, twists in the passenger seat to face me.

'Emily, I did want to have a little talk with you today.'

I nod.

'How long is it you've been having lessons with me now?'

I shrug. 'I'm not sure.'

'Well I'm sure. It's over six months.'

'Is it?' I have a feeling I know where this is going.

'It is and, remind me, how many instructors had you had before you came to me?'

I mutter something into my chest.

'I'm sorry Emily. Say again.'

'Four.' It's actually six, but still.

'Four. Right. And in all that time you've never actually taken your driving test, have you?'

I shake my head. 'It's not my fault though. Some of those instructors weren't very good, and I'm definitely getting nearer, and I just think a few more lessons—'

'Emily, I'm not sure why I'm saying this. I mean the two hours I spend with you twice a week are probably the easiest bit of my job, but I don't feel right taking your money.' He smiles at me. 'You're more than ready to take your test. You've been ready since I met you. You were probably ready several years before that.'

It's not the first time this has happened, but he's wrong. The others were wrong too. I need more time. I need more practice. It's one thing driving when he's sitting next to me with the dual control. I can't go wrong then, can I? Doing it all on my own is completely different. 'I need a little bit more time.'

He shakes his head. 'I'm sorry Emily.' He sounds exasperated. 'We'll do the lessons you've already booked, but after that, unless you book your test, there's nothing more I can teach you.'

'But—'

He holds his hand up. 'I'm sorry, but you're ready to drive on your own.' He smiles again. 'That's a good thing. You should be pleased.'

I nod. There's no point arguing with driving instructors when they get like this. I've tried before with Zoe, and Barry, and Carl, and Amanda, and Kelly. Darren, I got rid of, rather than him ditching me. He kept 'accidentally' touching my knee. I nod at Tony. I guess it's time to find a new driving school. Again.

Chapter Six

Dominic

Dominic rang the bell and waited. He was looking forward to the evening. Hopefully Emily would have calmed down from the shock of her father's new houseguest, because he had news of his own to share. He rang the bell again, grinning to himself.

'Hi!' Helen threw the door open in a flurry of flour and enthusiasm. She held up her fingers. 'Sorry. I was making pasta. Covered in flour.'

He leant forward and kissed her cheek, trying not to coat his clothing in cooking debris. 'You make your own pasta? Seriously?'

Helen nodded. 'I thought it might be cheaper.'

'And is it?'

She laughed. 'Not if I have to chuck it out and use regular pasta anyway.'

Dominic followed his hostess into the living room. He'd known Helen for years, since she was his student in fact, an earnest, passionate twenty year old who ... He shut down the train of thought. He knew too well where it always led.

'So Dominic, this is Alex. Alex, Dominic.' The man lounging on the sofa hauled himself to his feet and shook Dominic's hand. He was slim, with a shadow of stubble across his chin. He looked familiar but Dominic couldn't place him.

'Hi. And you're ...' Dominic's voice tailed off. What exactly was he trying to ask? There was a man in Helen's living room, a man who looked very much at home. He knew he'd been distracted with his dad's condition recently, and tired from driving back and forth up the M6 for hospital visits, but he was pretty sure he'd have remembered Helen moving a boyfriend into her home. 'So you and Helen are …' His eyes flicked from Helen to Alex and back again.

'No!' The stranger sounded horrified at the notion. 'No. Definitely not. We're practically related.'

Dominic glanced at Helen, who smiled as she offered an explanation. 'My mum is Alex's godmother.'

Alex interrupted. 'And vice versa.'

'Alex is taking over Professor Samson's classes for the rest of the year, and he's renting Susie's old room.'

Dominic nodded. Suddenly the fug of the vaguely familiar face cleared. 'You're a grad student! I've seen you around.'

'Yep.'

Helen laughed. 'You've seen him around the university? A rare sight.'

Alex flicked his middle finger in Helen's direction. 'I'm on campus loads.'

Dominic sat down in an armchair in one corner of the room. 'Well you must be doing well if they've offered you Samson's job.'

Alex shrugged. 'They were kind of desperate. Did you hear how he died?'

Dominic nodded. The entire university had heard how Samson died. The only thing that had stopped Professor Midsomer actually having a heart attack over the whole thing was the fact that the man had had the decency to do it during the university holidays.

Dominic accepted the offer of a beer and sipped. It was odd talking to Alex tonight. A young man setting out on the career that Dominic was tiring of. 'Actually I've got something to tell everyone this evening.'

Helen looked curious. 'What?'

It was tempting to tell them in ones and twos, but he was

using tonight as his dress rehearsal. If he could get through the big announcement once, then he might have a fighting chance of repeating the feat with his parents. He shook his head. 'When Emily gets here.'

'Right.' Helen nodded. 'I see.' She looked around the room for a second. 'I'd best get back and finish in the kitchen.'

Dominic was left alone, in the living room, with this new Alex person. What to talk about? He nodded, in what he hoped was a friendly, relaxed sort of way. Alex responded with a non-committal sort of noise, accompanied by a shoulder shrug. Dominic was on the verge of raising his eyebrows and nodding again, more vigorously, possibly adding a vague, 'So …' when the doorbell rang. Oh thank the Lord.

'I'll get it.' Alex jumped out of his seat as if it had been wired to the mains. Dominic smiled to himself. Well, at least it wasn't just him who was feeling awkward. Presumably it would be Emily at the door. He glanced at his watch. It looked like her driving lesson had finished early. He hoped she hadn't broken another instructor.

Chapter Seven

Emily

I ring the doorbell and wait, pulling my coat tight around me. It's starting to snow, for the first time this winter. Eventually the door opens.

'Oh my God! It took you long enough. It's bloody freezing out here.' I glance up and stop. The person answering Helen's door isn't Helen. I take an involuntary look down the street. No. I'm definitely at the right house. There is a man answering Helen's door. I've been friends with Helen for nearly seven years. I don't think I ever remember her so much as going on a date, let alone having a man who was familiar enough to be allowed over the threshold. 'Who are you?'

He stands back to let me come in. 'I'm Alex. I'm Helen's sort-of-but-not-really cousin.'

'You're a boy.'

He nods. 'I know.'

I don't know why I'm surprised. Helen said *her friend Alex* was moving in. I'd assumed it was a girl Alex. Helen isn't somebody I'd expect to be keeping a boy squirrelled away. I sneak a proper look at him as I take my coat off. Skinny, and dressed to accentuate it in a tight shirt and narrow jeans. He's a bowtie and a pair of statement spectacles off being able to play Doctor Who.

'So you're the new Susie?'

'I am.' He looks at me as he answers. I've never seen eyes like these before. Dark brown, almost black. When I was little I watched *Gone with the Wind* at my childminder's house, and I remember her saying that Rhett Butler had 'bad boy eyes'. I didn't know what she meant; I do now.

I realise that I'm staring. Then I realise that he's staring back. I should say something, but no words come out of my mouth. I'm still staring. I have to look away. If I look away now, then this second in this hallway will just be a single moment that passed. And a single moment is nothing.

I push past him and into the living room. Dom's already here. He has nice eyes – bright and blue and open. I try holding his gaze, and wait for the butterflies I must feel to come, but Helen bustles in from the kitchen and he turns away. She's wearing the feminist apron I bought her for Christmas last year. It says 'Well-behaved women seldom make history' on it, which Helen said she loved, although she's probably the best behaved woman I know.

'Did you meet Alex?'

I lean down to kiss Dom's cheek before I answer. 'You're not shagging him are you?'

'Ew.' Her face scrunches up in disgust. 'We're practically related. He's just the lodger.'

To be honest I wish she would shag someone. Her whole life is books and work. It can't be enough.

'Anyway, dinner is served.'

The three of us follow Helen into the kitchen and take our places around the table she's managed to squeeze into the limited space. She dishes out pasta in a thick tomato sauce into bowls and passes them round.

'That's huge.'

Helen looks at my plate. 'It's a perfectly healthy amount.'

I shake my head. 'It's all carbs,' I mutter, before I give up. Helen and I don't see eye to eye about what constitutes healthy eating.

Dom sits beside me. 'How was your driving lesson?'

I pout, but don't answer.

'What happened?'

'I need a new instructor.'

I see Dom and Helen exchange a look. 'How come?'

I shrug. 'He just doesn't want to teach me anymore.'

Helen sucks the air over her teeth. 'What happened?'

'Nothing.'

I can feel them both looking at me. I know what they've assumed about the whole driving thing. They must think I'm so bad that instructors are scared to get in the car with me. I could try to explain, but what would I say? He won't teach me anymore because I'm too good. I don't fancy my chances of getting anyone to believe that, and if they did, it would be two more people hassling me to take my test, and I'm not ready. I need more time.

'I didn't learn to drive til last year.' Alex pipes up from the other side of the table. 'I had two lessons when I was seventeen, and then I spent the rest of the money my mum gave me for driving on going to see The Killers.'

Dom laughs. 'Maybe it's time for you to give up, Em? I mean, if you want to.'

It would be easier. I'm definitely not ready to do it on my own yet. I shake my head. 'I'm sure I'll get the hang of it,' I offer as brightly as I can.

Helen, thankfully, changes the subject. 'Anyway, Dominic what was it you want to tell us?'

I look at her. The confusion must show on my face.

'Apparently, Dominic has a big announcement, but he wouldn't share until you got here.'

Something clenches in my stomach. We've been together a year, haven't we? Courting for a year and then ... And then what? He can't be going to pop the question here though. I force myself to breathe. She said 'announcement' not question. That means that if I was involved I'd already know. I turn towards my boyfriend. Calling him that, even in my head, feels wrong. There's nothing boyish about Dom. He's big, not fat, but tall and solid, and a tiny bit older than me. Nearly eleven years older. I've always preferred older men. They know how to look after you. 'So?'

'Right. Yes.' He sounds nervous. 'So it's not really an announcement. Nothing's finalised yet, but ...' A phone rings. We all stop and do the obligatory 'Is that mine?' dance, even though most of us know full well that it's not our ringtone. Dom delves in his pocket and holds up his mobile. 'Sorry. Excuse me.'

He gets up and strides into the living room, pulling the door closed behind him.

'Well that was anti-climactic,' I joke.

Helen starts to clear the bowls and cutlery away, leaving me at the table with Alex. He picks up the bottle of red and fills his glass. I hold mine out so he can do the same. It would have been polite of him to do the lady's glass first.

'So what do you do for work?'

'I'm a PhD student, but I'm covering some lectures this term.'

'What courses?'

'Samson's modules.'

Professor Samson. Right. 'Did you hear how he ...?'

'Yep.' That's disappointing. It's the most incredible piece of gossip that's ever happened at my work, but because it's so incredible it went round the whole university in about seventeen seconds. I hardly got to tell anyone.

Alex is blatantly looking me up and down. I catch his gaze and raise an eyebrow.

'I'm sorry. It's just ... well you and Helen. You don't look like natural friends.'

'What do you mean?' I know exactly what he means but it's fun to watch people try to express it sometimes.

'Well, she's all Germaine Greer and you're more ...' he pauses '... well sort of Malibu Barbie.'

'That's ridiculous!'

'In a nice way.'

'Apologise this second.'

'Why?'

'Well that's not even a good Barbie. I had a presidential candidate Barbie, and a pilot Barbie.'

He holds his hands up. 'You know what I mean though. You're all prettied up, and Helen, well the apron she was wearing before is probably genuinely the smartest thing she owns.'

I laugh. 'I bought her that.'

'I rest my case.' He grins. Those eyes shift from brown to black and back to brown when he smiles. 'So how come you're mates?'

Helen wanders back over to the table. 'Ah, the how we met story? Do you want to or shall I?'

I take a deep breath. 'It was my first week working in the department.'

Helen butts in. 'And my first week as a graduate student, and they did a joint induction meeting thing for new staff and graduates.'

'It was meant to be for academic staff really, but there were only two of us in the admin office, and I don't think they knew what else to do with me, so I got sent on it as well.'

Helen jumps in again. 'And it was so boring.'

I nod. 'Boring like you wouldn't believe. There was all this stuff about thesis supervision, and periodical submissions and graduate seminars.'

Helen shakes her head. 'That was fascinating, but then there was all this stuff about where to collect your photocopying and how to add credit to your print account. I was losing the will to live.'

'Anyway, at the end they asked if there were any questions.'

I see Alex close his eyes. 'She didn't ask a question, did she?'

'She did.'

'Was it to do with why the department persisted in endorsing outmoded gender roles?'

I nod. 'It was.'

Alex smiles. 'And that inspired you to want to be her friend?'

I shake my head. 'No way. My dad pulled me to one side, and said "She's going to be trouble, that one" and asked me to keep an eye on her.'

Helen laughs. 'So we're not really friends. Em's undercover for the patriarchal elite.'

'Only then you found out that the stuff about photocopying and print accounts was actually quite important, and decided that a friend who knew all that might be useful.'

'Invaluable. Anyway, who wants to be friends with people like themselves? I'm like myself already. Difference is good.'

It's true. It shouldn't work, but difference *is* good. I encourage Helen to treat herself to nicer stuff than she'd ever choose for herself, and she looks after me. Underneath all the feminist rage, she's a total mother-hen, is Helen.

She's looking towards the door to the living room. 'Do you think Dominic's okay?'

He has been gone a while actually. 'He's probably fine. Did I tell you I tried to talk to my dad about Tania?'

Alex is looking blank. Helen jumps in. 'Emily's dad came home from a conference with a new fiancée in tow.'

'It's insane. She's a cocktail waitress. They have nothing in common. Anyway, he wouldn't listen. Wouldn't even talk about it.' I tried three times last night and again this morning. He changed the subject every time.

Helen is still peering anxiously towards the living room door. 'Are you sure Dominic's okay?'

I'm about to go and check on him when the door opens. His face is pale and he doesn't make eye contact as he walks back to his chair and sits down.

I touch his arm. 'Is everything all right?'

He looks at me for a second, and then at Helen, and then back down at his phone. 'No. It's not. My father died.'

Chapter Eight

Alex

Alex waited in the living room while Helen saw her guests to the door. Unsurprisingly, the evening had ground to a halt after Dominic's news. So far as Alex could gather, the call had been from his mother. Dominic's father had had a heart attack that morning, but she had decided it was best not to worry her son, until a second heart attack, massive and fatal, struck a few hours later. And that was that. Ignoring doctor's orders and eating bacon and eggs at breakfast time; no more for this world by dinner. Alex shuddered. Life was fleeting.

Helen came back in and sat beside him on the sofa. She exhaled hard. 'Well that was less fun than I intended.'

Alex smiled. 'Was Dominic all right?'

'I don't know. I think he was in shock.'

Alex paused. He'd known Helen an awful long time, through the phase where their mothers would dress them up in matching outfits and make nauseating plans for how they'd end up together one day, through the phase where she was the older girl at secondary school that at least one of his mates fancied, and onto this new phase where she saved him from wrathful ex-housemates. He felt he'd got to the point where he could expect an honest answer to a question. 'So you and Dominic?'

Helen's face closed up slightly. 'What about us?'

'Well, what's your deal?'

'I don't know what you mean.'

The look on her face disagreed, as had the look on her face most of the way through dinner. There was something going on there and Alex liked knowing what was going on. 'Come on. I've seen you at the beach in your pants. You can tell me.'

She shrugged. 'There's nothing to tell. Nothing's going on.'

He thought his way around the edges of her denial. 'So you'd like there to be something going on?'

She shook her head. 'He's with Emily.'

'And if he wasn't?'

'But he is.' Helen stood up. 'So that's the end of the story.'

She went into the kitchen and ran the hot water into the sink to wash up. Alex followed her. 'But you like him?'

Helen stared at him. 'You're not going to let this drop, are you?'

He pulled himself up to sit on the last remaining bit of free worktop amongst the debris of Helen's dinner preparations. 'Nope. Tell me. You like him?'

'Honestly?'

Alex nodded.

'I more than like him. I've been in love with Dominic Collins since the first time I saw him.' Helen didn't stop moving dishes into the hot soapy water as she spoke. For a person telling heartfelt tales of unrequited love and passion, she was surprisingly matter of fact.

'Wow.'

'It sounds ridiculous, doesn't it?'

Alex held up his finger and thumb squeezed close together. 'Little bit.'

'It's how it is though. He was one of my third year lecturers, and from the moment he walked into the class I've been completely and utterly in love with him.'

Alex's jaw dropped open. Third year? But that was ... 'That's nearly ten years.'

'Yep.'

'And you've never done anything about it?'

'Once. Almost.'

Alex shook his head. He considered himself something of a world expert in the allied fields of flirtation and seduction. They were areas where 'almost' was synonymous with 'no'.

Helen turned away from the washing up for a second and picked a tea towel from the radiator to throw at Alex. 'Make yourself useful.'

'I'll dry if you tell me the whole story.'

'Of what?'

'Of the almost once time.'

She sighed. 'It was nothing. It was a moment. He was my lecturer and I was talking to him after a lecture. There was nobody else around.' She shook her head. 'I don't know. For a second it seemed like he might be going to kiss me or something, but ... anyway, it was a long time ago.'

'That's it?' Alex was incredulous. It barely even rated as a story to tell.

Helen nodded. 'It was a moment though. You must have had moments where it seemed like something could happen.'

Alex nodded. Of course he'd had moments. They usually immediately preceded conquests. What Helen was suffering from was a failure to convert her intangible moment into something real. 'What about the ten years after that?'

'It was never the right time.'

'For a whole decade?'

Helen washed the last of the dishes in silence, and pulled out the plug. 'Anyway, he's with Emily now, and they're very happy, so no point dwelling on the past.'

'And you're sure they're happy? Dominic and Emily?'

'Of course. Why wouldn't they be?'

Alex shrugged. 'I don't know. He just didn't look like her type.'

'Like I don't look like her type of friend? People can

surprise you.' Helen dried her hands. 'Why are you interested anyway?'

'I'm not.' So what if Presidential Candidate Barbie was cute? She was his landlady's friend and a senior colleague's girlfriend. He'd already lost one home over that sort of mistake. A repeat performance might give people the impression these things were somehow his own fault.

Chapter Nine

Emily

The faces are here again, spinning around and around me. Dad, and Dom, and Helen, and Mum. The faces whoosh around and then one by one they disappear into the dark, until it's me and Mummy and, like always, she's just out of reach.

I open my eyes, and sit up in bed. I force the air into my lungs and tell myself that it's only a dream. A dream can't hurt me. I look at the clock. Quarter to six. I lie down, flat on my back, eyes up to the ceiling. There's another two hours before I need get up for work. I should close my eyes and go back to sleep, but I don't. If I close my eyes the blackness will come back. Everyone will be beyond my reach, and I'll be completely alone. If I was at Dom's I'd wake him up. I'd lean across and whisper, 'Dom, are you awake?' and I'd keep asking a little bit louder and then a little bit louder, and a little bit louder, until he woke up. I'm not at Dom's tonight. After he found out about his dad, he said he wanted to be on his own, which I respect, of course, even though I don't understand. Why would you ever want to be on your own?

Sleep isn't going to happen, so I drag myself out of bed and pull my dressing gown on. I'll get a cup of tea and put the TV on for company. I pad down the stairs, but stop in the hallway. There's music playing in the living room. Not proper music, weird wind-chime stuff like they play when you go for a spa day. I push the door open as quietly as I can and take a look. Tania. Of course. Bloody Tania, playing plinky-plonky music in the middle of the night.

She's wearing black Lycra trousers and a pale green vest, and her hair's all piled on the top of her head. I take the opportunity to peer at the hair at the back of her neck that's normally hidden, but even there I can't see any grey strands. She's very well put together, is Tania. She's standing at one end of the rug, with her hands pressed together in front of her chest like she's praying. Then she lifts her arms and bends forwards from her hips reaching down to touch her toes, but she doesn't just touch her toes. She puts her whole hands down flat on the floor. That's bendy for somebody so old. I watch as she kicks her legs backwards and pushes her bum up towards the ceiling to make an upside-down V shape with her body. She looks ridiculous. She lifts one leg off the floor, so she's balanced on one foot and her hands.

'Morning Tania!'

She flinches as I come into the room and her elbow crumples under her sending her face-down into the rug.

I rush to her side. 'Oh my God! Are you okay? I'm so sorry.'

She wriggles into a seated position. 'I'm fine. I didn't think anyone else was up.'

'Couldn't sleep.' I haven't decided what to do about Tania. She can't marry Dad. She's only known him five minutes. It's been me and him my whole life. It's my job to look after him, but if I look like I'm trying to split them up people will act like I'm the one being unreasonable. I need to find out a more about her. Friends close; enemies closer. That's the approach.

I smile my sweetest smile. 'I was going to make a cup of tea. Do you want one?'

Tania turns off the horrid music and follows me into the kitchen. 'I'll have a peppermint one. It's much more energising, and less caffeine.'

'And here's me thinking it was the caffeine that gave you the energy.'

Tania shakes her head. 'It's terrible for you. You have no idea what caffeinated drinks do to your insides.'

She's probably right. There are some horrible toxins in food. I'll have to remember to Google what caffeine does to my insides later. Right now though, I don't want to let her win. 'Well, I'll have a coffee.'

She doesn't reply. I open the cupboard, but the coffee's not there. There's a neat little case of funny herbal tea bags with names like 'Raspberry revitalize' and 'Citrus soothe' but no coffee. I look back at Tania. 'What have you done with the coffee?'

She leans past me and reaches up to the very back of the very top shelf, and pulls the jar down. 'Out of sight, out of mind. You'll be amazed how little you miss these things when they're not staring you in the face.'

Sod the getting to know my enemy. Right now, I want to smash my enemy in the smug, freakishly line-free face with the coffee jar. I don't. I'm biding my time. I put the kettle on and open the fridge to get the milk. I stop. What she's done to the cupboard is nothing compared to what she's done in the fridge. I scan the shelves. I did an online shop the day before Dad came back. There was bacon, two steaks, a pack of sausages. I look again. I definitely bought cheese, proper cheese not the low-fat cottage variety that's there now and butter, proper old-fashioned butter, which is what Dad likes. 'Where is everything?'

For the first time since she scraped her face off the rug, she looks a tiny bit uncertain. 'I had a bit of a clear out. Theo said you wouldn't mind.'

I lift the milk, semi-skimmed – one of the only things that seems to have survived the cull – from the back of the door, and force myself not to explode. I smile brightly. 'It's just that those were some of Dad's favourites.' I pat Tania sympathetically on the arm. 'I guess you've not known him that long, have you?'

She steps away from my hand. 'But he's not getting any younger, is he? We've got to take care of his health, haven't we?'

We're both quiet for a second, standing opposite one another in the kitchen, both wearing cheek-achingly bright and cheerful smiles, neither one of us backing down. So that's how it's going to be, is it? I turn away and pour water over her sanctimonious mint teabag. Well, at least we both know where we stand.

Chapter Ten

Alex

Alex opened his eyes and carried out his customary first-thing-in-the-morning checks. Whose room was he in? He glanced around. His own. Excellent start. Did he remember the night before? He certainly did. Dinner with Helen and her friends, cut short by Dominic's bereavement. Teasing Helen over her hopeless infatuation with Dominic, and then into town to meet up with a mate for drinks before the weekend was officially over. So far so good. How hungover was he? Alex pulled himself up onto his elbows and tipped his head from side to side. No nausea. Only the slightest hint of a headache. Not too hungover, he concluded. And finally, the big question. Who else was in his bed? A cursory look around confirmed what he already suspected. A blonde head on the pillow beside him. It was shaping up to be a good day.

The blonde head raised itself from the pillow. 'Is it morning?'

Alex grinned and slid himself out of bed. 'Certainly is.' He grabbed his boxers, jeans and shirt from the floor and pulled them on, before gathering up an armful of female attire. It was quite small attire he noted – blonde-head was facing an uncomfortably scantily-clad walk of shame. He chucked the clothes onto the bed. 'Wait here.'

Alex headed downstairs and peered into the living room. As he expected, Helen was already up. Now clearly it was none of Helen's business who he spent the night with, but she was something of a specialist in the delivery of heartfelt speeches about developing self-respect and owning one's own sexuality, and he didn't want to build up a reputation for offering his overnight guests a good time at night and a sermon in the morning. He stopped in the doorway and listened. Helen seemed to be on the phone, and she seemed to be quite angry about the fact.

'No, but now I've got a new lodger, so I've got rental income again ... No. I know. I used to have a lodger, but she moved out, which I told you six weeks ago and you reassessed me then ...'

Alex had no idea who she was talking to but it sounded like it could take a while. He leaned around the doorpost and peeked into the room. Helen was sitting with her back to the door. Excellent. He ran back upstairs. Blonde-head was sitting on the edge of the bed, pulling her boots on. She looked up as he came in. 'So I'd probably better ...' She gestured towards the door.

He nodded. She followed him down the stairs, and slipped out the front door, stopping on the doorstep. 'So you could call me?'

Alex nodded again. 'Sure.'

Blonde-head frowned. 'So I'll give you my number?'

'You gave me it last night.' He started to push the door closed.

'I don't think I ...'

'Bye then.' The door clicked shut. Alex turned back into the house. Helen was standing in the hallway.

'You really are the most incredible tart.'

Alex shrugged. 'We all work with the talents we're born with.'

'Were you trying to hide her from me?'

Now Alex felt a bit stupid. 'I wasn't sure if you'd mind.'

'What do I care? You can stick that where you like. So long as you pay your rent and do your half of the washing up, we're fine.'

'Cool.' He followed his landlady back into the living room. 'Who were you phoning?'

'Tax credits. They claim I never told them Susie moved out, so now I've told them you're moving in they think there are three of us.' She flopped onto the sofa. 'For the amount of money I get, it's barely worth the time on the phone.' She peered at her new lodger. 'You've only got one module this term?'

'One and a bit.'

Helen closed her eyes. 'I've got four. That's …' Her voice tailed off as she moved her finger in the air, drawing the calculations on the space in front of her. 'That's not enough money.'

Alex shrugged. 'I've still got a bit of my bursary left, and we can economise.'

Helen looked around the rather drab and very empty lounge. 'I'm not sure how. I'm already wearing cardigans over jumpers over cardigans instead of putting the heating on.'

'I don't mind the cold.' Alex peered out of the window to make sure blonde-head had definitely left. 'It discourages people from staying too long in the morning.'

'I need to get a proper job.'

Alex shuddered at the thought, but Helen was his friend and respecting your friend's right to be fundamentally wrong-headed about ideas like work ethic and commitment was part of friendship. 'Fingers crossed for Samson's old post then.'

Chapter Eleven

Emily

'Are you sure you don't want me to come?' I'm curled up on Dom's bed, flicking through the TV channels. He's packing his bag to go to Stockport for his dad's funeral. At least he's supposed to be packing. So far he's just walking round the room picking things up, and putting them down somewhere different.

He shakes his head. 'It's probably not the best time for you to meet my mum.' He holds his one and only suit up for my inspection. 'Is this all right? It's not black.'

I nod. 'I think it's fine. I don't think people worry about wearing black so much these days.' I have no idea whether that's true, but it seems like the most helpful thing to say.

'I think my mother probably worries about stuff like that.'

'I'm sure she won't mind.'

His expression doesn't change. 'You haven't met her.'

I don't answer. This isn't the time to start a row, but I'm very aware that I haven't met Dom's mother. I hadn't met his father either, and now he's dead. I hope Dom isn't simply banking on me outliving all the relatives he doesn't want me to meet.

He starts to fold his suit. I stand up and take it off him. 'Don't you have a suit carrier?'

He shakes his head.

'Then put a bin liner over the hanger and hang it up in the back of the car. It'll get all creased in your case.'

He goes to the kitchen to get a bin bag. He's not normally this biddable. It feels like the real Dom has gone into hibernation somewhere in the middle of the Dom-shaped shell that's still walking around and packing bags and getting on with things.

'Are you sure you don't want me to come?' I don't know why I keep asking him. This is at least the fifth time this evening. It's the only helpful thing I can think of to do. It's the girlfriendly thing to do, isn't it? I should go with him for moral support. He should want me to go with him for moral support.

He shakes his head again. 'I don't want to put you out.'

Chapter Twelve

Dominic
Two Days Later

'Cup of tea?' Dominic half stood from his seat on his parents' patterned sofa, hoping for a few moments relief from the feeling that the air itself was pressing down on his shoulders.

His mother shook her head. 'They'll be here soon.'

Dominic glanced at the clock. Eleven in the morning. The service was at 11.45. The car to collect them to follow his father on his final journey would be here at twenty-five past. Twenty-five minutes that felt like they were stretching away to the end of days. Maybe he should have brought Emily. Her brightness might have taken an edge off the sense of insipid despair that overcame him every time he visited his parents' home. He tried to picture her here, but his brain wouldn't do it. It was as if he was trying to draw a character from a different world into this setting; his mind rejected the contradiction. It wasn't that his mother wouldn't like her. He had no doubt that his mother would be overjoyed with the professor's daughter. Maybe that was what unsettled him. The idea of his mother falling over herself to do things properly for his la-di-da girlfriend. The idea that he'd be the returning hero coming home from the big bad world with his prize.

He sat back and willed the silence to pass more quickly. He'd suggested that the whole family meet up here before the service. His dad's brother and his wife. Maybe even their children too if they've managed to drag themselves away from their own lives for long enough to pay respects to their distant and not well-loved uncle. His mother had pooh-poohed the idea. More than one car coming to the house wouldn't do. His father, apparently, would have been dismayed at the ostentation.

Dominic stood and paced across the room, stopping to take a look out of the net-curtained bay window at the front of the house. It was the sort of workaday terraced street that seemed destined for either descent into slum status or creeping gentrification. Either way, Dominic thought, Mother would remain, increasingly isolated and out of place. He paced back again. Everything in this room was a memory. The carpet that hadn't changed since he was a school boy. The collection of figurines on the mantelpiece which his mother painstakingly moved to dust beneath every week, and then put back in their precise allotted positions, where they would sit unnoticed and unloved until the following week. Even the television was the same as when he was a boy. Dominic had installed a digital receiver box for his parents, but they'd refused his offer to buy them a new TV. The current set hummed to itself for five minutes after you switched it off, and every time it was switched on, but was deemed 'good enough for us' by Dominic's mum.

He paused next to the empty chair opposite the television. His father's chair, which he fancied would always be empty now. His mother would never get rid of it, but at the same time, would never consider sitting there herself. Like so much else, it would stay frozen in this moment. He looked at the chair, trying to picture the man, but the image in his mind was fuzzy. He couldn't see the cold blue of his father's eyes, or the shape of his nose, or the tone of his skin. The chair was just a chair.

'Are you sure you don't want me to stay longer?' It was a conversation they'd already had multiple times, but Dominic couldn't bear the quiet any longer.

His mother shook her head. 'You've got to get back to your work.'

'They can manage without me for a few more days.' It was true. It was only mid-January. His full teaching schedule didn't kick in until the following week. He was supposed to have office hours for students to drop in this week, but before lectures had even started the chances of anybody needing to see him urgently were slim. There was no rush at all for him to get back to work.

'No. You should get back. You're a professor now.' She said the word like it was something she'd learnt from a foreign language, over pronouncing every syllable. 'It's what you've always wanted.'

Dominic paused. This wasn't the time, but in another sense it was as good a time as he would ever get, because being an academic wasn't what he'd always wanted. It was what had always been wanted for him, and he'd assumed that, as the feelings around him were so strong, he must feel the same. What Dominic really wanted was change. 'Actually, I've been thinking about that and—'

'Your father was so proud of you.' His mother wasn't listening to him. She was trapped in her own story of his imagined life. 'All those extra hours he worked to pay for your school. All those years when the pair of us didn't have so much as a day out to see the illuminations, let alone a holiday, so that you could get where you are now. A proper professor. It makes it all worthwhile.'

Dominic swallowed.

'Sorry.' His mother dabbed the corner of her eye. 'What were you saying?'

Dominic shook his head. 'Nothing.' He was, after all, a product of his parents' sacrifice, and that meant that he had responsibilities to people other than himself. He had a responsibility to have everything they'd wanted for him.

The good career. The nice house. The perfect family. It wasn't all about him. There were the years of work and expectation from the father he'd be letting down; the father to whom he would never now be able to explain. A sound in the street caught his attention. The black outline of the hearse appeared like a shadow through the net curtain. And so it was time.

Chapter Thirteen

Alex

Alex mooched along the corridor on his way to the hourly-paid lecturer's office. He'd never had an office before, even a one eighth share of a communal office. He must, in his own small way, be growing up. The offices in the department of history were arranged in spurs, off a central long corridor. How far you were placed from the central hub by the main entrance was a fairly direct signifier of your importance within the department. Accordingly, Professor Midsomer had an office with its own reception area where Emily maintained a guard position, directly off the main corridor. Alex glanced through the door to see if she was at her desk, but the office was empty. He shook his head; he wasn't even sure why he'd looked.

Dominic Collins's office was the second one along off the first spur. The hourly-paid lecturers were at the far end of the furthest spur, between the cleaners' cupboard and the office of an emeritus professor who hadn't actually been spotted in person for several years. The received wisdom was that he had probably died, and his family had omitted to let anyone at the university know. Anyway, an office was an office, and for Alex it was a step-up in the world.

He glanced down the first spur as he passed and saw a student banging enthusiastically on a closed door. Alex paused. 'Are you all right there?'

The young man was staring intently at the door. 'Can I help you with anything?'

The student pointed at the door. 'I'm here to see Dominic. Professor Collins.'

'I don't think he's here.' Alex remembered. The funeral. 'Actually he's not in at all today. I think he's back tomorrow.'

'Okay.' The guy leaned back against the wall for a second before sliding down to sit on the floor.

'I don't think you can wait here.' Alex grinned. 'Maybe come back in the morning.'

'Right. Only I can't get into my room.'

Alex didn't want to know, but curiosity got the better of him. 'Why not?'

'No key.'

'Right. Is it a room in halls?'

The boy looked at Alex as if he'd performed a small feat of genius. 'Yeah man.'

'So have you asked the porters to let you in?'

The boy shook his head. 'Gotta have ID. No ID. 'S'all like in my room.' He looked back at the door. 'Professor Collins usually sorts this sort of stuff out for me.'

Did he now? Alex shrugged. 'I think you're going to have to try to persuade the porters this time.'

'Or the girl!' The student jumped up off the floor.

Alex was confused. 'What girl?'

'The girl in my room.' The boy's brow furrowed. 'She wouldn't let me in.' He stared down at his own feet for a second. Alex followed his gaze. Greying socks. No shoes. 'Do you think the girl in my room might have my shoes?'

Alex found himself shrugging again. 'It's possible.'

'Right.' The boy set off, apparently in pursuit of his lost footwear and the mysterious girl.

'Hold on. What's your name? Do you want me to tell Professor Collins you were looking for him?'

The boy nodded. 'Yeah. Nice one. I'm Nick. Nick Bottomley. Dominic's my pastoral thingy.'

'Pastoral supervisor?'

'Yeah. Can you tell him "thank you" as well?'

'For what?'

'He got me one of those grant things for when you've spent all your money.'

'A hardship grant?'

'Yeah, but you can tell him I won't need another. I've got a job.'

Alex nodded. 'Great.' He watched the boy shamble off down the corridor. Pastoral supervision was one of the many and various obligations of the departmental staff. It usually amounted to a cursory meeting with the student twice a year. It looked like Dominic had got himself landed with a rather more high maintenance charge. Heaven help whoever had had the misfortune to employ him.

Alex was still grinning to himself as he finally arrived at the shared office. It was deserted, apart from Helen, sitting at one of the four computers. She looked up as he came in. 'What you smiling at?'

'I just met one of Dominic's students.'

'And why's that funny?'

'Nick something. I think he was stoned.'

Helen laughed. 'Nick Bottomley probably. It's impossible to tell whether he's stoned. I taught him for a whole term last year and he's basically like that all the time. Once he turned up to a seminar with no trousers.'

'What?'

'He was already sat down when I got there, so I didn't notice til the end. He walked out, cool as anything, in T-shirt and boxer shorts. Dominic swears he has hidden depths.'

Alex shook his head, and looked around the room. It appeared to have been furnished by the method of chucking in all the decrepit and mismatched furniture that nobody else wanted, and suffered from the lack of care common to communal spaces where nobody felt personally responsible for keeping things nice. 'So this is our office then?'

Helen followed his gaze. 'It is. Shared by eight people and we have four desks, three computers, and three functioning chairs. It's not exactly palatial.'

'Four computers,' Alex corrected her.

'Nope.' Helen pointed towards the desk in the farthest corner of the room. 'That one's only a monitor. And you should be thanking me for telling you that. Normally we just let newbies waste ten minutes working it out for themselves.'

Alex sat down on a wobbly office chair. 'Isn't it easier to work from home?'

'But then you miss out on the gossip and everything.'

'Everything being the chance that you might run into Dominic?'

Helen turned back to her computer, studiously not answering his question. 'They've sent an all-staff email around about Samson dying.'

'Does it mention the orange and the asphyxiation?'

Helen frowned at him. 'No.'

'Does it mention recruiting his replacement?'

She shook her head. 'No. It's the usual stuff. *Sad news, deepest condolences to his widow.* You know the sort of thing.'

Alex looked around the office. The mishmash of rejected furniture and second-hand computers was depressing. He sighed. 'Lunchtime?'

'Yeah.'

Chapter Fourteen

Emily

I need to do something about Tania. I've tried to be nice to her. I've tried to talk to Dad about the whole insanity. They've had nearly a fortnight for the whole thing to fizzle out. It's time to take action.

I leave work early, so I'll be home before Dad comes in. I shout 'hello' as loudly and cheerily as I can manage as I come through the door, and wait for a response. Nothing. Tania's not here. I run upstairs and into Dad's room. I haven't been in here since She arrived. It hasn't changed much, but there are touches here and there, traces of Her. I fling open a couple of drawers. His clothes. His clothes. Her clothes. I pull a few things out and look underneath. I'm not really sure what I'm looking for. Whatever it is it's not in the first drawer. I try the others, but there's nothing incriminating. Clothes, a few bits of cheap jewellery, some toiletries. Something doesn't feel right about that. I can't put my finger on what. I survey the room, trying to commit it to memory, waiting for the moment to strike when the thing that's out of place pops to the front of my attention. That's how it always works on TV. The detective character has a little niggling feeling that something's not quite right, and then five minutes from the end he has a revelation and the whole mystery becomes clear. I wait a minute, but no revelations are forthcoming.

'Anyone home?'

Tania's voice travels up the stairs. Shit. I scan the room to make sure I haven't left anything out of place and dive into the hallway, just as she comes into view. She glances at the swinging door behind me. 'Were you in our room?'

I shake my head, and push past her to go back downstairs. Not that there's any reason that I shouldn't go in there. It's my house. I've lived here since I was a baby. She's the interloper, not me.

I hear the click as she pulls the bedroom door shut before she follows me. 'Where have you been?' She doesn't have a job and, so far as I know, she doesn't have any friends around here.

She smirks. 'I'll tell you when Theo gets in.'

I let her go off into the kitchen, no doubt to prepare another of her deadly dull meals for Dad. I flick my phone on. Nothing from Dom. I texted him this morning before the funeral and got a two line reply. Nothing since. My stomach contracts. Dad is, apparently, set on marrying Her, and Dom doesn't like having me around enough to introduce me to his mother. I can feel the blackness closing in. Breathe. Slow deep breaths. I tell myself everything is going to be okay. Dom is dealing with his dad dying. He's bound to be preoccupied. Everything will get back to normal soon. And there's no way my dad's actually going to go through with marrying Tania. It was a holiday romance. One way or another he'll realise that. They can't be serious about getting married. They'd be talking about wedding plans if they were.

I tell myself that again and again in my head, but I can't stop thinking about what it will be like if they do go through with the wedding. Tania won't want me living here. What if Dom carries on going off me as well? What if, in the end, everyone does leave me and it's just me and the darkness and nothing else? The feeling of being alone competes with my hostility towards Tania. I almost go into the kitchen and make chit-chat. At least she's somebody. At least she's here. I put the telly on instead and turn the volume up high to drown out my thinking.

Dad comes in just after six. I stay firmly seated in the lounge so I don't have to watch them getting all teenage up against the kitchen worktop. It's disgusting, and it's not like him at all.

'I've poured you a drink Emily.' Tania bears down on me clutching two champagne flutes.

I take one from her. What's she up to? 'What are we celebrating?'

She waits for my dad to sit down, and perches herself on the arm of his chair. 'We are celebrating the fact that I think I've found the perfect wedding venue.'

Dad sits up straight. 'Really?'

'Really. It's called Arden Manor. It's about half an hour out of town – beautiful old manor house, with grounds. It's absolutely gorgeous, and it's just about within the budget we talked about.'

I feel myself tense. Wedding venues? Budgets? When have they been discussing all this?

My dad's eyebrows rise. 'How "just about" within the budget?'

Tania drops her head and looks through her lashes at him. 'Very nearly just about. I promise. And I've had another idea too.'

'Go on.'

'Well, they've still got the midsummer weekend free at the end of June, and so I thought, what if, instead of having hen and stag parties, we had a big midsummer's eve party on the Friday night for everyone, and then the wedding on the Saturday?'

The end of June. That's only five months away. 'I thought it took years to plan a wedding.'

Tania waves her hand. 'It doesn't have to. Five months is plenty of time, and I love midsummer's eve. All the folklore about the solstice, and the long light evening. When I was a little girl in Penzance, my grandmother used to tell me stories about old Cornish midsummer traditions. They call it Gollowan, and there were fireworks and parades. And you're called Midsomer as well! It'll be the Midsomer Midsummer wedding.'

Penzance. She had a grandmother in Penzance. I file the fact away in my memory for later. It sounds like it'll take more than hope to stop this happening, and knowledge is power. She stops talking, keeping her eyes fixed on my dad. 'So what do you think?'

Eventually he nods. 'I think it sounds perfect.' He raises his glass. 'To the Midsomer Midsummer wedding!'

Part Two

Spring

Chapter Fifteen

Dominic

'Hush. Hush. You're okay.' Dominic stroked his girlfriend's hair on the pillow beside him.

Emily opened her eyes sleepily. 'What happened?'

Dominic smiled. 'You were kicking the duvet off. I think you were having a bad dream.'

She peered around the room for a second, and shook her head. 'I'm fine. Sorry. Did I wake you up?'

Dominic shook his head. 'I've been up ages.' He held the clock up for her inspection. 'If you want a lift to work you need to get dressed.'

'I'm gonna go in later.'

Dominic raised an eyebrow. It was the first proper day back after the Easter break, and they had a full departmental meeting at nine. 'I thought you were doing the minutes.'

Emily shrugged. 'I've got stuff to do.'

Emily had had 'stuff' to do a lot recently. Dominic wondered if he ought to ask. It was two and a half months now since his father passed away, and since Emily had been lumbered with a new wannabe stepmother. He wondered if they ought to be talking more to one another about how they were feeling. There were only two problems he could see with that idea. He hadn't been raised to wear his heart on his sleeve, and he didn't have a clue what he was feeling anyway, about his father, about his future, about his career. Everything had crystallized to one moment in Helen's hallway when he'd answered the phone and been told his father was dead. He gave Emily a squeeze which he hoped communicated more than he was able to put into words, and kissed the top of her head. 'Are you okay?'

'How do you mean?'

How did he mean? He wasn't quite sure. 'Just generally.'

She nodded.

'Good. I guess I'll catch up with you later then.'

The meeting, when he arrived, was an unusually long and boring one, in a life that seemed, to Dominic, to be increasingly filled with long, boring meetings. Professor Midsomer had already talked at length about the challenges facing the department, and the whole university, in the new funding model and the need to attract more students with higher A-level results. The Vice Chancellor was talking a good game on that point right now, with Theo nodding vigorously at his side. Dominic didn't fancy their chances. Kids with As at A-Level didn't pick the University of the South Midlands, unless they were taking a peculiarly subtle approach to teen rebellion against an Oxbridge educated parent.

A piece of paper drifted into his peripheral vision. It was blank apart from a series of dashes and a question mark at the top of the page.

_ _ _ _ _ _ _   _ _ _ _ _?

He grinned, and wrote the letter E at the foot of the page. That filled in two blanks. He remembered exactly when he and Helen had started passing notes during meetings. It had been a graduate seminar with a visiting professor. About fifteen minutes into the professor's presentation Dominic had noticed that the man's fly was undone. Approximately eight seconds later a piece of paper ripped off Helen's pad had appeared in front of him. The message simply read: *I can see his pants*. As a comment on the argument in front of them it was neither big nor clever. It was, however, accurate. Since then Helen's hastily scribbled comments had tended toward the more academic, but that first one stuck in his memory. The note passing had quickly progressed into puzzle setting, especially when Helen was as bored as him. It kept them both awake if nothing else. He looked at the game in progress, and followed the E with an S. One more blank completed. T and A got him the upright and the crossbar of a gallows, but a lucky guess at I, followed obviously by N and G got him back on track.

_ E _ _ I N G   _ E _ _ S?

It still didn't make sense. He raised an eyebrow at the puzzle setter sitting next to him.

The door crashed open at the back of the room. 'Sorry!'

It was Emily. He glanced at his watch. In an odd sort of way he had to admire her brazenness. She'd been awake when he left for work, and still managed to roll in a clear two hours late. That, he supposed, was the benefit of working for your dad.

She bowled across the room, and plonked herself into a seat next to her father who smiled indulgently. The Vice Chancellor's lips pursed slightly, and the poor doctoral researcher who'd been stuck taking minutes slid their pad and paper across the table to Emily. She waved at Dominic across the table. He nodded trying to hit a balance between professional and affectionate. Dating at work was a minefield. Dating the boss's daughter was worse. Part of him wished Theo disapproved terribly. Then they could keep the whole thing secret. It would be easier.

Dominic looked back at the pad in front of him. R, T, O and U took him further down the road to the hangman's noose, before L and D filled in enough gaps for him to finish the puzzle. He wrote the W and B straight in.

WEDDING BELLS?

He paused for a moment, wondering what she was driving at. Theo was getting married soon, but everybody knew about that. Most of the department were going. It was old news. He glanced at Helen, who shifted slightly in her seat and pointed her biro towards Emily.

He pulled the sheet of paper back towards him.

WHO SAID THAT? He scribbled.

IT'S TRUE?

He paused, wondering if his brain would present a clear answer to the question if he allowed a sufficient period of silence. Nothing came. Dating for fourteen months. She had a drawer in his bedroom and a spare toothbrush and selection of potions in his bathroom. He wasn't twenty-one anymore. It was getting to the point where he was expected to put a ring on it. And why not? He liked Emily. She was exactly the right sort of wife for the life he had. But he hadn't actually popped the question yet. Something was holding him back. What was the phrase they used for relationship statuses online?

IT'S COMPLICATED.

'Professor Collins?'

Theo was looking directly at him.

Dominic smiled broadly. 'Yes?'

Next to him, he could hear Helen stifling a giggle. It must be obvious that he had no idea what was happening in the meeting. His only hope was that nobody else was following things closely enough to notice.

'You were going to share some thoughts on the issues with the second year elective timetabling?'

'Right.' Dominic looked around the room at his

colleagues. Not an attentive face amongst them. He'd be better off putting the whole timetabling plan in an email for them to ignore at their leisure, rather than forcing them to come together and ignore him en masse. Nonetheless, they were here, and like it or not, he was a full professor now. 'Committee rooms and drinks parties' – that's where his doctoral supervisor had told him academic careers were made. Dominic wondered if he needed to start paying more attention at both.

He rambled valiantly for a few minutes about second year timetables, before inviting opinions from the floor. Given the fact that nobody appeared to have been paying the slightest attention, a surprising number of opinions were forthcoming, and the first two or three were actually relevant to the subject. As the debate degraded into the traditional moaning about the quality of the coffee in the senior common room and the arcane rules about photocopying allowances Dominic zoned out again.

'There was one thing before we finish.' Theo was calling the discussion to halt. Dominic dragged his attention back into the room. 'As you all know, Professor Samson passed away recently ...' Theo paused to allow the inevitable murmurings about the whys and wherefores. 'That does mean that we have an academic vacancy in the department. Just to confirm that we will be advertising that vacancy during the coming term with a view to having someone in post for the new academic year.'

Chapter Sixteen

Emily

The meeting descends directly to gossip at that point, which is to be expected. It's a room full of historians; they're not used to having stuff that's actually going on now to talk about. It's fine for me. I don't have to bother minuting gossip, so it gives me a chance to think about the rest of the morning. It wasn't very successful. It turns out that if all you know about a person is that they're called Tania and they might have once lived in, or near, Penzance, it's really hard to find out anything else. So far as I can tell she's not on Facebook, or Linkedin, or Twitter, or even Friends Reunited, which, to be honest, I didn't realise was even still a thing, but it is, and she's not on it. That seems odd. Everyone's on some sort of social network these days, aren't they? Even my dad's on Facebook. It's excruciating. He had a whole phase of typing 'lmao' after everything because he'd seen other people do it. I had to tell him what it meant.

I look up. Dom looks bored by the whole meeting. Dom looks bored a lot of the time lately. He hasn't said anything or done anything, but I can feel him drifting away. Fourteen months. Fourteen months we've been together and it's perfectly nice, but it's not moving forward. I need it to move forward. I can't lose Dad and Dom all at the same time. I need a two-pronged plan: to get rid of Tania and keep hold of Dom.

At the other side of the table, Dom whispers something to Helen sitting next to him. She laughs. They were writing notes to each other when I arrived, like naughty school children. That gives me an idea.

I catch up with Helen in the corridor as people are drifting away. 'Coffee?'

'Sure.'

We find a quietish corner in the main canteen. I'm not quite sure how to phrase this without sounding like a lunatic. 'You're friends with Dom, aren't you?'

'Yeah.' She sounds wary. 'Why?'

I'm not sure how to put it into words. How do you explain that you need help making your boyfriend fall in love with you? 'And he likes you, doesn't he?'

'I don't know what you mean.' She's staring down at her coffee.

'I mean that you've known each other ages, haven't you? And you get on?'

She glances up. 'It's not like that.'

'Like what?'

She's running her finger up and down the side of her mug. 'I mean we're just friends.'

I can't help giggling. Bless her. Obviously, I didn't think there was anything going on between them. I mean, Helen's lovely and all, but she's not the girlfriend type. Seriously, before we started hanging out I don't think she even shaved her legs. 'No. I know. I meant as friends.'

'Right.' She looks up. 'Good. Okay.'

'But you talk, don't you?'

She nods.

I take a deep breath. I'm going to have to come out and say it. 'I think Dom's going off me. How do I get him to fall back in love with me?'

She laughs awkwardly. 'I'm sure he's not going off you.'

'He is. Since his dad died he's been really distant.' I can hear the whiny edge of desperation in my voice. 'You've known him forever. What does he like?'

I see her cheeks tinge pink.

'I mean I know what he likes in that way! But what does he like, you know, in a person?'

She shrugs, staring back down at her coffee. 'I don't know.'

'Please.'

'Maybe. I don't know.' She stops. 'Isn't it best to keep your relationship between the two of you? You should talk to him if you're worried.'

I shake my head. This is why Helen is single. If I talk to Dom about it he'll know how much I need him to stick around. You can't let the man see that. Neediness is a total turn-off. 'I thought we were friends.'

She purses her lips. 'We are.'

'Then what's wrong with helping me? You're not going behind his back. You're helping me make him happier. What's wrong with that?'

She sighs, but I can see that she's coming round. 'Well, maybe you need to get him involved in something you're doing. You know, like a shared interest.' She looks up. 'He loves teaching. He loves helping people, so maybe something he could help you with. Make him feel needed.'

It's brilliant. I can't believe I didn't think of that. One idea strikes me straight away. And then another. Dom will get to feel needed, without me being needy, and I'll get to kill two other birds with the same stone. It's perfect. I can feel the darkness receding. It's going to be okay. I'm going to hold everything together and I'll never have to be alone. 'Thank you!' I jump up. 'Better go. Dad gets all weird if I'm away from my desk for the whole day.'

Chapter Seventeen

Helen

Helen watched Emily walk away from the table and across the dining hall. Emily thought she was being a good friend, but Helen was a horrible friend. If there was a secret to getting Dominic Collins to fall in love with you she patently hadn't discovered it. She was in no position to offer advice to anyone else.

She closed her eyes for a second. She needed to think. Emily's argument was perfectly sensible. Helen and Dominic were friends. They did get on well. Maybe she did know what he liked and what made him happy. What she had to accept was that there was more to someone being in love with you than that. There was a certain *je ne sais quoi*, that Emily apparently possessed and Helen didn't. That had always been the way. Plain Helen. Clever Helen certainly, but she'd never been the girl that boys gravitated towards, and she'd honestly never cared. She'd seen friends lose all sight of who they were in pursuit of a man, and then have the same man squash their hopes and dreams. Helen would never do that. She knew exactly who she was. That was the beauty of unrequited love. It was stable. It hurt, but it hurt a consistent, manageable amount. Of course, if Dominic did get serious about Emily, that would have to change. The relationship was common knowledge at work and she'd heard more than one colleague speculate that Theo wouldn't be the only Midsomer getting married soon. And Dominic hadn't denied it, had he? He hadn't confirmed it either. Helen closed her mind to the faint voice of optimism. He'd been seeing her best friend for over a year. At some point, even the most ardent devotee had to accept that hope was lost.

That implied moving on. It implied not thinking about him last thing at night, and first thing in the morning. It implied not coming into the office when she wasn't working, on the off chance of seeing him. It might even imply going out on dates with Other Men. The thought turned Helen's stomach. She had a flashback to her most recent date. Four years ago with a civil engineer from Leighton Buzzard, who'd been foisted on her by Susie. They'd established over appetisers that he loved speedway and she loved Katherine Mansfield and Vita Sackville-West, and they shared no obvious common ground in between. Nonetheless, he'd ended the evening with an enthusiastic two-handed boob lunge. Nothing about the experience had made her think the hunt for requited love would be any less soul-destroying than staying at home and keeping the candle she held for Dominic burning brightly. Well one step at a time, she thought. Helping Emily could be the start of moving on. There was no need to rush into the rest of it.

Chapter Eighteen

Emily

I leave Helen at the table. Ninety per cent of the plan has already come together in my head. It's going to be perfect. Dom will get to feel helpful and supportive, which will make him feel extra protective of me, and I'll get to work out what to do about Tania and a get brand new, totally free driving instructor. It's genius.

I stop at the counter on my way out of the canteen. Dad likes a snack after long meetings. I glance at my watch. It's before twelve. That means they'll still be serving his favourite. I order a bacon sandwich on white bread with extra brown sauce. What Tania doesn't know won't hurt her, will it?

At the door to the office I stop. There's somebody sitting at my desk spinning idly in the chair. 'Comfortable there?'

The spinner stops, looks up and smiles. Alex. I haven't seen him properly since the day Dom's dad died. I tell myself I haven't thought about him either. 'You weren't here. I decided to wait.' He points. 'Your parcel is dripping.'

The brown sauce has breached the napkin I've wrapped round the sandwich, and is running onto my hand. 'Wait there.' I run into Dad's office and deposit the sandwich.

He frowns. 'Tania doesn't think I should have too much red meat.'

I wink at him. 'Our little secret then.'

Back in my own office Alex has stopped spinning in my chair and is now going through my in-tray. I snatch the handful of papers off him and put them back on the 'To Do probably at some point' pile. 'What can I do for you?'

He shrugs. 'So, let me get this right? You live with your dad and work for your dad?'

'Yes. And?'

He shakes his head. 'And nothing.'

I move around the desk and wait for him to vacate my seat. He stands up slowly and, rather than waiting for me to sit down so he can get past, he slides between me and the wall. For a second our bodies contact all the way from the shoulders down to our knees. Our eyes lock together. I could lean forward just a fraction right now and kiss him. It would be so easy. I don't, of course, but just for a moment I'm aware that I could. He's smiling. I have no idea whether I'm smiling too. I'm struggling to remember to breathe. It's a very very long second, and then it's over.

He moves to the other side of the desk. 'They said I had to bring my bank details and national insurance number in. Apparently that's why I've never been paid and you're the person to fix it.'

'I'm the person.' I'm staring at him with my mouth wide open.

'Good.' He puts a sheet of paper with his name, a sort code and account number scrawled on it, and his national insurance card on the desk in front of me.

I'm still staring. Must stop staring. Must pick up piece of paper and do things with the paper. I can't for the life of me remember what things. Breathe Emily. Breathe. Bank details. Yes. 'I have to put them on the ...' I point at the screen on my desk. I have to put the details into the screen box thingy.

'I can wait.'

'No.' I grab a notepad and write down his national insurance number. 'I mean you don't need to. I've got everything I need.'

He shrugs. 'Fair enough. I'll see you later then lovely Emily.'

I nod. He walks out of my office and straight down the corridor opposite. I watch him. I can't stop watching him. I shake my head. I don't like skinny boys. I like real men, like Dom.

Chapter Nineteen

Alex

Emily was hot. Alex turned the thought over in his head as he walked down the corridor. He was sure she hadn't been quite as hot when he'd met her before, but then she'd had Dominic Collins in tow, and the whole evening had turned a bit death and bereavementy, which was enough to take the edge off anybody's hotness mojo. Of course the level of Emily-hotness was an entirely academic issue. She was going out with Dominic, and having a crack at her would be in contravention of Alex's brand new rule about not sleeping with girls with boyfriends. Or, at the very least, not sleeping with girls whose boyfriends he knew.

He ambled the length of the building considering this conclusion, and realised that he was actually disappointed. That was unusual. Normally he was a devotee of the plenty more fish in the sea theory of sex. One rejection or missed opportunity was neither here nor there. There would always be other girls and other chances further down the line. Disappointment that a girl was already off-the-shelf was an unfamiliar emotion.

He stuck his head round the door of the hourly-paid lecturers' office. As he'd hoped, Helen was in there. Excellent. That meant he could probably wangle a lift home. He also had news. She had her headphones in and was engrossed in work, sitting at the far end of the office with her back to the door. Alex watched his friend for a moment, and a plan started to formulate. Helen was in love with Dominic. Obviously, she'd tried to make out it was no big deal, and she'd definitely said she didn't want him to

71

get involved, but that didn't change the fundamental truth. Helen was in love with Dominic. Therefore, if Dominic was single that would be good for Helen. Logically, the only way to achieve that would be to do something to split Dominic up from his current girlfriend. Thinking things through, Alex reasoned, sleeping with Emily could be seen as an act of friendship, rather than an unutterably terrible idea.

He ambled across the office and flicked his landlady on the back of the neck. She jumped in her seat. 'What?'

'I have gossip.'

Helen pulled the headphones out of her ears. 'I don't gossip.'

'Bollocks. Anyway, it's more news than gossip.'

'Go on.' Helen's gaze didn't shift from her computer screen.

Alex leant on the desk to face her. 'I came from Emily's office, and guess what she had on her desk?'

'What?'

'The draft advert for the new permanent lecturer's job.'

Finally he had her full attention. 'And?'

'Like I said. Modern or early modern, not medieval. You're a shoe-in.'

Helen shook her head. 'Levine'll apply.' Doctor Levine was the longest standing hourly paid lecturer, a rather boring fastidious little man, in Alex's opinion. 'And they'll have external applicants.'

Alex sighed. He did adore his not-quite cousin, but sometimes her realism and practicality were exhausting. 'You'll definitely apply though?'

'Probably.'

'Definitely. And I'll help. We'll make a whole campaign plan.'

Helen frowned. 'Why do you care?'

'We're friends.'

She narrowed her eyes. 'And that's the only reason?'

Alex nodded. 'And, you know, I don't really have anything better to do.'

'What about your PhD?'

Alex pulled a face of mock horror. 'I thought you knew me better than that.'

Chapter Twenty

Emily

Dominic pulls the car up outside my house.

'Are you sure you don't want to stay tonight?' he asks, glancing at the overflowing box of papers on the back seat. 'I've only got a bit of work to do.'

'It's okay. Thanks for the lift.' I lean across to kiss him goodbye and stop. I've got a plan. I need to put it into action. 'Actually, I wanted to ask you something.'

'Yeah?'

'It's about my driving.' A look flashes across his face. He covers it quickly, but it's too late. I saw the horror. 'What was that face for?'

He shakes his head. 'What face?'

'I need more practise.'

'So you'd better find a new instructor then, hadn't you?'

What did Helen say? Make him feel needed. Right. I open my eyes as wide as they'll go. 'It's really hard with an instructor I don't know. I was thinking maybe it would be better with somebody I already trust.' I run my finger up his arm. 'I thought maybe you could take me out sometime, just to practise.'

He grimaces. 'I don't know. My dad tried to teach me to drive. It was awful.'

'Did you fight?'

He shakes his head. 'I wish. Every mistake I made, I could feel the disappointment. At the end he actually said ...'

'What?'

'It doesn't matter.'

'Tell me.'

'He said, "And I thought you were supposed to be clever." And then he got out of the car and never mentioned it again.'

I stick out my bottom lip. 'But we wouldn't be like that. You already know I'm dippy.'

'You're not dippy.'

'You'd really be helping me out.'

He shrugs. 'All right. We'll do an hour and see how it goes.'

I fling my arms round his neck. 'Thank you!' I plant a massive kiss on his cheek, and he moves his face to kiss me back full on the lips. I get out and watch him drive away. It's working. Helen was right. If I can make him feel needed he'll love me again and everything will be all right.

Dad's car is already outside the house, which is a surprise. He normally works at least another hour after I finish for the day. That's good. He won't like it if Tania's pressuring him to come home earlier.

They're sitting together at the dining room table. Tania has a lined A4 pad in front of her, and most of the table top is hidden under stacks of bridal magazines and brochures. I plaster the smile that I seem to wear more and more across my face. 'More wedding plans?'

My dad nods. 'Tania wanted to get the guest list sorted out.'

Tania nods. 'Less than three months to go. We need to sort out the invites.'

Less than three months. It's actually nearer two, which is still seven weeks longer than they'd known each other when they got engaged. I lean across the table and pick up the pad. I skim my eyes down the list. A selection of aunts and uncles and distant cousins. A few old friends of my dad's who I remember from when I was a kid. Pretty much every university colleague he's ever had. I flick the page and scan to the bottom of sheet two. David Levine. Helen Hart. Alex Lyle. My mind jumps back to the moment in my office. My whole body pressed against his. I shake my head. Bad boy eyes. Not what I need in my life. Not somebody I could rely on. 'Alex?'

My dad nods. 'I've invited everyone from the department.'

I shrug. 'I didn't know you even knew who he was.'

'Well I don't really, but Tania thought we ought to invite everybody rather than pick and choose.'

I take in the length of the guest list. It's not Tania that's going to be paying though, is it? Something else strikes me. I scan again, looking for names I don't recognise. If I can find some of her family or friends, maybe I can find out some more about the mysterious cocktail waitress from Penzance. There aren't any. Every single person on this list is a friend, relative or colleague of Dad's. I hand this list back to Tania. 'So I guess you've still got to do your half?'

She swallows and flicks her eyes towards my dad. I knew it. She's hiding something. 'I don't have much family.'

'None at all?'

She shakes her head, and laughs uneasily. 'Just call me poor little orphan Tania.'

My dad wraps an arm around her shoulder. 'It doesn't matter. We're your family now, aren't we Emily?'

I nod, but I'm worried. No family at all. No friends. Whatever it is she's hiding, it must be something big, and somehow I've got to find out what it is. Dad's not used to dating. When I was little I once asked whether I'd get a new mummy, like Jodie Henderson at school got a new daddy. He laughed. He said I was the only girl in his life. He's so trusting, and in a few weeks, he's going to marry a virtual stranger. It's up to me to look after him now.

Chapter Twenty-One

Emily
Five Days Later

Dom has driven us to a business park on the outside of town. It's Saturday so the place is all but deserted, with the exception of two other learner drivers pootling about the empty roads and car parks. We swap seats, and I feel him watching me as I fiddle with the seat back and mirrors.

'So I want you to pull out, drive along this street and then turn left.' He points towards a turning about a hundred metres in front of us. 'And then pull in somewhere round the corner.'

'Okay.' It feels a bit weird driving Dom's car. It's bigger than the standard driving instructor super-tiny, super-economical models, but I think I do all right. I pull in and stop around the corner.

Dom grins. 'Pretty good. Right. Shall we do some manoeuvres then?'

I pull into an empty car park and, after a couple of misfires that I put down to it being a much bigger car than I'm used to, I successfully bay park in three different spaces of Dom's choosing. I also manage to turn the car in the road and make short work of reversing around a corner.

'You're pretty good.'

'Thank you. I told you. I just need more practise.'

Dom shrugs. 'Do you though? I mean I know we've only done manoeuvres but you seem fine. Are you sure you wouldn't be better off putting in for your test?'

I shake my head. 'I'm not ready to do it on my own yet. It's different with an instructor. They've got the dual control thing, so it's not all on me.'

'But I don't have dual control, and you've been fine today.'

He's right. I have. That's Dom though. There's something very safe about being with him.

'Do you want to drive home?'

I shake my head.

That's another good thing about Dom. He doesn't push me. We swap seats again and I settle into the passenger side for the drive home, blocking my ears to Dom's chuntering about what on earth I've done to his seat position and mirrors. I think I hear the term 'long-armed midget' under his breath.

I like Dom driving us places. I like watching his hands on the wheel, while I sit back and let him take us where we're going, all calm and in control. I snap myself out of the lull. There was another point to today, besides the driving lesson. Another chance for Dom to feel needed and a step towards finding out what secrets Tania's hiding. 'How do you research someone?'

'What?' He sounds confused by the question.

'How do you find out about somebody? Like about their past?'

He glances at me before flicking his eyes back to the road. 'Someone historical?'

'No. Someone still alive.'

'Erm, well I presume you've tried Googling them?'

'I didn't find much.' I didn't find anything.

'Okay. Have you tried local papers?'

'I don't think she's from around here.'

'She?'

'Tania.'

His eyes flick towards me again, but he's stuck concentrating on driving. Maybe I should have lied.

'Why don't you just ask her whatever you want to know?'

Sometimes, for a very clever man, Dom can be really stupid. 'Because she's hiding something.'

'What?'

I sigh. 'I don't know, do I? She's hiding it.'

'Well, the history centre at the main library holds local papers for all over the place, so if you know where she's from, you could try that.'

Penzance. She said something about Penzance, but that's still all I've really got to go on.

'And some of the indexes of births and marriages are online now. I can send you the links. Or you can look those up at the history centre too, at least for the South West. You might have to pay though.'

'That's fine.' It'll be worth whatever it costs, if I can find out the truth and get Tania out of my dad's life forever.

Chapter Twenty-Two

Dominic

Dominic dropped his girlfriend in town, as requested, and waited for her to disappear into the crowd before he pulled away. Should he have tried to discourage her from interfering? So far as he could see, Tania's past was none of Emily's business. He could imagine his mother's horror at the idea of interfering in someone else's relationship. *It's not my place* ... that's what she'd say. His ringing mobile interrupted his thoughts. 'Hello.'

'Dominic, it's your mum.'

'I can see that. Hold on.' He pulled the car in at the side of the road and switched his phone off speaker. 'Is everything okay?'

He heard his mother sigh on the other end of the phone. 'Well I don't like to grumble.'

Dominic closed his eyes and zoned out slightly as his mother launched into an extended anecdote about the mother of somebody who was in Dominic's class at primary school, and had now apparently been caught shoplifting from the discount supermarket. Dominic couldn't escape the impression that it was the cheapness of the produce stolen, rather than the actual shoplifting that his mother disapproved of. Tittle-tattle about strangers was much more his mother's style than actual messy involvement in her loved ones' day to day lives.

His mind wandered. He didn't remember the kid whose mother she was talking about, but he remembered the school vividly. The pictures in his mind of primary school were fiercely technicoloured. The reds of bloodied knees.

The fluorescent yellow of school dinner custard. The green of dinner ladies' overalls. The blue of the big mats they hauled out across the hall at the start of PE. Secondary school was different. More austere. More ordered. The memories were calmer. They didn't scream with life.

He knew why he was thinking about school. It was both a missed opportunity for the future and a turning point in his past. Thousands of pounds, that they could ill afford, his parents had spent to send him to a fee-paying secondary school. Thousands of pounds worth of expectations now sat on his shoulders. Thousands of pounds that had led all the way to his full professorship. Thousands of pounds his mother would think were being thrown back in her face if he walked away now.

Dominic forced his attention back to his mother's voice on the end of the line.

'Well I'll let you get on,' she muttered. 'I know how busy you are.'

'It's not that bad.'

She tutted away his disclaimer. 'No. No. You've got to keep working hard. You always do. You're your father's son. No doubt about that.'

No, thought Dominic, no doubt at all.

Chapter Twenty-Three

Emily

The house is quiet when I come in. At first I think there's nobody home, but Tania's sitting in the conservatory, still in her yoga gear with an old V-necked pullover of my dad's over the top. There's a pile of bridal magazines on the table, but she's not looking at them. She's sitting there, staring out at the garden. Friends close, enemies closer, I remind myself.

'Hi! What are you up to?'

She looks up when I speak; I think that's the first time she's noticed that she's not alone. 'Oh. Emily, when did you get in?'

'Couple of minutes ago. Where's Dad?'

She turns her head away from me and stares out towards the garden. 'He had to go into work.'

I sit down on one of the obligatory wicker conservatory chairs and pick a magazine up from the table. 'He's a busy man.' I put my best sympathetic face on. 'It must make planning the wedding tricky.'

She looks at the magazines in front of her. 'It's a lot to think about.'

'Well why don't I help you?' I pull a notepad from under the magazine mountain and find a pen in my handbag. 'What is there still to do?'

'Why are you helping?'

'What do you mean?'

She narrows her eyes. 'You don't like me.'

I don't even miss a beat. 'Of course I like you. I haven't really had chance to get to know you. This will give me chance.'

She gives me a tiny smile. 'I thought you hated me.'

Her voice is quivering. It must be hard, coming into someone else's home like this. I shake my head. It's not that I hate her. It's that I have to protect my dad. It's not personal. 'Of course I don't. So what have you already done?'

She pulls her knees up in front of her, so she's sat in a tightly coiled ball on the sofa. 'Well I've got a venue, and I've ordered the invites.'

'Excellent. What else do we need?'

She slides her feet onto the floor and leans forward. 'There was a checklist-thingy.' She rummages through the magazines for a minute before pulling one to the top, and flicking to the centre pages. As promised, there is indeed a checklist-thingy: *Everything You Need To Organise For The Perfect Wedding!* It's an eight page pull-out. Eight pages of things you, apparently, need to organise for the perfect wedding, most of which, it seems, should have been done months ago. I can see why she might be a teeny bit overwhelmed. 'Wow.' I skim through the magazine. 'Apparently you're supposed to have four separate outfits.'

'What?'

'One for getting ready in. One for the day. One for the evening, and one for going away.'

Tania shakes her head. 'I'm going to have one dress. I'll wear it all day.'

'Even to get ready?'

She laughs. 'I can do my make-up in my pyjamas I think.'

I read on a bit. 'No. You can't. You can't do your make-up at all. Somebody has to do it for you. In fact if we've got a couple of months to go, you should be having your first make-up trial in about a fortnight.'

'Don't be silly. I've been doing my own make-up for forty-eight years.'

Forty-eight. Yeah, right. And the rest. 'Well you can't for the wedding.' I smile as sweetly as I can. 'And we'll need

to sort out dresses. Have you thought about bridesmaids?'
I try to make my voice casual, like I'm not bothered about
the answer, but she must have at least one old friend who
she wants with her at the wedding, maybe even a sister.

'Actually yes.'

Bingo.

'I talked to Theo about it. I'm not going to have hoards
of bridesmaids, but I would like one.'

Excellent. Just one. That must be her best friend.

'Emily, I was hoping you'd be my bridesmaid.'

What? My mouth goes dry. I've never been a bridesmaid
before. When I was about seven I had a princess dressing-up
dress, and I used to march up and down the garden grabbing
handfuls of whatever plants I could reach, pretending to be
a flower girl. I used to imagine that I had lots and lots of
aunties and cousins and big sisters and that I was going to
be a bridesmaid for all of them.

'Emily?'

Of course I should have been expecting this. She's
marrying my dad. She has to ask me, doesn't she, to keep
him happy. It doesn't mean we're friends.

It's good though. Well, not as good as her revealing that
she has a sister who she's kept hidden in a mental institution
for the last forty years, since she was hideously scarred in a
teenage fight after which Tania stole her identity and went
on the run. But it'll do. It gives me a perfect opportunity to
snoop around Tania a bit more. 'I'd be delighted.'

She leans toward me. I let her hug me. If it wasn't Tania,
it would almost be nice.

When she sits down, I pick up another of the bridal
magazines. She's turned some corners down in this one. I
turn to the first marked page. It's a picture of a dress. The
model is young with loose blonde curls falling around her
shoulders. The dress is one of those wafty, floaty numbers

that women of a certain age think are 'forgiving' but actually you have to have the figure of a twelve-year old boy to carry off. I turn the corner back up. 'You'll be wanting something a bit more structured, won't you?'

She doesn't answer.

I let my eye run over her figure. It's actually pretty incredible for her age. All the yoga must be having some effect, but still, she's not twenty-five. I'm struck by the terrifying thought that she might look better than me, before I remember that there isn't going to be a wedding. My dad's going to come to his senses, and the whole situation will blow over. I flick a bit further through the magazine.

'What's going on here?'

I didn't hear Dad come in. Tania jumps out of her seat and practically launches herself at him. 'Emily's agreed to be my bridesmaid.'

Dad smiles. 'Wonderful, and wonderful to see you two getting on.'

I smile back. 'Of course we're getting on. I'm going to help Tania plan the wedding.' I keep smiling. 'You're so busy with work. We can hardly expect you to drop everything to pick buttonholes can we?' I stand up and link my arm through Tania's at his side. 'You can leave everything to us.'

Chapter Twenty-Four

Alex
Two Days Later

The click of Helen's key in the lock was Alex's signal to jump up and hit *Play* on the CD player in the corner of the living room. It was practically an antique, but given his landlady's freakishly frugal lifestyle he decided to count himself lucky he wasn't having to fire up the gramophone. The distinctive strains of 'Eye of the Tiger' blared out.

'What the ...?' Helen stood in the doorway and surveyed the scene in front of her. In addition to the music there were a few decorative changes to the room, most of which had involved Alex printing out motivational slogans from the internet and blu-tacking them to the walls. There was also the flip chart in pride of place in front of the fireplace.

'Where did you get that?'

Alex considered answering and decided against. She'd find out next time she had to teach in the small seminar room off the main departmental corridor. 'Come in. Come in.' He ran forward and grabbed her hand, dragging her into the room.

'What's going on?'

'This is "Operation Get Helen That Job" headquarters!'

She peered more closely around the room. 'Why does it say "You're all woman!" above the TV?'

'It's inspirational.'

'How?'

Alex shrugged. 'It was on a website of inspirational sayings.'

'But you're not all woman.'

He sighed. 'It's not aimed at me.'

'What does "Be your own cheerleader" mean?'

'It means that you're allowed to big yourself up a bit.'

Helen looked bemused.

'That's not really the point. Look. Sit down.'

Helen did as she was instructed and took a seat on the couch.

'As I was trying to explain, this is now the official headquarters for Operation Get Helen That Job.' He turned over the first page of the flip chart to reveal a cartoon of Helen in full academic dress surrounded by the trappings of her new found wealth. There were dollar signs, and a bright red convertible. Across the bottom was another inspirational slogan: 'Visualise your success.'

'Did you draw that?'

Alex nodded.

Helen laughed. 'You have too much free time. And I don't really want a flash car.'

'I know.' Alex looked at the drawing. To be fair he might have done a better job of visualising Helen's dreams if she had dreams that extended beyond buying a new cardigan. He handed Helen a pile of A4 papers. 'Here we have job description, person specification and a copy of the job ad. The sections highlighted in yellow are where we have weaknesses to tackle.'

He gave Helen a second to catch up on her reading. 'You've highlighted outgoing.'

'I have.'

'I'm outgoing.'

'When's the last time you went out?' Helen opened her mouth. 'Work doesn't count.'

'That isn't what it means. It means your personality, for networking and stuff.'

Alex nodded. 'I know, and you are not a sociable animal. We need to work on that.' He carried on talking before she could issue any further objections. 'The situation is as follows ...' He turned a page on the flip chart to reveal a sheet he'd written up in advance and talked her through the numbered points. 'One – you need to earn more money. Two – you're not prepared to move to a different area to do this, because of your ridiculous infatuation with Professor Collins. Three – that basically means you have to get this job, because if you don't it'll probably be another ten years before another one comes along. Do you concur?'

Helen nodded mutely.

'Good. Then we move onto the action plan.' Alex turned to another prepared flip chart sheet. 'In addition to the obvious stuff, like filling in the application form, there are four prongs to our approach. One – interview practise. Two – Dominic Collins. Three – the Community Dig weekend, and finally, four – what on earth are you going to wear?'

'What about Dominic?'

Alex sighed. So predictable. 'You need to ask for his help.'

'With what?'

'To put in a good word. You're friends, aren't you? You need to make the old boy's network work for you.'

'You're asking me to collaborate with the methods of the male elite.'

'Yep.'

She opened her mouth to object.

'We got a red notice for the phone bill this morning. I added it to the pile.' Alex pointed towards the growing mound of final demands, balanced next to the TV. 'You can't afford principles, I'm afraid.'

Helen nodded uncertainly. 'What's the Community Dig?'

Alex grabbed another piece of paper from the coffee table. It was a flyer for the university's community archaeology day. 'They need volunteers to help. It'll show that you're a team player.'

'It'll be outside.' Helen pulled a face. 'With mud, and weather, and outside things.'

'And every other hourly-paid lecturer in the department will be there, in their brand new waterproofs wielding specially purchased tiny trowels desperate to make a good impression. That means you have to be there too.'

She looked over the flip chart again. 'I do not need help picking an outfit though.'

Alex sighed. 'Yeah. You do.'

She stuck out her chin. 'I'm sure they're going to be appointing based on suitability for the post, not on fashion choices.'

If Alex left her to her own devices she'd probably turn up at the interview in something beige with holes in the elbows. 'You don't have to do the full power dressing thing, but Homeless Crazy Lady isn't a good look for a job interview.'

Helen furrowed her brow but didn't argue. She glanced around the room at the massed products of Alex's endeavours. 'What were you supposed to be doing today?'

Alex looked at his feet. 'Going to the library.'

Helen laughed. 'Well I suppose your procrastination on my behalf is appreciated.'

He grinned. 'I don't have much choice. My mother told me that if I messed up living with you she was disowning me.'

'Are you sure you're not going to apply?'

He shrugged. 'They want a modernist. I told you. Anyway, it's a ...' Alex dropped his voice down to a horrified whisper. '... permanent job. Not my scene at all.'

The house phone rang, from three different points around the house. Helen pulled herself off the sofa and went to the dining room to answer the oldest and cheapest of the three phones; the basic, physically-plugged-into-the-wall model that actually worked.

Chapter Twenty-Five

Helen

The phone call was from Emily. Helen was pleased to hear from her. She could be an independent witness to Alex's madness. 'I've just had a whole motivational presentation about applying for Samson's old job and ...'

'I don't think it was enough.'

What wasn't enough? Helen paused, trying to match up Emily's answer to what she'd been saying. It didn't help. 'Sorry?'

'I got Dom to help me with a driving lesson. It was fine. I thought it was fine, but what if it was too little? What should I do?'

Helen still wasn't following the conversation. 'What?'

'You said I had to make him feel needed. So I got him to give me a driving lesson.'

'Right.' A driving lesson? Helen was not expert in matters of the heart, but even the most basic reading around the subject would probably tell you that driving lessons weren't romantic. She pulled the phone cord away from the wall and sat down on the floor.

'So what do I do now?' The anxiety in Emily's voice was only just below the surface.

Helen didn't want to get drawn back into this. However much she told herself she was being a good friend to both Emily and Dominic, she couldn't quite get the tiny devil Helen off her shoulder. Tiny devil Helen thought she was being pathetic. Actually tiny devil Helen thought Emily was being pathetic. 'You know you shouldn't have to make him love you.'

'What do you mean?'

'Well if you're unhappy talk to him.' Helen paused. She was preaching the value of honesty and openness. She was a hypocrite. She gave tiny devil Helen a hard look. 'Sorry, but you're his girlfriend. You know what he likes.'

'Please Helen. You said you'd help.'

Helen took a deep breath. Emily could make her own choices, and those choices should be respected by her friends. So, what could she suggest? 'Well his family are a big deal to him. Obviously he was totally in awe of his dad, but family generally is a big thing.' The devil popped back up. 'But you must know that. I bet you've met them loads.' Emily had never been taken to meet the parents.

'Well he knows my dad quite well.'

Helen sighed. She couldn't do it. Being bitchy for her was a moment of spite followed by days of guilt and self-recrimination. Her belief in the sisterhood ran too deep. 'Yeah, but in a work way. Maybe you could invite him to something with your dad and Tania outside of work.'

'Don't say Dad and Tania.'

'Why not?'

'Because they're not a proper couple. It's a moment of insanity. It won't last.'

Helen didn't reply. Professor Midsomer was engaged. It sounded like it might well last. 'Okay, well your dad anyway. Make Dominic feel part of the family. He'll appreciate that.'

'Are you sure?'

'Yeah.' Of course she was sure. She'd undertaken a decade long study of the character of the man. She was just too cautious to ever shift her theories into action. They wrapped up the conversation, but Helen didn't move. Maybe Alex wasn't the mad one after all. At least he had a plan for her future. She pulled herself back to her feet and marched into the lounge. She picked a marker pen from the tray at the bottom of the flip chart and turned the pad to a new page. In capital letters she wrote a new heading. OPERATION GET OVER DOMINIC.

Alex watched her from the sofa. 'Seriously?'

She nodded. 'He's with Emily.'

'Which you said you were fine with?'

'I am.'

Alex raised an eyebrow.

'I'm not fine yet. But I'm going to be. I need a plan.' She stopped and stared at the rest of the empty flip chart. 'I'm not sure what the plan should be.'

Alex jumped up. 'You need to get back out there.'

'Out where?'

'Out dating. You need to meet new people, to help you forget about the old people.'

Alex grabbed the pen and wrote 'speed dating' and 'internet dating' on the paper.

Helen shook her head. 'I'm not sure. I've been on dates. Dating people are weird.'

'Not all of them. The trick is to meet enough. If you meet enough people, some of them are bound to be acceptable.'

Helen wasn't sure. The whole notion sounded horrendous. She liked familiar people. She liked people she already knew. Meeting new ones was traumatic.

Alex slung an arm over her shoulder. 'We'll start with speed dating.'

'We?'

'Definitely.' He nodded.

'I don't need a chaperone.' She glanced at her lodger. 'Not one that's going to be better at it than me anyway.'

He laughed. 'So you'd rather go on your own?'

Well obviously not. 'Together then.'

'Together. One for all. Like the Muskehounds.'

Chapter Twenty-Six

Dominic
Two Days Later

Dominic looked round the gaggle of students crammed into his office. They were second years, all of whom had expressed some level of interest in doing their final dissertation in Dominic's subject area. For his first few years as a lecturer he'd met with each new potential dissertation student separately. Eventually it had dawned on him that he was spending half an hour with each student and the conversation only varied for about forty-five seconds between each session. He told himself that putting all the students together into a group was efficient, rather than symptomatic of his growing lack of interest.

'So, let's start by you each telling me what area specifically you were thinking of working on?'

He glanced around the room. Four straight History students. One History and Politics, and one History and Drama. He made a mental bet with himself. Four witchcrafts, one Thomas Cromwell and a Shakespeare. Undergraduate dissertation topics were nothing if not predictable. He turned his gaze to the first student in the circle, and raised an eyebrow.

'Er ... maybe like witchcraft.'

'Very good.' He turned to the rest of the group. 'Any more votes for "maybe like witchcraft"?'

Three nods. As he expected.

'And you Cecily?'

'Well I've been reading Wolf Hall and ...'

Dominic zoned out. At least Hilary Mantel was saving

him from a witchcraft clean sweep. He mentally ticked off "Thomas Cromwell."

'And you Nick?'

Nick Bottomley – joint honours history and drama student – was the student who Alex had found in the corridor a few weeks earlier, no longer in possession of his shoes. Dominic had been forced to acknowledge that that wasn't a one-off occurrence. If he was entirely honest, Dominic was stunned that Nick was still on the course, and managing to attend at least some sessions fully dressed and in the general vicinity of 'on time'.

Nick was working his brain towards the act of speech. 'So like, yeah, like witchcraft, yeah ...'

Dominic frowned at losing his mental bet. He thought a joint history and drama student was a safe bet for a Shakespeare dissertation.

'... but like not like the actual real witches ...'

Actual real witches?

'... more like witches in Shakespeare ...'

Of course.

'... and that. Sort of like about how witches are depicted in plays, but like not just witches. Like the whole supernatural – you know fairies and stuff too. Yeah.'

Dominic watched Nick lean back in his seat, clearly exhausted by the depth of academic rigour in his previous, like, sentence.

'Very good.' Dominic listened to his own voice starting his annual pep talk on how to approach the undergraduate dissertation, the admonishments to start early and not leave it to the last minute (which would almost certainly be ignored), the encouragements to come and see him as their supervisor if they felt anxious or pressed for time (which he could only hope would be taken on board). He finished, as he always did by handing out formal dissertation proposal forms, where the students would detail more clearly their area of research, the sources they planned to use, and would explain what was original about their approach. Anything more specific than "like real witches and that" would be progress.

'Professor Collins?'

He turned. Nick was loitering in the doorway.

'What's up?'

'I wanted to say like thanks and that. For the hardship fund thing.'

Most of Dominic's students had Mummys and Daddys they could run to when money ran out. Dominic was aware that Nick's mum was a lone parent with two younger children still at home. Spare cash to bung in the direction of the one who'd already moved out wasn't a luxury she could offer. 'Do you remember what else we talked about?'

Nick nodded. 'Yeah. Like budgeting and that. I've got a part time job. I wanted to say thank you for that as well. For the thingy.'

'The reference?'

'Yeah.'

The official policy of the department discouraged students from working during their second and third years. The official policy of the department wasn't written by someone who was strapped for cash.

'What's the job?'

'Waitering. For like posh parties. Really posh parties, where they eat weird shit.'

Jolly good. Dominic had no doubt that any really posh party would be improved by what he was sure was quite an individual approach to the handing out of the weird shit.

Nick wandered off. A few seconds later Dominic saw him wander back past his door in the opposite direction. At least being a waiter wouldn't be too complex, he thought, and it had been nice of him to take a minute to say 'thanks.' Dominic smiled, and then stopped. He was proud of something he'd done at work. He might actually have made a tiny difference to somebody. He didn't get that feeling very often.

A knock on his office door disturbed the train of thought. 'Come in.'

Emily popped her head round the door. 'Sorry. I wasn't sure if you had anyone in here.'

Dominic shook his head. Emily pushed the door shut behind her and strutted towards him. She stopped directly in front of his chair and swung one leg over his thighs so she was straddling him, before she leant forward and kissed his lips.

'Em ...'

'What?'

'Not here.'

She pouted slightly. 'Why not? We've done it here before.'

Dominic closed his eyes. It was true. They had. One afternoon last summer when the department was all but deserted. He shook his head. 'That was different. I'm working. Your dad's probably sitting about ten metres that way.'

She stood up and folded her arms. 'Fine.'

Now she was upset, which wasn't what he wanted either. He was aware that he'd been drifting recently, and he was aware that he was dragging Emily with him. He was telling himself the feeling started when his father died, but maybe that was a lie. Regardless, he needed to feel like his life was on track. He wanted to feel anchored, safe, certain, under control. 'I'm sorry. I'm a bit preoccupied.'

She unfolded her arms. 'I actually came to ask if you wanted to come for dinner with Dad and ...' She paused. '... and Tania.'

Dominic was surprised. Apart from his summons, along with pretty much everyone else Theo knew to the great surprise engagement party, he wasn't usually invited to Midsomer family gatherings. 'Any particular reason?'

Emily shook her head. 'I thought you might want to come. I mean family's important, isn't it? And you're important to me and ...' Her voice tailed off.

It was good, he thought, to be important to someone. He nodded.

'Next week then? Thursday? Or the weekend after if that's easier.'

Dominic shook his head. 'Thursday's fine. Actually I'm probably going to see Mum that weekend.'

'Right.' Emily started towards the door, and then stopped and turned back to face him. 'Maybe I could come too.' She stopped again. 'Or not. I mean, it's not a big deal ...'

Taken by surprise twice in one conversation. There was anxiety in Emily's voice. It wasn't her fault his head was all over the place. 'I'll have to check with her, but okay. Why not?'

'All right.' She skipped back over to him and kissed him on the lips. 'I'd better get back.'

He watched her walk out of his office, and took a very deep breath. This was good. This was what he wanted. Taking Emily to meet his mother was exactly the sort of thing that somebody whose life was moving forward would do. Whatever fancies he'd been harbouring about changing his lot, the moment had passed. It was time to get back on the right track.

Chapter Twenty-Seven

Emily
The Following Week

Tania has hired a wedding planner, Mia. She claims it was my dad's idea but it's like being in an episode of *Real Housewives*. There are samples of everything. Dress fabrics, table cloths, flower options, menu cards, party favours. It's exhausting. We're sitting in the conservatory looking at napkins with Mia. Smiley, perky Mia who doesn't appear to be aware of what a complete joke this whole thing is.

'Er, that one.' Tania jabs a finger at a plain white napkin.

Mia crinkles her nose. 'White? With an ivory gown?'

'Okay.' Tania shrugs. 'Ivory then?'

Mia nods. Apparently that's correct. 'Ivory sheen or ivory matt?'

I stare, with Tania, at the two napkins Mia has pulled to the top of the pile. For a second I'm almost starting to sympathise with the enemy. That's a thing isn't it? Hostages get it; when they've spent too long with their captors they start to get emotionally involved. I'm not here to support Tania. I'm here to find out more about her so I can stop my dad from making this ridiculous mistake.

Tania is still staring at the napkins. 'I don't really mind.'

Mia laughs. 'Oh come on. I know brides. Everything has to be perfect.'

'That matt?'

Mia nods. 'Excellent.' I guess that must have been the right answer then. Honestly, I expected wedding planning to be a lot more fun than it is. Of course it's different for Tania – Dad's far too busy to be expected to spend time on planning the details. If me and Dom get married, we'll be doing all this together. I try to picture Dom choosing table decorations. The image in my head cracks a little, but I don't let it break.

'Now, one last thing.'

I feel Tania shift in her seat next to me. This is Mia's third 'one last thing.'

'The guest list?'

'I thought that was all done.' I'm sure Tania ordered the invitations weeks ago.

'Quite. Quite.' Mia arranges her face into a sympathetic half smile. 'It's just that most couples like to keep it quite even between the sides.'

My ears prick up.

'What do you mean?'

Mia leans towards us. 'Well it's up to you, Tania, but I did just wonder if you wanted to add any of your family at all?'

'No.'

Mia doesn't respond straight away, and I let the silence hang there. Maybe Tania will feel pressured into saying more. She shifts again in her seat, turning her face out towards the window. I follow her gaze. It's grey and drizzly outside. Mia taps her fingers against her folder.

'Okay.' Mia eventually moves on. 'Just one last thing.'

Tania's eyebrows shoot up. 'Really last thing?' She glances at the clock. 'Only we've got people coming for dinner.'

Mia laughs slightly. 'It's about the entertainment for the pre-wedding party.'

'The Midsummer's Eve Party?'

'It's just that circus performers and magicians are a very specific request.'

Tania nods. 'You said it wouldn't be a problem.'

'Well it is quite short notice.'

Tania slumps back in the seat. 'You promised you could arrange it.' She sighs. 'The party is important. Magic and folklore and midsummer – I can picture it all.'

'Why's it so important?'

Tania smiles without looking at either of us. 'My grandparents were circus performers you know. I mean a long time ago before I was born. They were known as The Amazing ...' She stops suddenly and looks at me and then at Mia. 'Sorry. It was a long time ago.' She turns back to Mia. 'Circus performers and magicians. That's what we're paying for.'

Mia squirms. 'Well perhaps if I had a slightly more generous budget to offer?'

Tania nods. 'Fine.'

Of course Tania's happy to spend more money. It's not her money, is it? It's Dad's. Circus performers though. That's unusual. I add it to my mental list of what we know about Tania. Cornish grandmother. Circus family. Worked in a cocktail bar. It's still not a very long list.

Chapter Twenty-Eight

Dominic

Dominic rang the doorbell at precisely 7.43p.m.

The instruction Emily had given him was 7.30p.m. for eight, and he'd been pacing the adjacent streets since twenty past seven. *Never be too early*. That had been one of his father's many number one rules for life. Apparently if you were too early *they* would know you were keen and have the advantage over you. Dominic was unclear about who the great never-specified *they*, of whom his father lived in fear, might be, but was increasingly concerned that Dominic, himself, might have become one of them.

Theo's fiancée answered the door. Dominic arranged his face into a smile and held out the bottle of wine he'd bought on the way. She took it off him and glanced at the label. Dominic wondered whether it was good wine, and whether she would know any better than him if it wasn't. He was more of a beer man himself.

'Lovely.' Tania smiled at the wine and smiled at Dominic. 'Come in.'

They negotiated the niceties of greetings and jackets being taken and squirreled away. Not being allowed to hang up one's own jacket seemed, to Dominic, to be the middle class's way of ensuring their guests stayed a respectable amount of time. "You can't leave," the gesture intimated. "We have your coat."

He settled himself on the sofa while his hostess excused herself in the direction of the kitchen. So, here he was. All on his own. Where was Emily? Where was Theo? Was he early? Had he committed the sin of looking too keen after all? He glanced around the room. It was a room. It was what his mother would term, "a bit modern", but that simply implied that it had been decorated in a style this side of 1983. Actually the house, he guessed, was Georgian. It was a big, generous town house, that had probably only cost Professor Midsomer a few thousand pounds back in the 1970s. Dominic tried not to think about what percentage of his academic's salary got eaten up by the mortgage on his much smaller home every month.

A photograph on the fireplace caught his eye and he stood to take a closer look. It was a town, with what looked like a Roman amphitheatre in the background. Tania and Professor Midsomer were standing together in the centre of the frame, hands clasped, huge smiles across their faces.

'Where we met.'

'I'm sorry.' Dominic dropped the photograph back onto the mantelpiece and turned.

Professor Midsomer was standing behind him. 'That's quite all right.'

He moved to shake the younger man's hand. 'They were wonderful days.'

Dominic glanced back at the picture, and remembered the story from the engagement party. 'Verona?'

Tania's voice cut in from the doorway. 'On holiday.'

'I wasn't on holiday!' There was a touch of indignation in her fiancé's tone. 'It was a conference.'

She laughed. 'Of course. It looks like he was working hard, doesn't it?'

They fell into silence. Dominic swallowed. He was supposed to be making a good impression on Professor Midsomer, but was without his usual artillery for impressing the boss. Bringing a copy of your most recent published work to dinner seemed wrong, and it wasn't really the right moment to launch into a Powerpoint outlining strategies for improving student retention. What could he do that would say, 'good enough for Daddy's little princess'? Conversation. He probably ought to try to make some.

'So ... Professor.'

'Oh, call me Theo for goodness sake.'

'So, Theo.' Theo? Of course he knew the professor's first name. It was just that he'd never actually heard any of his colleagues use it. Anyway ... 'Theo, erm, wedding plans going well?'

Theo laughed. 'Oh Tania has all that under control.'

Tania nodded. 'Actually, we're sending out the invitations this week.'

Theo smiled. 'And Emily's been helping.' Theo gestured for Dominic to sit on the armchair before joining his fiancée on the sofa.

Tania nodded. 'Yes. Emily's been very involved.'

A noise came from the doorway. 'Well, Daddy doesn't have time for things like wedding planning, do you?'

Theo chuckled indulgently, as Tania turned slightly away and stood. 'I'll check on dinner.'

Emily watched her stepmother-in-waiting leave the room, before taking her place on the sofa next to her father.

Dinner, when it was served, was a Quorn mince chilli with corn bread. Emily rolled her eyes. 'You know Daddy likes steak.'

Tania popped on a smile. 'His arteries might not agree.'

Emily turned to Dominic. 'It's crazy. Yoga and Reiki and half of what we eat seems to be made of seaweed!'

'Well this is delicious.' It really was. He wouldn't have known it wasn't beef if Emily hadn't kept going on about it.

Emily continued. 'And what was that thing you were doing when I came in on Saturday?'

Tania's face coloured slightly. 'Meditating.'

'Yeah but with all the scarves and stuff.'

'Colour meditation. Different colours invoke different moods. That was green.' Tania raised her gaze towards Emily. 'It's for serenity.'

Dessert was brought and eaten. Theo started a conversation about a research paper he'd recently reviewed, allowing Dominic to chime in on safer ground. It was a paper about the cultural significance of the image of the bowman in medieval popular culture. Dominic listened to himself arguing that the notion of the principled bowman was a Tudor construct, and had one of those out of body moments. He sounded interested, passionate even, but the Dominic listening was bored senseless by the Dominic talking. The bowmen were all several centuries dead.

He made his excuses soon after dinner. Being in the midst of someone's family felt good, but also alien. It reminded him of visits to his aunts' and uncles' houses when he was younger. They always felt a few degrees warmer than his own home. He liked that feeling. If he ever had a family of his own he wanted it to feel like that. He wanted children running in and out and no stress about people being too loud or too clumsy.

Emily walked him to the porch, and paused, leaning on the door frame. 'Thank you for coming.'

'Thank you for inviting me.' There was something else he ought to say. 'And sorry.'

She looked up, straight into his eyes. 'What for?'

'I know I've been a bit off since my father ...'

'I know.' She took his hand. 'We're okay though, aren't we?'

He understood what she was asking. That was one thing he and Emily definitely had going. He understood her need for reassurance, even if neither of them ever spoke of it out loud. 'Of course we are.'

He kissed her lightly on the lips. 'You could come

back to mine, if you wanted? I can give you a lift to work tomorrow.'

She nodded. 'Give me two minutes to get some stuff.'

He waited on the doorstep looking out into the cold, black sky. For a second he fancied he could feel himself spinning away into the night, cut loose from his moorings, drifting beyond his own control.

'Are you ready to go?'

Emily was back at his elbow. He nodded, and gripped her hand. It was something, at least, to hold onto.

Chapter Twenty-Nine

Helen

Helen pulled her jacket tight around her as she walked, trying to keep the hint of drizzle off her clothes. It was early evening, and the city centre was quiet. 'So I've been doing some reading about this.'

Alex groaned. 'Of course you have.'

'Well there's nothing wrong with being prepared.' She paused to wait for the road to clear before they crossed. It was speed dating night. Helen's personal idea of hell. She tried to stop her brain dwelling on the sleaziness and hint of desperation about the whole idea. She hadn't had a date for four years. Maybe desperation was appropriate. 'Anyway, women are generally more selective than men at speed dating events. But that's cancelled out by the sitting down bias.'

'What?'

'Well, as I understand it, normally one gender stays sitting down and the other moves around. The sitting down people generally end up being much choosier than the moving round people. So it's better to be sitting down basically.'

'Right.' Alex stopped outside a bar. 'I don't think you get to decide that though.'

Inside, tables were set out around three sides of the room, with the bar at the far end. Alex raised an eyebrow in Helen's direction. 'Drink?'

She nodded. 'Just a coke.'

He shook his head. 'You're not having a *drink* drink?'

Of course she wasn't. She needed to keep a clear head to assess the potential candidates. She surveyed the opposition.

There was quite a wide variety in terms of age and looks. Some women had gone for the full make-up and mini-dress combo. Others, like Helen, had gone for jeans and a nice top. Well it was quite a nice top. It was second-hand, but completely free of holes and obvious stains. The point was that she wasn't horrendously underdressed. Alex returned with her drink. 'See anyone you fancy?'

Helen looked around again, this time focusing on the male half of the gathered throng. It was a varied bunch. Some of them looked relatively clean and presentable. She shrugged.

At the bar end of the room a woman tapped her pen against a glass for attention. She welcomed everyone to the event and ran through the ground rules. You got four minutes with each person. Everyone had a sticker with their personal number on it, and everyone had a card where they had to place a tick or a cross by the matching number to make it clear whether they were interested in contacting that person again. The woman kept going. 'So we're going to have the men sitting down this time and the ladies moving around.'

Helen cursed under her breath. She'd been banking on having the sitting down advantage. No matter. Best foot forward and all that. She found herself numbered F15, while Alex was M4 which meant they were starting at opposite ends of the room. She raised her glass in his direction before going to find her first date. 'Good luck.'

Alex scowled. 'I don't need luck.'

Helen's first date was older than her, dressed in a dark blue blazer with gold buttons, and a hair colour that Helen suspected owed a lot to a box of Just For Men. He shook her hand vigorously. 'I'm Doug. I'm from Tewkesbury. Now let's get down to brass tacks. Are you one of those gold-diggers?'

'What?'

'You know, those girls who are all teeth and tits, looking for a sugar daddy?'

Helen was outraged at the very thought. Obviously there was a lot more to her than teeth and tits. The latter weren't even slightly on display in her chosen outfit. 'No!'

'Oh.' Doug from Tewkesbury looked disappointed. 'Right.' He looked around the room. 'Do you think there'll be girls like that here though?'

It was a long first four minutes. Followed by a clear twenty-four minutes of men who were perfectly pleasant in some ways, Helen supposed, but were quickly ruled out of consideration on the grounds of:

1. Having too big a head;
2. Weird teeth;
3. A tendency to say 'like okay' at the end of every sentence;
4. Wearing a horrible shirt;
5. Unruly facial hair; and
6. Looking freakishly like a young Tony Blackburn.

All of which were sensible and valid reasons for rejecting them. Helen maintained a very clear idea of what her preferred date would be like. He'd be intelligent, but not pretentious. Tall, broad across the shoulders. Dark-haired. Ideally, he'd be working in a similar area to her. If she had an absolutely free choice, she thought, she did like names that started with a D.

The string of rejections brought her round to Alex. This would be like having a break in the middle of the horror.

He grinned as she sat down. 'How are you doing?'

She shook her head. 'I haven't ticked anyone yet. You?'

He held up his card. He'd ticked them all.

'You can't choose everyone.'

'Why not? They were all girls. They all had boobs. What's not to like?'

Helen wasn't sure Alex really had the right approach to finding his life partner.

'You seriously didn't pick anyone?'

Helen shook her head. She started to list the shortcomings of her dates so far.

Alex held up his hand. 'Can I summarise this as "they weren't Dominic Collins"?'

Somewhere behind Helen a whistle sounded. Time to move on.

Chapter Thirty

Alex

Alex watched Helen move on to the next table and turned his attention back to his incoming date. She was a woman. She had boobs. It was all good. He flashed his biggest smile and set about asking questions about her. He was genuinely interested. That was one thing he didn't understand about his landlady. Meeting new people was brilliant. How anyone could get stressed about meeting people was beyond him.

By the end of the evening he'd ticked everyone except Helen and one girl who'd told what turned out to be quite a racist anecdote about her hairdresser. Sixteen women that he'd be happy to meet again. Not bad going for one evening in a nice bar. The deal was that everyone's responses were collated, and then you got a text or email with the contact details for all the people you'd ticked who had also ticked you.

Alex's phone buzzed about ten minutes after they'd left the bar. He scanned the message and grinned at Helen. 'Sixteen for sixteen.'

'They all ticked you?'

Alex nodded.

'How?'

He shrugged. 'Girls like me.' It was true. It wasn't something he'd particularly dwelled on, but he'd never in his life struggled to pull. He just chatted to women. It seemed to work.

Helen's phoned trilled in her pocket. She didn't answer it.

'So? That might be your matches.'

'I know what it'll say.'

'How?'

'It'll say no matches.'

'You don't know that.'

She pulled her phone out and read the message. 'No matches.'

'What?' Alex was incredulous. Helen wasn't pin up hot, but she was smart and funny and he'd seen some of the men who'd been there. Some of them were desperate.

'I only ticked one person.'

Alex shook his head. 'Which one?'

She looked sheepish. 'You.' She shrugged. 'I didn't fancy any of them, but I was too embarrassed to hand my sheet in completely blank. I figured you were safe.'

So step one of Operation Get Over Dominic may not have been an unmitigated success. Well not for Helen at least. Alex had sixteen phone numbers to call. For him the getting over Dominic was going excellently. In fact, there was nothing to stop him calling one of them right now. It wasn't that late. He could suggest a drink, and then … whatever. An unfamiliar feeling built in Alex's chest. He was reluctant to make the call. Too much time with Helen must be having an effect. There wasn't anything else it could be. It wasn't the image of Presidential Candidate Barbie that kept popping into his head. It couldn't be. Getting hung up on her would be insane. Not only was she very taken, but Alex knew that he knew prettier girls, and smarter girls, and much much less spoilt girls. If he was going to get hung up on someone, which he wasn't, it wouldn't be Her.

Chapter Thirty-One

Helen
Two Days Later

'Why do we have to go?' She held up the cream invitation card for Alex's inspection.

'Because they'll notice if we don't.'

Alex was sprawled across the sofa. Helen shoved his feet along and sat down. He was right. They would notice, but what did it matter if they did. She turned the invitation over in her hand. Thick, cream card, with a dark red ribbon. The whole thing opened out from the centre to reveal black lettering surrounded by a red and gold border. 'It's all weekend. How do you make a wedding last all weekend?'

'It's not all weekend.' He took the invitation from her hands. 'It's Friday night until Sunday morning.'

'That's all weekend.'

'It might be fun. A weekend in a luxury manor house.'

Helen pursed her lips. 'It's a pimped up hotel.'

Alex waved the printed information sheet that came with the invite. 'Wedding guests get twenty per cent off.'

'We'd need a hundred per cent off.'

'It's only money.'

Helen was sure he only said things like that to wind her up. She pointed at the red bill mountain. 'It's not only money. It's the gas, and the council tax, and the mortgage.'

Alex grinned. 'My name's not on the mortgage.'

'Well, your rent then.'

Another grin. 'I have an understanding landlady.'

'Well I'm not going. I can't afford it.'

'You have to go. Remember your motivational sayings.'

Helen glanced at the wall. 'I'm all woman. I'm still not going.'

'You are currently seeking promotion. Your boss has invited you to his wedding. Every other hourly paid pleb in the department will be there, all gussied up, overpriced gift in hand, desperate to impress. You can't not go.'

She considered his argument. 'I think teaching quality and published research are more important than wedding presents.'

Alex laughed. 'Seriously, sometimes it's like the motivational sayings were all for nothing.'

'How is going to a wedding "being the change I want to see in the world"?'

'Well this is just the sort of event that successful permanently-employed Helen will get invited to all the time. This is you living that dream.' Alex scanned the flip charted list, still standing in pride of place in the lounge. 'Have you asked Dom to put a good word in for you yet?'

Helen shuddered. Normally a cast iron reason to spend time with Dominic was something she would pounce on, but this was different. This was going cap in hand, asking for a favour, rather than earning things on her own merit. 'It feels like taking advantage.'

'Well yes. It's not what you know; it's who you know. Hence the obligatory wedding attendance.'

'We can't afford it.'

He shrugged. 'Any bits of credit card left that aren't over the limit?'

'Maybe.'

'Then we should go. It's an investment in your future.'

She rolled her eyes. He might have a point though. Her current financial situation could scarcely get worse. Maybe throwing everything at this job was her best option. 'Where's the RSVP?'

Alex handed over the card.

'You've already filled most of this in.'

'Well I'd already decided you were going.'

'And you're going too?'

Alex nodded.

'Why?' She knew that Alex was even more broke than her and he wasn't in the running for the job.

Alex shrugged. 'Might be fun.'

'He'll be there.'

'Who?'

'You know who. He'll be with her.'

'I thought "her" was your friend.'

'She is.'

Alex stood and turned over the flip chart to the 'Getting Over Dominic' page. 'Look. You had a whole plan.'

Helen shook her head. It had been a stupid plan. Ten years of him not looking twice at her hadn't cured her obsession. A few four minute mini-dates were hardly likely to do the trick. 'S'not working.'

'Because you're not doing it.'

She folded her arms.

'You said you'd try online dating.'

'It's cringeworthy.'

'It's that or speed dating again.'

She closed her eyes. 'Maybe I could stay as I am.'

'Dominic's with Emily.'

'Well that's as maybe, but I love him. I love how clever he is. I love how much he cares about the people around him. I love that you can depend on him, and he's honourable and kind. And I love how hard he works for his students.' She paused. 'And I love his eyes. They're clear and blue, and sort of trustworthy. I'm sorry. I just love him. It is what it is. There's nothing I can do to change it.' She looked at Alex. Lucky, happy Alex who didn't understand. 'You just love who you love.'

Chapter Thirty-Two

Emily

I sit in the car and let myself be hypnotised by the lights of the car in front of us. Dom's got the news on the radio, but I don't want to hear about people dying and fighting. I want to be still. 'Can I turn this off?'

'Sure.'

It's Sunday night. We're on our way home from Stockport, which apparently is different from Manchester. Dom's mum was quite vociferous on that point. 'Do you think it went okay?'

Dom nods. 'Yeah.'

'You sound surprised.'

'No.' His eyes are fixed straight ahead on the road. 'Mum liked you.'

'Do you think?' Doubt starts to creep in. I thought it went all right. I accepted all the food and drink I was offered, even the vegetables that appeared to have been on to boil since the beginning of time, and the pudding that came out of a tin. I didn't say a word about the separate bedrooms, but maybe I could have done more. Helen was right. Family's important. I'm not sure I did enough to make her like me. One comment sticks in my head. She asked me about work, and I explained that I was a personal assistant. *'Oh. Like a secretary?'* she said. *'So you're not a career woman?'* 'I thought she wanted someone more career focused.'

Dom laughs. 'Oh god no. She's very traditional. She'd hate me to be with somebody who put work before family.'

'But she sounded so proud of your career.'

He doesn't answer for a second. 'By traditional, I mean

incredibly old-fashioned. I think her and Dad always had a plan for me, and a traditional marriage to a nice girl is definitely part of it.'

I keep staring straight ahead. He mentioned the M-word. We've never talked about that before.

'They sacrificed so much to send me to this fancy school. It was a bus ride and then a train and then another bus every day to get there, and if there was problem with the trains my dad had to take half a day off work to take me to school, and there was always a plan that I was going to do better than they did, have a better life than they did.'

I keep listening. I saw the pictures at his mum's house. Dominic in school uniform – the whole works, with a cap and everything. The photo was in pride of place on the mantelpiece next to Dominic's graduation, and then Dominic's PhD graduation.

'They were so proud when I got my PhD, and then when I got a lecturing job, but it was weird.'

'Weird how?'

'Sometimes I feel as though they worked so hard to make me different from them that we ended up with nothing left in common.' He stops talking for a moment and swallows. I glance over at him. He's still staring straight at the road but his eyes look wet. I've never seen Dom cry. 'Sometimes I think I let them down. I think they had in mind that I'd be married with kids by now.'

'There's nothing wrong with that.'

'No.'

I daren't look at him. 'It would be nice to have kids. I can picture me with children and a husband and a house. The whole thing.' These are the things that everybody wants, aren't they? Not flirtations, or maybes, but something guaranteed. 'I'd want to be a proper mummy though. I want to be looked after and look after a family. And I'd have a house with a garden big enough for a climbing frame, and near to my dad, maybe even with an annex he could live in when he got old. I'd have my whole family around me. I think I'd feel safe then.'

'Don't you feel safe at the moment?'

I don't answer.

He tries a different question. 'What do you have bad dreams about Em?'

I've never told anyone this before. I keep staring at the road in front of us. 'I dream that everyone's left me. I dream that I've been abandoned.'

He moves his left hand off the steering wheel for a second and strokes my leg.

'I don't like people leaving me. I like things to be settled, you know, secure.'

'I know.' He glances over at me. 'So how many children are you picturing?'

I've thought about this. 'Three. I don't want an only child.'

'Why not two?'

'Two would fight with each other.'

'But with three, won't one be left out?'

I think about it for a minute. 'Four?'

He laughs. 'Then I think we're going to need a bigger house.'

We? He said we, didn't he? The tense, bubbly feeling that lives in my tummy subsides a tiny bit for the first time in a very, very long time.

Chapter Thirty-Three

Emily
May
Three Days Later

I sip my wine. It's my second large glass of the 'one quick one' Helen and I planned to have after work. Are two glasses going to be enough to make sure I sleep tonight? The dreams are coming more often recently, rather than less. Always the same. Always surrounded by people I know and then one by one they slip away until it's just me and Mum, and I can never get to her. I end up alone in the dark. Every time. I yawn. Across the table Helen grins. 'Keeping you awake?'

'Sorry.'

'Why so tired?'

Because I barely sleep a night without waking up in a cold sweat. I don't say that to her. I know what she'd say. Either she'd tell me that it was just a dream and not worth getting worked up over, or she'll take it seriously and start talking about therapy and counselling, which would be worse. Counselling's for if there's something wrong with you. I'm fine. 'Just a busy weekend. We went to Stockport.'

Helen nods. 'Must be weird for Dom now his dad's not there.'

I suppose it must. We didn't really talk about it. I remember what we did talk about. 'He sort of suggested getting married.'

'What?' She opens and shuts her mouth for a second. 'He proposed?'

'Not exactly, but it's on the cards.' I let the solidity of the idea of being Mrs Collins calm my anxieties for a second. 'Thanks to you.'

'What do you mean?'

'Well you said I needed to get him more involved in family things. It's working.'

She nods, a little tiny nod, but she doesn't smile. She should be smiling. This is good news. She's supposed to be happy for me. 'I thought you'd be pleased.'

'I am.' Now she smiles. 'Sorry. I'm a bit preoccupied with work. I've got my job application to finish.'

'How's it going?'

'I've already done it once, but Alex said it wasn't good enough and made me start again.' She sounds a bit miffed. 'He made me take out all the bits critiquing the gender bias in the questions on the form.'

From anyone else I'd assume she was joking, but it does sound like something Helen would do. She's not great at letting a point of principle drop. It's nice that Alex is helping her. I sometimes feel bad that I've got Dom and she's on her own. I let the idea that I've got Dom linger in my head. I'm safe. I've got a plan for the future, and nothing is going to knock me off course.

'Hello ladies.' Alex is standing right in front of our table. I didn't see him come in, but now he's here. Whatever I was thinking about vanishes from my head the second he catches my eye. Just for a moment, there is only Alex. Then he turns his head away and grins at Helen. 'Your carriage awaits.'

Helen gulps her remaining wine. She's going to offer me a lift, isn't she? There's no sensible reason to say no. I consider, 'I can't be in the same car as him. I don't trust myself not to lick his face,' but decide against mentioning that out loud. In the end I smile and nod and I follow them into the street.

His car is the epitome of a clapped-out student banger. It was probably black at some point in the past but now it's a uniform dirty grey, interrupted only by the dark orange of rust above the wheels. I walk to the passenger side and correct myself. It's not uniform grey – the passenger side door is green and clearly started life on a completely different vehicle.

'Do you mind going in the back?'

I shrug. As I squeeze myself through the child-sized gap between the front and back seats I do mind a bit, but being in the back means that there's no chance of accidentally brushing my hand against Alex's as he changes gear. Being in the back is safe.

It's about fifteen minutes' drive from the pub to my house. For the first two minutes, it's fine. Helen is nattering to Alex and I just look out of the window at the city trundling by. Minute three is when I stop looking out of the window and let myself look at him. I tell myself that what happened in my office was a silly moment of flirtation, and that if I look at him properly I'll remember that he's not my type at all. I can see his hands on the steering wheel. He's wearing a T-shirt and his arms are just slightly tanned, enough to turn all the little hairs blond rather than brown. I've been telling myself that he's weedy, but his hands on the wheel look strong and in control.

I keep staring until minute six, and then I force myself to look away. I'm still safe here in the back. Looking at someone's arms isn't wrong. Even thinking about kissing them is okay. I'm not actually going to do it. I know that really he's just some friend of Helen's who I barely know, and what I do know about him is that he flirts with every girl he meets, and sleeps with nearly as many. I look out of the window. We're coming up to the new bridge. It's not new, of course. It's just one of those things that they have in every town that was new once, and the title stuck. I must come over this bridge, either with Dad or Dom or on the bus, pretty much every day. I look out of the back window of Alex's antique car and I can see the railings and the river below.

Minute seven. That's when I realise I'm not safe at all. The whole idea of safe rushes out of my grasp. It's hot in the car. Too hot. I want to rip my clothes away from my skin, to try to find some cool air. I scrabble at the back window, but it only opens a crack. My throat gets tighter. I know that soon I'm not going to be able to breathe at all. It's not safe here. I can't breathe. I close my eyes and try to wish myself somewhere else. There's a layer of sweat all over my body. I'm burning up, and then all at once I flip from white-hot to icy cold.

'Emily? Em? Are you all right?'

I open my eyes. Helen is twisted around in her seat staring at me. I need to tell her about the breathing and the hot and the cold but I can't make the words.

'Alex pull over.'

'I can't stop on the bridge.'

I close my eyes again. Helen's still talking but it sounds a very long way away. I tell myself that I can manage this, that it's just another bad dream, and soon I'll wake up and it will all be over. All I have to do is keep breathing and wait for the darkness to go away.

The car slows to a stop and I feel the air around me shift as Helen throws her door open. I let her guide me out of the car and into the day. We're in the supermarket car park not far from the bridge. I lean against the bonnet and stare at the floor. Nice, solid, grey floor.

Helen touches my arm, but it's Alex that speaks. 'Do you think you're going to be sick?'

I shake my head.

'Any dizziness? Headache?'

'No.'

'And you can see normally?'

I nod.

'Can you look up for me?'

There's something capable and reassuring about the way he's talking to me, like a girl hyperventilating and losing the power of speech in the back of his car is completely run-of-the-mill.

'Well you're looking a better colour.'

'I feel a bit better.'

Helen extends her arm around me. 'You should have said you got car sick. I wouldn't have made you sit in the back.'

Car sick?

Alex frowns. 'Do you think that's what it was?'

I nod quickly. I don't feel sick, but car sickness sounds much better than explaining that I looked out of the window and just stopped breathing. Saying that might make it sound like there's something wrong.

Chapter Thirty-Four

Helen

At home Helen turned on her computer and waited for the antique machine to boot and find the internet connection. Emily and Dominic were talking about marriage. It wasn't surprising. It confirmed what she already knew. Her decision to get over Dominic had been quite right. Her only failing was not doing better at it. Speed-dating had been hell. Online dating was next on the list.

She typed and clicked her way to one of the sites she'd seen advertised on TV. It looked friendly enough, proclaiming proudly that forty eight thousand members were currently online in her country. Surely one out of the forty eight thousand must be an acceptable Dominic-substitute. She picked a username and password, confirmed that she was a woman seeking a male partner, and clicked Register. This was easy. Now presumably she just waited for the men to find her. Apparently not. From the numbered headings on the screen in front of her it appeared that there were twelve more screens of questions about her and her lifestyle and preferences. She hadn't got anywhere near to a member of the opposite sex yet and she already felt weary.

She took a deep breath. Question 1: What sort of relationship are you looking for? A) Serious, b) Casual, c) Let's wait and see, or d) I'm not looking for a relationship. Helen let out an involuntary 'Ew' of distaste when she realised what the people in the fourth group were looking for. She selected 'Let's wait and see,' and moved on.

The next screen presented her with twenty-seven different

words she could pick from to describe her personality, but only let her select one single characteristic from the list. Well that was preposterous. People were complicated. She wondered if there was an option to write a discursive essay on the nature of personality. There wasn't. She scanned the options. Well she wasn't 'superstitious' and only a mad person would pick 'high maintenance' or 'possessive.' That got it down to twenty-four. 'Alex!'

She yelled down the stairs and waited to hear his footsteps. He stuck his head round the door. 'What's up?'

'Would you say I was more adventurous or more quiet?

Alex shook his head. 'Neither. Why?'

She turned the screen for him to look at. He clapped his hands together. 'Well you don't want to put carefree or up for anything. They basically mean slutty. So does adventurous actually.' He skimmed the rest of the list. 'You're quite stubborn.'

'I'm not putting stubborn.'

'Fair enough. How about generous?'

Helen shrugged. 'Thoughtful?'

'Boring. Put generous.'

'Am I particularly generous?'

'You've been advising your friend on how to spice up her relationship with the man you're in love with.'

'Not spice up exactly.'

Alex gave her a pointed look.

Helen clicked on the 'generous'. The progress bar at the top of the screen edged imperceptibly forward. 'You're not going to let me finish this on my own, are you?'

Alex shook his head. 'You were going to put adventurous. You need my help.'

He got no argument. Helen needed all the help she could get.

'I might sign up myself.'

That was surprising. 'I didn't think you were looking for anything serious.'

Her housemate had his gaze fixed to the floor. 'Not serious necessarily, just something to take my mind off ...'

'Take your mind off what?'

Alex shrugged. 'Nothing. Forget it.'

Helen turned her attention back to the screen.

'Do you think Emily was okay?'

The change of subject was unexpected. 'How do you mean?'

'In the car.'

Helen shrugged. 'She said it was just car sickness.'

Alex didn't reply.

'Why?'

'No reason.' He shook his head. 'Come on. Let's find you a love life.'

Helen wondered if there was something else on his mind, but before she could ask Alex was pulling the mouse out of her fingers and clicking through the screens, confidently selecting a range of virtues for her dating profile. She might not be doing very well at being her own cheerleader, but at least she had someone to do it for her.

Chapter Thirty-Five

Dominic
One Week Later

Dominic preferred working with his office door propped open. It was an old habit. Absolute quiet had never suited him, and he loved the noise of campus. It was the summer term, and the warmer days and lighter nights seemed to lift the mood, so the atmosphere was a mixture of pressing deadlines, summer barbecue and building hangover. It suited Dominic. It made him feel nineteen again.

Dominic scanned the document on the screen in front of him. It was his final draft of a journal paper based on his research into sixteenth century crime and punishment in the Welsh borders. He'd got lots of interesting material on the treatment of sex workers and the rates of sexual crime in the period, but his journal paper focused on witchcraft. Dominic rolled his eyes. He'd written his undergraduate dissertation on witchcraft more than fifteen years ago, but it never fell out of academic fashion.

His email pinged. He kept meaning to turn the notifications off and close his email while he was working. He kept meaning to; he never did.

He clicked on the notification window. Dr Hart. Subject: Urgent meeting.

He smiled and picked up his phone, dialling the extension for the Sessional Lecturers office. Helen answered on the second ring.

'You didn't answer my question.'

'What question?'

'From the staff meeting.'

'That was weeks ago.' He was stalling.

'You still never answered.' She paused. 'So you and Emily, wedding bells?'

He sighed. 'We're not engaged.'

'Really?'

He shrugged, which wasn't much help over the phone. 'I don't know.'

'Well have you proposed to her?'

'No.'

'Then you're not engaged.'

Dominic rubbed his eyes. He wasn't engaged, but marriage had been mentioned. That crossed a boundary. It wasn't a conversation you could take back. You couldn't sit down with your girlfriend and tell her that the discussion had been purely theoretical. He wasn't sure he would want to anyway. Marriage. Children. Career. Those were the things he was meant to have, and Emily had been sweet lately. She'd been kind to his mum, and he knew how scared she was of being alone. He had the ability to take some of that anxiety away. You could measure a man, Dominic's father had always said, by how he treated the women around him. Dominic didn't want to be the sort of man who strung his girlfriends along. 'What do you care anyway?'

There was a pause on the line. 'I don't. I hate to be behind on the gossip.'

'You detest gossip.' It was one of Helen's most admirable qualities. Most people claimed to dislike gossip, but only as a social nicety before embarking on a full-blooded character assassination. Helen genuinely meant it.

'I actually wanted to talk to you about work.'

'What about it?'

Three hours later, Dominic settled into the usual table in their usual pub. It was where all the staff from the university came.

Close enough to stagger back to offices after overlong lunches, but not so close – and slightly too pricey – to be a student hangout. He sipped his pint of something with a stupid name. Vicar's Vice or Curate's Curiosity or something similar. He was early and Helen was late. Dominic could remember when he was always the one who was late for drinks after work, always trying to squeeze in one last thing before he left the office. These days he was out of there as early as possible.

He flicked through his phone while he waited. One text. From Emily, in reply to a message he'd sent her earlier after discovering that Theo and Tania's Midsummer Ball was going to be fancy dress. He skimmed the message. *Don't worry about it. We can sort costumes nearer the time if we have to*. If we have to? That didn't sound like Emily had seen the folly of interfering with her father's affair.

'So how was your day?'

He jumped as Helen plonked a glass of plonk on the table and sat down next to him. 'You know. Same old, same old.'

'Well that's being a historian. There's a lot of old to get through.'

'How about you?'

Helen shrugged.

'You said you wanted to talk about work?'

She nodded. 'It's about the vacancy.'

He raised an eyebrow in question.

'Since Professor Samson ...' Her voice drifted off. '... you know with the orange ...'

He nodded. 'And the duct tape.'

'Yeah. I just ...'

'You just wondered about applying for his job?'

'Yeah. Sorry. Is that bad?'

Dominic shook his head. 'Not at all. I've never understood why you insist on hanging about around here. You could have got a post somewhere else years ago.'

Helen didn't answer. 'Maybe.'

'So why do you need to talk to me about it?'

'Well, Professor Midsomer likes you. I wondered if maybe ...'

'You want me to put a word in?'

She nodded.

'Course. Don't see why the old boy network shouldn't work for girls.'

'Women.' She corrected him automatically.

'No. Then it'd have to be old man network. That would be to help you make sure you got into the nicest retirement village.'

'You're reckoning without the centuries old linguistic belittling of women through the normalisation of infantilising language.'

Dominic didn't respond. It was an argument they'd rehearsed many times before. 'Whatever. I'll see what I can do.'

'Thank you.'

They sipped their drinks in silence for a minute.

Dominic broke the quiet. 'What made you ask me about wedding bells?'

'Just a rumour.'

'Nothing Emily's said?'

'Would it bother you if she had?'

The question was asked casually, without making eye contact. Dominic stared at his pint. 'No. I just prefer my private life to be private.'

Dominic took another sip from his drink. He glanced at Helen. Her head was still bent over her drink, but he could see the shock of untamed curls, and the shape of her button nose, and the slightest hint of the beginning of freckles across her cheek. He'd known her since she was twenty years old, and he would swear she hadn't changed the slightest bit. She was still every bit as preoccupied with work and study as she'd ever been. Never one to be reckless. Never one to waste time on whims and romantic ideas. If she had been, might things be different now? He looked away. Maybe he should learn from Helen. He cared for Emily a great deal. Romance faded. Compatibility, shared plans – those were the things that lasted. Something else niggled at the back of his mind. 'It's funny.'

Helen looked up. 'What is?'

'You going for promotion. A couple of months ago I was thinking of packing it in.'

'What?'

'I was going to resign.' It was the first time he'd actually said it out loud. The decision had been made. He'd been all set to tell his friends, and family, and then his father had died and something had changed. He couldn't exactly put his finger on what, but somehow letting the man down to his face had seemed easier than letting down a ghost. He shook his head. 'It was a whim.'

'Are you sure?' Helen looked concerned. 'I mean if you want to talk about it?'

Dominic shook his head. 'It was a silly idea. I'm fine.' He glanced at his watch, and then drained his pint. 'I'd better get going. I've got assignments to mark.'

He paused. 'Are you going to this stupid archaeology thing at the end of the month?'

Helen pulled a face. 'I've been trying not to think about that.'

'It's a chance to make a good impression if you're serious about the job.'

Helen grimaced. 'That's what Alex says.'

'Right. Alex. Yes.' Why shouldn't Helen be getting advice from Alex? She could be friends with whoever she chose. She could have a relationship with whoever she chose. He smiled as broadly as he could manage. 'Guess I'll see you there, if not before, then.'

Chapter Thirty-Six

Helen

You have four new messages.

Helen opened her email and scanned the subjects. One special offer on carpets and three messages from potential internet dating suitors. This was good. Getting messages from single men was what internet dating was all about. This, she supposed, was what she'd signed up for. She clicked on the first message. It seemed innocuous. The sender was called Carl, and was a naturalist, living in Gloucestershire. He was thirty-two. He owned his own home. So far, so good. He'd also attached a picture. Helen clicked on the image and waited for it to open on her ages-old computer. The photo was, presumably, of Carl, standing in a garden holding a football. He had dirty blond hair and big hazel eyes, neither of which distracted from the fact that he was stark bollock naked. Helen closed the picture and re-read the email. Not naturalist, naturist. Well, that would teach her to read more carefully in future.

She opened the second message. This one purported to come from a Mikey B, and was shorter with no picture. She identified two spelling errors and an incorrect apostrophe in the first sentence. The second sentence was a question. Helen could tell that because it started with the word 'Wot.' Another no, Helen decided.

Message three was the longest. It started with a paragraph praising Helen's great beauty and announcing that the sender, Juan, had felt a great connection with her from the moment he clicked on her profile. By the fourth paragraph Juan was explaining that he would be very keen to come to England to explore this connection further, if Helen could first see her way clear to lending him £500 for the flight which he would, of course, pay back as soon as he landed in the UK.

Helen shook her head. Maybe she had been right all along. Maybe her infatuation with Dominic wasn't a symptom of her hopeless lack of get up and go. Maybe all the men in possession of good fortune had already snagged themselves a wife, not that Helen was looking to embrace the outmoded institution of marriage, or expected to be financially supported by a partner. The point was that she was rapidly moving towards the conclusion that there simply were no other acceptable single men out there. Although Dominic wasn't a single man, she reminded herself. The memory of a time when he had been single sat at the front of her mind. That one forbidden moment between a student and her teacher. She could still recall the scent of his aftershave, the crisp blue of his shirt, the look in his eye. Or could she? It was a ten year old memory of a man not actually kissing her. Maybe she'd crossed the boundary between memory and fantasy a long time ago. It didn't matter. Then he'd been her teacher. Now he was her friend's boyfriend. Always off limits.

It didn't look like jumping into the dating scene was going to be enough to cure her infatuation. She couldn't have Dominic. She didn't want anyone else. She needed to fill her head with things she could control. Her research. Her career. Perhaps she should take up a hobby. Helen sighed. She was turning into a cliché. The blue-stocking spinster. The only thing missing was the houseful of cats.

Chapter Thirty-Seven

Emily
Three Weeks Later

The Big Community Dig is the centrepiece of the Faculty for Humanities and Social Sciences' claim to be engaging with the local community. Basically, it's an archaeological dig on a former car park in the city centre which is apparently destined to become a block of luxury apartments, but because we're 'engaging with the community' we have special activities for kids and displays of finds from other nearby digs, and pretty much everybody who works for the faculty has been forced to don their wellies and come and stand in what is essentially a massive muddy puddle.

I look around the site. Even Helen is here. Helen is not a digging-in-mud sort of person. She's a libraries and museums sort of person. She's standing at one edge of a group who are waiting to get their instructions for the day from one of the archaeology professors. Looking more closely, I notice that all the hourly-paid lecturers are here, apart from Dr Sandys who's about eighty. Aside from Alex, they've all applied for the permanent job as well. Such a coincidence that that would happen at the same time as a sudden upsurge in team spirit.

Fortunately I'm saved from actually having to get my hands dirty, by dint of having brought a clipboard with me to hold. It's a brilliant trick. Stand anywhere, looking vaguely purposeful and holding a clipboard and people will assume that you're incredibly busy. At the moment I'm standing with my dad, who is far too important to be expected to go near actual mud, and Dom who's managed to wangle himself onto 'showing round local dignitaries' duty, and is also saved from having to wield a trowel.

I try to pay attention to the introductory speech the archaeology professor is making. I almost feel sorry for him. He's probably had a team working here for weeks and now he's got all these amateurs clomping across his beautiful site. Eventually, he splits the 'volunteers' into smaller teams and dispatches them to different trenches, each one with an archaeology grad student to keep an eye on them.

I whip round the side of the group and grab hold of Helen before she ends up knee-deep in mud. 'You must really want this job.'

She rolls her eyes. 'This wasn't my idea. Alex made me come.'

Alex. I find my eyes scanning the crowd looking for him. He's at the other side of the site. His hair's all sticking up, and the waterproof he's put over his uniform skinny jeans looks like he rescued it from a charity shop reject pile. 'Why's Alex bothered about what you do?'

'He's obsessed with helping me get this job. He thinks turning up here will make a good impression.' She leans towards me. 'To be honest it's knackering. He's got formal interview practise scheduled for most of next week, and I haven't even definitely got an interview yet.'

'Right.' I smile. 'He must really care about you.'

She shrugs. 'Guess so. Anyway I'm going to need a break at some point. I wondered if you wanted to go costume shopping together?'

Costume shopping? 'What for?'

'Er, for your dad's party. The fancy dress ball.'

Oh. That. 'I guess.'

She slips her arm through mine and walks me a few metres away from the general rabble. 'I thought you'd be excited about the wedding by now Em.'

I shake my head.

'What's wrong? Tell me.'

'She's not right for him. I keep trying to say something, but he doesn't want to hear it, and Dom thinks it's none of my business but it is my business. I know him better than anyone, and she won't make him happy.' I can feel my fists clenching. 'She won't.'

I wait for her to tell me I'm making a fuss. That's what everyone thinks. I tell myself that's why I haven't actually followed Dom's advice and gone to the history centre yet, but that's not the reason. Actually going there and finding out the truth is the point of no return, isn't it? Whatever I find out, I'll have crossed a line.

'What makes you so sure?'

'Everything. You haven't met her. She's like something from a different planet to him. He's nice pullovers and good whisky. She's all spray tans and yoga and she knows about colour blocking. My dad shouldn't be with someone who reads fashion magazines. He should be with someone who bakes and sews and knows how to look after him.'

I see her start to laugh, but she swallows it fast. 'And if he managed to find this perfect 1950s housewife, would you be happy for him then?'

'Of course I would, if she made him happy.'

'You can't really do anything about it though, can you?' Helen rubs my arm. 'And it's been four months now. If it was a holiday fling I think it'd have flung by now.'

I shrug.

'So costumes?'

I suggest a day and time.

Helen pulls a face. 'That's the day before the party.'

'It'll be fine. The wedding planner's got a deal with the costume place. They're getting extra costumes in the week before specifically for us.' I walk away before she can suggest we go at the start of the week. If things go to plan there won't be a party and we can forget the whole costume thing anyway.

Helen excuses herself to go back to the dig. I hold my clipboard in front of me like a shield and make my way back to the little marquee they've set up to keep the rain off the important people.

Chapter Thirty-Eight

Alex

Soil. Mud. Trowel. Don't break the history.

Alex had only been about fifty per cent attentive to the introductory talk, but he reckoned he'd internalised the main points. He wasn't here for the archaeology anyway. He was here for something else entirely. He was sick of watching Helen mope. If she wasn't going to do anything about her feelings, it was time for a friend to step in and give things a little nudge. Emily was here, standing at the back of the little tent they'd set up to keep the important people dry. She was wearing pink wellingtons. Alex should hate that. It was such a twee little affectation. 'Look at me,' it seemed to say. 'I'm just a helpless ickle girl.'

And she wasn't a little girl. Helen had told him that there was four years between them, which meant Emily was only two years younger than him. A spoilt-rotten, pink-wellingtoned Barbie doll. A spoilt-rotten, pink-wellingtoned presidential candidate Barbie doll, he corrected himself. With a boyfriend, he added. There was something there though, something stronger and more vital than you'd expect at first glance. He remembered her leaning against his car, struggling to find her breath. He wasn't sure what happened. It wasn't just car sickness, whatever Helen thought, but whatever it was Emily had handled it. He'd watched her pulling herself back together. She might be a Barbie doll, but she was a doll with an iron core.

Alex put down his trowel and caught the trench supervisor's eye, gesturing in a vague way that he hoped suggested the intent to go to the toilet or for a cigarette or some other equally innocuous reason for leaving his post. Emily was on her own now. He walked towards her. Ten steps away, nine steps away – she was watching him as he closed the gap between them – eight steps away, seven steps away – she looked over her shoulder, scanning her eyes across the dig site – six steps away, five steps away, four steps away – he could almost reach out to touch her now – three steps away, two steps away, one step. He brushed his arm against her and caught her fingers amongst his own, and carried on walking. For a second he felt her arm pulling on his, before the tension dropped and she followed his lead.

'What are you doing?'

'I don't know.'

They walked to the corner of the site along the length of a fence with a gate at one end. It was chained shut.

'Come on.' Alex dropped her hand, climbed the gate, and jumped to the ground on the other side.

'Where are you going?'

'I don't know.' He stopped and turned back to face her. One of them was on the wrong side of the gate. His head and his body were giving him different messages about which of them that was. 'I can't stop thinking about you. You're always on my mind. I can't help myself.'

He stopped, trying to think of some better words. All of the things he'd said were true but they weren't why he was here. He reminded himself that he was only doing this for Helen. Helen loved Professor Collins. Alex was simply helping clear her path. He liked that idea; it would be the first time in his life that he'd used his powers for the greater good. He needed to say the right thing. Anything that wasn't a cliché or a song lyric would suffice. 'I really really want to shag you,' he said.

Chapter Thirty-Nine

Dominic

'Well you could try to look like you're having a good time.'

Dominic stood over the trench where Helen was scraping half-heartedly at the soil.

'I'm having a perfectly horrible time.'

He laughed. 'I know. Isn't it awful? I can't believe people actually do this through choice.'

She scanned his outfit. Jeans, but no wellies or walking boots. 'You're not exactly up to your elbows in mud though?'

He pulled a face. 'Course I'm not. I've already got a job.'

'That's not why I'm doing this.'

He raised an eyebrow.

'I happen to believe that this sort of event provides a valuable opportunity for the university to engage with the wider community.'

'Right. Well the bigwigs are making the rounds, so you keep practising saying that. You might almost sound like you mean it by the time they get to you.'

Helen followed his gaze to the next trench where Professor Midsomer was leading a group of men in suits around the site. 'Who are they all?'

'Well you recognise the Vice-Chancellor?'

She nodded. 'He's a geographer, isn't he? I don't really know much about geography.'

Dominic laughed. That was normal. Traditionally historians only found out which places were next to each other when they reached a decade when the countries in question had a war.

Helen was still staring at the bigwigs. 'I know the Pro Vice-Chancellor too.'

'Which one?' Dominic gestured towards the group. 'Red tie or purple?'

'There isn't a red tie. There's pink and dark blue.'

'That's not blue. That's purple.'

Helen shook her head. 'I know the pink one.'

'S'red. The other one's a Pro-Vice Chancellor too. Physicist.'

'And the woman?'

'Ah yes. The token woman.' He glanced down to see if Helen was taking the bait. She pursed her lips, but didn't bite. 'Vice Chair of the university governors. She owns a glass factory.' He didn't quite know why he added that. It wasn't as if Helen would instantly think, 'Oh, glass. Plenty to chat about there then.'

The group made its way over to the trench. Dominic stood back slightly, like a person who wasn't distracting the worker bees at all.

Professor Midsomer peered down. 'Ah. Dr ...' He tailed off.

'Hart. Dr Hart,' replied Helen.

'Yes. Yes.' He turned to his little touring party. 'Dr Hart is one of our up and coming talents.'

The group nodded. The Vice-Chancellor scanned his eyes across the trench. 'So lots of interesting finds, I trust?'

'Erm. Well ...' Helen glanced into her empty tray, as if she was hoping something might have materialised while she wasn't looking. 'It's still early days.'

'Actually, the lack of finds is a real positive.' The archaeology grad student in charge of the trench popped up all perky and smiling. 'Our plan of the site suggests that this would be an area with not many finds, so it's great to see the evidence on the ground confirming that.'

The bigwigs nodded. Token woman leant forward. 'And what was this area then?'

'We think it was a cowshed or stables. Definitely a building, but we don't think there was human habitation in this area.'

Dominic stifled a laugh at the look of horror on Helen's face. Essentially she was trowling through crap.

The group started to move away, but perky archaeology girl wasn't finished. 'Professor Midsomer, I was hoping I could have a quick word.'

Midsomer nodded, and the pair moved to one side of the trench, while the rest of the suits moved on. Dominic waited, trying to look like a person who wasn't listening. He glanced at Helen. He hoped he was doing a better impression of not eavesdropping than her. She looked like a meerkat on watch duty.

'I heard you had a vacancy for a lecturer coming up.'

Midsomer shook his head. 'In history, not archaeology.'

'My PhD is multi-disciplinary.' Perky girl was still smiling winningly. 'I thought I'd throw my name into the ring. It's such a great department, and the chance to work with you would be incredible.' She patted her hand on his upper arm. Professor Midsomer took an uneasy step backwards.

Dominic took a step towards them. 'But of course there's a lot of talent already in the department.'

Midsomer nodded. 'Well there'll be a recruitment panel and suchlike in due course.' He dropped his head and moved to walk away.

Dominic stopped him. 'Have you seen Emily?'

Midsomer looked around. 'She was here earlier. To be honest I thought she'd gone looking for you.'

Dominic watched his boss head off after the rest of the important people.

'Did you get a chance to talk to him about me?'

'Not yet.' Dominic grinned at Helen. 'Don't worry. I will.'

'Thank you.'

'And relax. They haven't even shortlisted yet.'

'Do you know when?'

'Should be next week I guess.'

Helen sighed. 'So too soon to get a whole load of papers published or make up some headline grabbing research?'

Dominic laughed. 'Probably. Right. I'd better go find Emily I suppose.' He smiled at his friend. 'Have fun in your cow shit.'

Chapter Forty

Emily

'I really really want to shag you.'

'What?' I know exactly what Alex said, but my brain is telling my ears that they must have misheard. People don't announce that they want to shag you, especially not people you've only met a couple of times before. It's ... I don't know, it's impolite.

He glances down at the floor before looking me straight in the eye. 'I said I really really want to shag you.'

I hear myself giggle, because he's joking obviously. You don't accost virtual strangers in public places and announce that you want to have sex with them. It's not a thing that happens. 'Don't be silly.'

'I'm not.' He's standing on the other side of the gate. 'You're beautiful.'

'I've got a boyfriend.' I decide to deal with the obvious objections first.

He smiles. 'So it's not that you don't like me?'

'That's not what I said.'

'So you don't like me?'

'That's not what I said either.' I stop. That could have been construed as flirting. I look at him properly. He's all kinds of wrong. Crazy, unkempt hair, Dr Martens that saw better days some time around the building of the Ark – he's the sort of boy I imagine my mother would have warned me about. Those eyes though. I've seen nice eyes before. Dom has lovely eyes. Alex doesn't. He has eyes you feel you could drown in.

He steps forward and climbs onto the gate. There are

four horizontal bars. He stands on the bottom one. 'You're beautiful, but you always look so bored.'

'I'm not bored.'

He laughs. 'You must be.'

'What do you mean?'

He tilts his head to one side. 'Well, everything's so simple for you, isn't it?'

I don't like what he's saying, but I don't walk away. I stick out my chin. 'You don't know anything about me.'

'I know that you live with your dad, and you work for your dad, and you're basically going out with your dad.'

'Don't be ridiculous.' Dom's nothing like Dad. I mean, they're both history professors, and they both try to take care of me, but there's nothing wrong with that. My dad's always been there for me. Ending up with somebody like that wouldn't be the worst thing in the world.

He grins again. 'I'm sorry. I must have been mistaken.'

'What?'

He shrugs and jumps back off the gate. 'I must have got the wrong idea. If you're perfectly happy with your life, then you wouldn't want to be wasting time with me, would you?'

'Exactly.' I turn as quickly as my legs can manage and start to walk away. Alex is behaving outrageously. Yes. That's it. I'm outraged. That's what I'm feeling. That's why my heart's pounding, and my cheeks are pink. There's nothing else. The picture in my head is still of those dark round eyes though. I tell myself it doesn't mean anything. Dom and I are real. We're serious. We're talking about marriage. If I did have the tiniest little hint of butterflies in my tummy that would be jitters, nothing more.

Chapter Forty-One

Alex

Alex watched her walk away. So much for pulling being his superpower, but then 'I really want to shag you' was possibly not his finest moment at the crease. He leant on the gate and watched her make her way back across the site. Even though she was wearing wellies she still tip-toed through the mud as if she couldn't bear the thought of getting messed up. And he'd hit a nerve, he realised, when he'd pointed out that she was basically dating her dad.

She was like a fairy tale princess, Rapunzel maybe, perfectly safe inside a tower that she didn't want to escape, but she was still trapped. Alex rested his head in his hands on top of the gate. He wasn't the Prince Charming type. He didn't save damsels. He didn't make everything better. He wasn't built of happy ever after. He'd taken a shot, and he'd missed. That was the end of this story. He looked up and saw Emily wrapping her arms around Dominic's neck on the other side of the site. His throat tightened, and he realised he'd clenched his fist.

Chapter Forty-Two

Dominic
June
Two Weeks Later

'Right. Anne Boleyn's marriage and downfall. It's a new area. Where do we start with a new area?'

There were eight students in front of Dominic, each staring at the floor more vigorously than the next. He picked on one at random. 'Camille?'

'Chronology.' She muttered the answer through lip piercing and fringe, but at least it was right. You couldn't understand history without understanding the basics: what happened when.

'Excellent.'

Dominic talked through the timeline of Henry's obsession with Anne, his disestablishment of the church in the pursuit of the marriage, her pregnancy and the birth of Princess Elizabeth, the hostility at court towards the new Queen, and her eventual fall from grace and execution. Some of them even managed to rouse enough interest to take notes. It wasn't much but it was probably the best he was going to get.

He set the students some reading for next time, and instructed them to be ready to discuss Tudor depictions of the Queen. This wasn't the sparkiest group, but every now and then a student did come up with an insight or a flicker of interest that was enough to keep Dominic going. The teaching was by far the best part of the job.

The students filed out and Dominic followed them, heading in the opposite direction at the end of the corridor to Theo's office. Emily wasn't at her desk but the boss's door was ajar and he could see through the crack that the Head of Department was alone at his computer. Dominic knocked.

'Come in.'

'Do you have minute?'

'Dominic! Of course. What can I do for you? Work or family?'

He paused for a minute remembering the other thing. One issue at a time, he thought.

'Er work.' Dominic took the seat alongside Theo's desk, so they were facing each other across the corner of the table – the traditional one-to-one tutorial position. 'It's about the lecturer vacancy.'

Theo's brow furrowed. 'Bit of a step down for you?'

'No. Well yes. It's not for me.'

'Ah, you've got someone in mind?'

Dominic nodded. This felt odd. He hadn't had any help from the old boys' network on his way up. Suddenly finding himself gazing down through the glass ceiling was unexpected. 'It's Dr Hart.'

Theo nodded. 'She's a good candidate.'

'Yeah. Well I wanted to make sure her cap was in the hat, name was in the ring.' Neither of those sounded right. 'You know what I mean.'

Another nod. 'Just one thing.'

'Mmm?'

'You and Dr Hart? Anything I should be concerned about?'

It took a second for Dominic's brain to send the outrage he definitely ought to have felt to his face. 'No! Of course not. What precisely do you mean?'

'Nothing. Nothing. Although, she was your student I recall, as an undergraduate.'

'Yes. So I've seen her progression.'

'And that's all?'

'That's all.' Dominic was emphatic.

'There were rumours.'

He shook his head. Was this really coming up again? There had been comments in the senior common room about her having a crush on Dominic back when Helen was an undergrad. A passing joke. Nothing more, and not even true. Helen had been far too preoccupied with study, both then and now, to look twice at him, or at anyone else so far as he could tell, but it had been enough to make Dominic extra-cautious. If she hadn't been a student, then maybe ... He stopped the thought in its tracks. She had been his student, and that was that. For years he'd found himself watching how he behaved around her. He'd been protecting both their reputations. 'Just rumours. Unsubstantiated rumours. Nearly a decade ago.'

'But still.'

'Still nothing. She was my student. Now she's my colleague, and a very good colleague. You should know better than to listen to rumours.' Dominic shook his head and fought to calm his tone of voice. There was still the other thing he had to talk to Theo about. He couldn't get into a fight with Emily's dad, not today, but at the same time he didn't want his boss thinking he got up to anything inappropriate with his students. Actually, he probably didn't want Emily's dad thinking that either. 'Anyway, what does the fact that she was my student have to do with anything? You've supervised plenty of the academic staff here over the years.'

'True. True.' Theo smiled. 'I apologise. I hear things, and maybe I react as a protective father, rather than your Head of Department.'

Theo was trying to placate him. Dominic knew he ought to let him. 'It's fine. Forget anything was ever mentioned.'

'Thank you.'

A change of subject seemed in order. Dominic paused. 'So are you all ready for the big day?'

Theo glanced around his desk. 'Well that's down to the bride, isn't it? I'm sure Tania has it all in order. I've got this post to fill and god knows what else before then anyway.'

'So you're interviewing before the wedding?' That was soon. Sooner than expected.

Theo grimaced. 'The day before. A week on Thursday. It's sooner than I'd like, but after that I'm supposed to be taking a few days off for a bit of a holiday with Tania, so best to get it all sorted.'

A few days for a bit of a holiday? Dominic wondered if his boss realised that that wasn't the most romantic way to describe your own honeymoon. He didn't comment.

'Anyway, you know when the interviews are.'

Dominic looked blank.

'You should have had an email about it, or a memo, or something.' Again Theo scanned vaguely around the papers on his desk as if it was entirely possible the memo in question was sitting right there.

'Why?'

'Because you're on the interview panel.'

'What?'

'We always have a current senior lecturer.'

'I thought Trevalyan was doing it.'

'No! Didn't you know? He had a heart attack.'

Dominic's thoughts shifted to his father. 'Is he all right?'

Theo snorted. 'He'll be fine. It wasn't even a proper heart attack. A minor cardiac incident according to the doctor, but he's still off for at least six weeks. Taking the piss if you ask me.'

Theo, Dominic had no doubt, would be reviewing funding applications and publication submissions from his hospital bed after a minor, or possibly major, cardiac incident. The word workaholic could have been coined for him.

It was a shame about Trevalyan though – well it was good for him that he was going to be fine. But if it'd been a proper heart attack there might have been two vacancies. Much better chance for Helen. Dominic put Helen out of his head. It was time to broach the other thing, wasn't it? He'd made his decision. He'd probably have made it months ago if his father's heart hadn't thrown everything he'd decided about his future into confusion. 'Actually there was something else I wanted to talk to you about.'

'Yes?' Theo had already returned at least half his attention to the computer screen in front of him.

'It's not a work thing. Er … maybe not here?'

Theo's gaze flipped back to Dominic. 'Nothing wrong?'

'No. No. It's good. I think it's good.' Dominic stopped himself talking. He did think it was good. He did. 'Maybe I could call round after work sometime?'

Theo nodded absently, attention fully returned to the computer. 'Of course. Of course.'

'Tomorrow?' Dominic tried to sound casual. Tomorrow was soon enough that he wouldn't get cold feet, but still gave him twenty-four hours to work out what he was going to say. 'About 7.30?'

'Yes. Yes.'

Chapter Forty-Three

Emily

I push my bedroom door shut and open up my laptop on the bed. Dad's still at work, and Tania's in the conservatory. While I'm waiting for the computer to boot, I have second thoughts and open the door a crack. That way I'll be able to hear if she comes upstairs. I'm not doing anything wrong though. I'm just finding out the truth. For Dad.

The email Dom sent me with links to family history sites is sitting in my inbox. I click to the first site and select the births section. There's lots of information I could put in. Mother's surname, precise date and place of birth, but I can only work with what I know. I type in the name: *Tania Highpole*, and select a date range that would allow her to be anything from forty-eight, which is what she claims, to sixty. I select Penzance as the place, because that's all I've got to go on. No results.

I click back and take the place out to search nationwide. Still no results.

Okay. Try to think, Emily. Maybe she's changed her name. Maybe she's been married before. She hasn't mentioned that, but she hasn't mentioned much. I change my search to Marriages, but all I've got is the bride's first name and a possible surname for the groom. No results again.

I'm not even sure what I'm hoping to find. Obviously she was born somewhere, and Dom did say that not all the records are online, so she might be forty-eight and from Penzance exactly like she says. But she's not. I'm sure she's lying. No guests at all for the wedding. No ties to stop her moving across a continent with a man she's only just met.

I have to find out what her big secret is. It's not snooping. I'm only looking at public information that anyone could access, and I'm doing it for Dad. He's not thinking straight. I'm looking after him.

Another idea strikes me. Passport. She came back from Verona with Dad. She must have a passport, and it must be somewhere in this house. I stand on the landing for a minute, and listen, but there are no sounds of movement downstairs. Tania must still be in the conservatory. Where would her passport be? My dad keeps all his important documents in a box in his study, but if she's not who she says I reckon she'll have kept hers private. I sneak into their bedroom. Where would she hide it? I run through all the obvious places. It's not in her underwear drawer. It's not on her bedside table. I kneel down and peer under the bed. There's a suitcase. I stop for a second and listen. Still nothing. I pull the suitcase out as quietly as I can and open it up. Empty. I shove it back under the bed and stand up. Try to think like Tania. There must be somewhere. Everyone has somewhere that they keep their most personal things. I've got a jewellery box that I only keep presents from my dad in, and folded up in the bottom there's a birthday card from my 5th birthday, written in my mum's writing, and a photo of her holding me when I was a new-born baby.

That's what I'm looking for. I'm looking for Tania's memory place. I scan the room again. There's no jewellery box or chest. I open and close the drawers again. There's no envelopes stuffed underneath her clothes. There's nothing. So far as I can tell, Tania is a woman with no memories at all.

Chapter Forty-Four

Dominic

Dominic sat in the same spot on the same couch as he had a few weeks earlier when he'd come for dinner as Emily's boyfriend. He could see his knuckles whitening from the intensity of his grip on the arm rest. Relax, he told himself. You're happy to be here. Lucky to be here. Lucky to have made it to university. Lucky to be on this path. He'd built the career. He'd bought the house. He'd found a girl he cared about deeply. Things were all mapped out. Dominic reminded himself, again, to smile.

Theo came into the living room carrying two mugs of tea. 'So what can I for you?'

'It's actually about Emily.' Dominic paused. 'You know I'm very fond of your daughter.'

Theo smiled. 'A bit more than fond, I'd have thought.'

'Mmm.' This was harder than he expected. He knew Emily was close to her dad, and he knew that this was the traditional way, but really? Asking the father's permission first? He took a deep breath. 'As I said, I am very fond of Emily. You know that I have a good job, so I can provide for her, and I would always try to care for her and protect her.'

Theo nodded, but gave no response. Right. In for a penny and all that.

'I would like to ask you for your blessing to ask Emily to become my wife.' There. It was done.

Theo was still smiling. 'Of course. Of course. It's what I've been hoping for. You're just the sort I hoped she'd end up with.' Just the sort? That wasn't true, was it? He was a scally. A kid from an estate. An interloper. He'd learnt the language, adopted the manners, bought the clothes of the sort of man Theo thought he was, but it wasn't real. Or maybe it was. Maybe the little boy with bloodied knees had been buried so deeply he'd simply withered away.

'Well, I think this calls for more than tea.' Theo stood up, set down his cup and poured two glasses of whisky. 'Welcome to the family.'

Chapter Forty-Five

Emily

Banished from my own home. Dad said he had a work thing at the house and I had to go out. I guess that's how things are now. Tania's there to play hostess, and I'm surplus to requirements.

I don't know where to go. Dominic's busy this evening, and he wouldn't tell me what he was doing either. I could go to a girlfriend's. I don't really have that many girlfriends. Helen. There's Helen. I could go and hang out at Helen's house to see Helen. Just Helen. That would be the only reason. I call a cab on the departmental account to get me there. I knock and wait.

'Oh. Hello.'

It's not Helen. It's Alex. He's wearing a round-necked top with buttons open at the neck. He's got a leather cuff around one wrist. I don't like jewellery on men. I like my men to be proper old-fashioned men. The cuff draws attention to his arms though and in my head I'm back in the car watching him drive, just before I had my ... little episode. I drag my eyes away from his forearm and try to focus on his face. That brings us eye to eye. That's worse. 'I was looking for Helen.'

Alex leans on the door frame. 'She's not here.'

'Right.'

'She babysitting for her sister. She's staying overnight.'

'Oh.' I knew that. I'd forgotten. Obviously I'd forgotten. I'm only here to see Helen. 'I was at a loose end.'

'You should have texted. I can come play with you.'

I shake my head. I couldn't have texted. That would

be like me asking him to do something. I'm not that sort of woman. I'm a woman who's run into him completely accidentally.

'So do you wanna come in?' He moves out of the doorway.

I shuffle past him, still avoiding eye contact, trying to brush as little of my body as possible against him.

He shows me into the living room.

'Why does it say "You're all woman" on your wall?'

'Oh nothing. It was for a thing with Helen.'

There's a flip chart standing in the corner. I wander over to it and start to open the pad. 'What's this for?'

'Nothing!' He pulls the page out of my hand, and holds it shut. 'Drink?'

'Why can't I look?' I pull against his hand and open the pad to the first sheet. There's a cartoon of Helen. 'What's this?'

'I drew it.' He glances down at the floor.

'It's good.' It really is. My dad took me to Paris when I was a teenager. All along the river there were guys offering to draw your picture. Funny cartoons with the Eiffel Tower in the background for the tourists. This is not like that. It really looks like her, for starters. 'Is this what you didn't want me to see?'

'Sure.' He pulls the page out of my hand. 'I don't like showing people stuff I've drawn.'

I drop the page and sit down. 'Why not? That was fantastic.'

He shrugs. 'Embarrassed I suppose. I'm not that good. Anyway, drink?'

I nod.

'Wine? We've got red out of a box that's nicer than you'd think, or white that Helen won in the raffle after the university quiz last year. I'd go for the red. The raffle white has the look of a bottle that may not be on its first re-gifting.'

I smile. 'Whatever you recommend.'

He bows his head ever so slightly. 'Very good madam.'

He comes back with two glasses of wine, and sits next to me on the sofa. That was my fault. I should have sat on the chair, and then he wouldn't have had the option. I probably ought to make my position clear.

'You do know that I didn't come to see you, don't you?'

He nods.

'And nothing else is going to happen between us. The thing. Before ...'

'Me asking you to shag me in a disused car park.'

'I meant it when I said no. It can't happen again.'

'So we're not going to shag?'

I shake my head, but there's something in his voice that doesn't sound like he's taking me completely seriously. 'I mean it.'

'I accept the challenge.'

'It's not a challenge.'

'Fair enough.' He spins round to face me on the sofa and crosses his legs. 'What are we going to do then?'

I haven't thought about that. 'Well, we could ...' I tail off. What could we do? All I know about him is that he's quite keen to shag me, and chatting about that might send out a mixed message. 'We could do friend sorts of things.'

'Right. So you braid my hair and then we'll have a pillow fight?'

'Don't be silly.'

'Well what do you do with your friends?'

I shrug. 'Normal stuff. What do you do?'

He shrugs too. 'To be honest I've not got that many friends round here apart from Helen. I sort of burnt my bridges with my last housemate.'

'What did you do?'

He folds his arms. 'What makes you think it was my fault?'

'Just guessing.'

He grins. 'Fair enough. I slept with his girlfriend.'

I don't reply straight away. At least that confirms that I was right about him. A nice forearm and two ridiculous jet-black eyes do not make relationship material. 'So what friend stuff do you and Helen do?'

'Hang out. I take the piss out of her for being uptight. She has a go at me for being a total flake.'

I feel a pang of something. It's a bit like the something I feel when I see Tania with my dad, but this is different. More visceral. More urgent. Definitely not daughterly. I can picture him and Helen sitting right where we are now, sipping their cheap wine and talking and laughing. The picture makes me feel like there's a knife being rammed into my belly. I take a gulp of my wine and remind myself, again, that he's not with Helen so it doesn't matter. And he's not with me either. That's the important thing. He's not with me, and I don't want him to be.

'Let's do that then. We'll hang out.'

'All right.'

And we do and after it stops being awkward, it's nice. He introduces me to something on telly called *Dog the Bounty Hunter* and I introduce him to the excessive amount of time that can be whiled away watching clips of different sorts of aerobics classes on the internet and imagining that you've done exercise. It's the sort of thing Dom thinks is a waste of time. Then we go on the website for the dog rehoming people and pick which dog we'd have if we were going to have a dog, and then he decides that having a dog is too much responsibility, and so we invent a whole business idea based around the concept of rentable doggies. And we laugh. A lot. To the point where it makes my eyes water.

'I bet my mascara's all down my face.'

'Yep.'

I grab a tissue from a box on the mantelpiece and try to stem the flow of grey-black tears. 'I must look ridiculous.'

'Yep.'

'Thanks.'

He shrugs. 'Doesn't matter though does it? If we're just friends, you're not trying to impress me or look hot, are you?'

Friends. Right. Of course. 'Course not.' I put the tissue down. Time to whack this ball back into his court.

'So friend, tell me something about you?'

'What do you want to know?'

'I don't know.' My thoughts keep switching to Dom. Dom who is the perfect fit for the life I'm going to have one day. 'Love,' I say. 'Talk to me about love.'

'What about it?'

'Well have you ever been in love?'

He does a sort of half shrug and pauses. 'No.'

'That was a long pause.'

'I thought I was once.'

'And ...'

'It was years ago. At sixth form. Jennifer Berkley.'

'What was she like?'

'Gorgeous. Tall. Blonde. Older than me. We sort of went out for about three months.'

'Sort of?'

'Well we didn't actually go out. We more sort of met up when we could.'

That sounds weird. 'What do you mean?'

'Well we weren't supposed to be seeing each other.'

I sit up straight. 'She had a boyfriend, didn't she?'

He shakes his head. 'No boyfriend.'

'Then what was the big deal?'

'She was my A-level English teacher.'

'You shagged your teacher?' That's so wrong. I'd never dare do something like that.

He nods.

'What happened?'

'School found out. She lost her job. I think I'm technically still grounded. It took me about three weeks to convince my parents not to go to the police.'

'Wow. Are you still in touch with her?'

He shakes his head. 'I tried ringing her and stuff at first but she wouldn't answer, and so I stopped trying. Actually, my brother saw her in the supermarket last year.'

'Did he talk to her?'

'I think he asked her where the bleach was. She works there now.'

'It's sort of romantic though. Forbidden love and all that.'

'It's not romantic. It was stupid. She lost her job. I nearly screwed up my education. We had nothing in common. We wouldn't have looked twice at each other in the street if it hadn't been forbidden fruit.'

He's right. Forbidden isn't exciting and romantic. It's stupid. It makes you do stupid things with people you have nothing in common with. 'Good that we're just friends then.'

He nods. 'And you've got Dominic, so you know all about love anyway.'

'Yeah.'

Chapter Forty-Six

Alex

Her voice said 'Yeah,' but her dipped head and avoidance of eye contact said something else.

Alex hesitated. This was his moment. She was vulnerable. He'd seen that before but now she'd come to him. All he had to do was make his move, and he was pretty certain she'd go for it. Emily and Dominic would split up. Helen would have her clear run and Alex would have made it all happen. That was the only reason he was thinking about it. He'd be a hero. A shagging super hero. He hesitated. 'Is everything okay with you two?'

'Of course.'

'You can tell me. I thought we were being friends.'

She laughed uncertainly. 'I don't know. Things were fine, and then his dad died, and everything went a bit off the boil.'

'Well he was probably upset.' Alex listened to himself. He was sticking up for her boyfriend. That was not a textbook pulling tactic.

She sniffed. 'I know. And things seemed to be going better. We made this whole sort of plan for the future. How many kids we might have. What sort of house we'd live in. All that stuff. But now I think he's avoiding me.'

Well that would be enough to scare anyone off, thought Alex.

Emily filled the silence. 'Like tonight, he wouldn't even tell me what he was doing. He got all weird when I asked him.' She shook her head. 'Dad's getting married. Dom's avoiding me. Sometimes I feel like I'm going to end up alone.'

Alex groaned.

'What?'

'Well listen to yourself. You're twenty-five. Why are you thinking about "ending up" anything? You should be having fun. Sowing wild oats. Drinking worryingly coloured shots. And so what if you end up alone? Being alive isn't a destination. It's a journey. It's about what you do on the way.'

'And who you do it with?'

'Exactly.'

She smiled slightly. 'So live in the moment?'

Alex grinned. 'The moment's all you've got.'

And this time he didn't hesitate. He leaned in, and paused for a second. She lifted her face towards him.

Chapter Forty-Seven

Emily

'No.' I push him backwards, and jump off the sofa. I've got my shoes on before Alex has managed to negotiate the transition to standing up. I grab my coat. 'I have to go.'

'Wait.'

I ignore him. All I can think is that I need to get out of here. The front door is locked on the latch. I fumble to open it, which gives him time to catch up with me in the hallway.

'Just wait.'

I shake my head. Finally, the door swings open. 'This didn't happen.'

'What? Nothing did happen.'

I look at him. 'The nothing didn't happen. Okay?'

He nods.

I stride down the street, not thinking, just walking. I make it to the end of the road and turn left and stride down the next road. I go right at the end, and along the next street. Then I turn left. Then right again. Then left. And then I realise that I don't know where I am. It's dark. It's unfamiliar, and I'm completely alone.

This time I feel it coming, but knowing what to expect doesn't make it any better. My throat tightens and my skin prickles to goosebumps followed by a flush of sweat. I try to swallow but every gulp makes me feel like I'm drowning. I know I have to breathe. I focus all of my attention on the voice in my head that's telling me to breathe. Nothing else matters. I drop to my haunches and then forward onto my knees, so I'm kneeling on the pavement thinking only one thing. Breathe.

Eventually my body responds. I pull the mouthfuls of lovely cool air into my lungs and close my eyes for a second before I look around. There's a street sign a few feet in front of me, and I've got my phone in my bag. I tell myself it's going to be okay. I just need to get back to people – real solid people I can rely on – and everything will be okay.

I stand up and call for a taxi, but that means I have to wait and waiting gives me time to think. I didn't kiss Alex. Nothing happened. I haven't cheated. I haven't done anything wrong. Another voice in my head is yelling at me that it's not that simple. Cheating isn't just the person you kiss or the person you sleep with. It's the person you share stuff with that you wouldn't share with your lover. It's wanting something to happen, even when it doesn't.

I close that voice down. I walked away. I did the right thing. I have a boyfriend. A boyfriend who has been a little bit distant lately, but who is good and kind and smart enough to realise that going round there and spending the whole evening with a man with stupid eyes is on the cusp of something much, much worse. Alex is a shiny bauble. Dom is what's real. We have plans together. We're going to have four children and a nice house and we're going to be a family. I don't want to be young. I don't want to be irresponsible. I want everything to be fixed. Forbidden moments are all well and good but you can't live a life of moments.

Chapter Forty-Eight

Helen

Helen balanced her sister's iPad on her knee. The baby was asleep. She had a glass of wine. If she was going to do this, it was as good a time as any. She logged back onto the dating site. She'd tried to explain to Alex that she was giving up after the first disastrous messages, but apparently that did not constitute her 'being the change she wanted to see in the world.'

One new message.

She opened the message. Andrew from Wiltshire worked for the Crown Prosecution Service, and loved theatre and hill walking. Helen sighed. Nothing too objectionable there. People would always need prosecuting, and the love of hill walking would at least get him out from under her feet for part of the time. She wondered whether working out how much time you could acceptably spend apart was the best starting point for a healthy relationship. A box popped up on her screen: *This user is online. He would like to chat with you. Live chat?*

She pushed the iPad onto the cushion beside her, and eyed it suspiciously, as if Andrew from Wiltshire might emerge fully-formed out of the screen. Did she want to live chat? One of her motivational sayings popped into her head: 'What would Alex do?' The actual printout had said 'What would Jesus do?' but Alex had crossed out the saviour of mankind and popped himself in his place. Alex would definitely chat. Actually Alex wouldn't be hiding behind an internet browser. He'd be out prowling the pubs and clubs, but Helen didn't fancy that. At least this way she didn't have to wash her hair and could down wine in copious quantities to calm her nerves. She pulled the iPad back onto her knee and clicked *Ok*.

A few seconds later a window opened on her screen and the first message appeared.

Hi.

Well that was inoffensive. Helen typed her reply. Hi.

So this is weird.

Yes. It was. I know. Is this your first time online dating?

Yes. How about you?

Same. First time.

Which seemed to put the ball back into his court. What on earth were you supposed to chat about on these things? What on earth did you chat about on a real first date? Helen tried to remember. All that came back to her was the certainty that she hated dates. She wasn't good at them. She was either too quiet, or too loud, or too dowdy, or trying too hard. She was terrible at chit-chat. Overall Helen suspected she was a bit of an acquired taste.

So tell me something about you?

That was a horrible question. She rehashed some of her profile information. I'm Helen. I'm a university lecturer. I'm twenty-nine.

What do you do for fun Helen?

She remembered Alex's insistence that reading journals couldn't be classed as a hobby. What did she do for fun? What was the most fun she'd had recently? Sitting with Dominic in the meeting at work? Probably not something she wanted to share. I like reading.

My ex loved reading.

Was talking about an ex this early in the conversation okay? Helen wasn't sure. She didn't have exes. She had Dominic.

How about you? Do you like reading?

A bit, but she loved it. She would devour books – 2 or 3 a week. Okay. This was definitely too much ex talk. Helen started to type but Andy from Wiltshire hadn't finished. There's still some of her books in my flat. Do you think I should take them back to her?

Helen took a big swig of wine. There was a feeling growing in her belly. Logically it ought to be disappointment. She paused and savoured the emotion. Not disappointment. Relief. How long ago did you split up?

About three weeks.

And do you know if she's seeing anyone else?

I don't think so.

Helen sighed. She was in friend and counsellor mode now. Much closer to her comfort zone than dating. Sorry to ask but why did you split up?

I was busy with work. We drifted apart. I probably could have paid her more attention.

Helen smiled. I think maybe you should take her the books. Three weeks isn't that long. Maybe you could talk to her about what went wrong too?

You think she might take me back?

Helen had no idea, but she knew what it was like to be in love with someone and be too cowardly to take a shot. It's worth a try, she typed.

Chapter Forty-Nine

Alex
The Following Week

Alex stared at the notebook in front of him. The words were in his writing, but he couldn't get his brain to make sense of the scribble. Across the dining table from him Helen shook her head. 'I thought you wanted to help me with this.'

'Sorry.' He tried to smile. 'Where were we?'

'I'd given you my brilliant "why I want to work here" answer. Traditionally at that point the interviewer asks another question.'

'Sorry.' Interview practice. That was the thing. He was helping Helen prepare for her interview. 'So why do you want to work here?'

Helen leant across the table and took the notepad from his hands. 'We've done that one. You should now be asking me ...' She skimmed through his notes. 'Where do I see myself in five years' time?'

Alex dragged his attention into the room and clasped his hands in front of him in a serious-interviewer sort of a way. 'So, Miss Hart—'

'Doctor Hart.'

'Don't interrupt the interviewer. It makes you seem snarky.'

'Well if they don't know that I'm a doctor I will be snarky.'

'And also unemployed.' Alex re-clasped his hands. 'So *Doctor* Hart, where do you see yourself in five years' time?'

Helen wittered something about further research goals, and working towards senior lecturer status. Alex zoned out.

Five years' time. In five years' time he'd be thirty-two. He did the maths in his head. When his Dad was thirty-two, Alex was already eleven. That meant that when his parents were his age, they had a six year old child, and a mortgage, and a sensible car. When his parents had been his age, they were already grown up. Alex was a child by comparison. It was the sort of realisation that he normally greeted with pure relief. He looked across the table. 'But really?'

Helen looked confused. 'What?'

'Forget the interview answer, where do you really see yourself in five years' time?'

Her brow furrowed. 'Well I want to extend my research in to domestic work and gender divisions. I'm really interested in male household roles, and how they were perceived.'

Alex shook his head. 'I said not your interview answer.'

'But that is what I want to be doing in five years' time.'

'Really?'

She nodded. 'What about you?'

Alex froze. 'I have no idea.' He closed his eyes for a second and tried to picture the future. He'd never been able to picture anything very much beyond his next meal, and he'd never wanted to. He'd meant what he'd told Emily. You had to live in the moment. Right now was all there was. Where did he see himself in five years' time? 'It's undecided.'

Chapter Fifty

Emily

The new library is clad in gold and silver panels. It's a concrete and bling nose-snub to the idea of austerity in public spending. I go in and make my way up the escalators to the history section. It's vast. To the left there are banks of computers, and two rows of other things that look like a picture of a computer drawn by someone from the 1960s. Off to the right are shelves of books, directories and newspapers.

In front of me there's a sort of high shelf with a computer on it, and a woman standing next to it. She looks bored. She also looks like she misses having a proper desk. She manages to smile as I approach. 'Can I help you?'

I take a deep breath. 'On your website it said you hold birth, death and marriage records for Devon and Cornwall.'

She nods.

'And local newspapers for Cornwall as well?'

'We do. Are you looking for something in particular?'

I explain that I'm looking for a particular person, and give her Tania's name and rough age.

'Is it a relative?'

I pause. 'My aunt. She was estranged from my dad's family. I'm trying to find out a bit more about her. Maybe track her down, get them back in touch.' I listen to my own voice telling its little lie. It's not because there's anything wrong with what I'm doing. This is all for my dad, but I can live without anybody else going on about how it's none of my business.

The woman nods. 'Well I can check the births, deaths

and marriages for you. What if I get you set up with some local papers to have a look at while I'm doing that?'

'Thank you.' I expect her to reappear with arms full of papers for me to flick through, but instead she leads me to one of the 1960s computers.

'Have you used a microfiche reader before?'

I shake my head. I realise that I have seen them before though. There are a couple shoved in a corner of the university library, but I've never known what they do. All the academics think I'm the genius though, because I can fix a copier jam in thirty seconds flat. The librarian gives me the two-minute tutorial in using the reader, which seems easy enough. Far easier than fixing a photocopier certainly. Then she shows me where the local paper films are kept. There's a whole drawer just for Penzance. They're arranged by date, with six months on each film. There's an index list but it only lists the main story for each edition. I don't even know what I'm looking for. This is going to take hours.

I decide to start by looking for a birth announcement. It's not much, but it would be a start. I find the films for the year Tania says she was born. It's laborious, and boring, but I manage to scan through the whole year. After the first couple of weeks I get an idea of where in the paper the birth announcements appear, and I get quicker at whizzing straight to them. There's nothing, and nothing else in the name Highpole either. No weddings, no baptisms, no funeral announcements.

The librarian taps me on the shoulder. 'I'm afraid I can't find the birth you wanted. Are you sure it was in Penzance?'

I shake my head. 'Not a hundred per cent.'

Maybe I should give up. Maybe everyone else is right. If Dad's happy, maybe that's all that matters, but I can't let it go. He might be happy now, but she's hiding something. He deserves to know what it is.

More in hope than expectation, I go to the index file, and flick through the pages, hoping something catches my eye. I start in 1965. That's two years before Tania says she was born. There's nothing that grabs my attention. I'm scanning through the pages on autopilot, barely even taking in what I'm reading. My stomach gurgles with hunger. I ignore it. At some point the librarian comes and asks if I'm okay. I must nod or answer or something because she goes away again. I keep going, scanning through the index. It's brain-numbing. I can't for the life of me understand how Helen and Dom do this sort of stuff for a living. I'm almost ready to give up, when I see something. A headline from 2001: *Circus Showman Dies*. Something Tania said rings the tiniest bell. Didn't she say her grandparents were in the circus?

I find the film and load it into the machine. My fingers are shaking from hunger and tiredness. I check the date on the index again. 5th October 2001. I find the right edition of the paper, and read the story.

Local politician, showman and circus proprietor, Jozef Polanski, also known as The Amazing Poldini, has died at the age of 82. Polanski was a well-known local figure, who served three terms as a local councillor after retiring from the circus business.

There are two pictures of Polanski. One, apparently recent, shows him in a suit unveiling some sort of plaque. The second shows a much younger man, dressed like a traditional circus ringmaster. I skim the rest of the story. There's nothing that suggests he had anything to do with Tania at all. The final line says that there will be a full obituary and tribute in the following day's paper. I scroll forward to the next day's edition, just to be thorough. The tribute is on page two and three. There are quotes from the mayor and from various local dignitaries. They use words like 'colourful' and 'one of a kind,' which I take to imply that they detested the man. I concentrate on the pictures. Some are recent – the local councillor in suit and tie. Others are older – showing Polanski the performer, but then there's one that stands out. It's another picture of Polanski, but this time in a shirt and cords standing in a garden. Judging from the clothes it was taken in the seventies or maybe early eighties. He's with a woman who I guess must have been his wife, and a teenage girl. I squint at the picture. The girl has dark hair, and she's young, but there's something about her face. The shape of her jaw, and lips and eyes. It's Tania. I'm sure it is. Gotcha. I read the caption. *Jozef with his wife, Albinka, and granddaughter, Tina Polanski.*

I read the rest of the article and then set about my search again. I was sure she was hiding something, but this is worse than anything I would have guessed. Once I know what I'm looking for I find everything I need in less than an hour. I want to run home and tell my dad straight away, but I force myself to think. I need hard evidence. I call the librarian over. 'Can I print from this thing?'

She shrugs. 'Normally, but it's not working. They're supposed to be coming to fix it at the end of the week. Friday.'

That's too long. It's Tuesday today. The wedding is on Saturday. The midsummer party is on Friday night. I need enough evidence to make her understand that this whole charade is over before then.

'I can print things for you when it's fixed. You could come in and collect them.'

'Could I send someone to collect them for me?'

She nods. 'I don't see why not. It's nothing confidential.'

I tell her someone will come in on Friday afternoon and I show her which articles I need. I skim through the details again before I set off for home. Oh Tina. I can certainly see why you changed your name.

Chapter Fifty-One

Dominic
Two Days Later

The first two recruitment interviews were uneventful. The panel of Dominic, Professor Midsomer and Mrs Addams from Human Resources ran through their questions and made cursory notes on the responses, but the candidates were unable to set the room alight. The first hadn't finished her PhD yet and was clearly way out of her depth. The next was an external candidate who seemed more qualified for Theo's job than for a basic lecturer's post. Dominic glanced at his application. Not currently employed. No reason given for leaving his last post. Clearly a story of some sort there, and not one Dominic wanted to deal with the fallout from. Two definite *Nos* to start the day.

Third up was the first internal candidate. Dr Levine had been a sessional lecturer for about a year more than Helen and taught eighteenth century culture, science and medicine. Dominic smiled and nodded and did his best to maintain an attentive face during the presentation. It was about Faraday and electricity, and ended with the claim that Dr Levine would electrify the teaching and research in the department. Dominic fancied he could almost hear Professor Midsomer wince.

Mrs Addams asked her questions first, opening with the classic, 'And why do you want this post?' followed by the equally timeless, 'And what skills do you think you would bring to the role?' It was the traditional interview opening one-two, and Dr Levine, predictably, didn't fluff his lines.

Professor Midsomer was next up with his questions

about teaching practice and how the candidate would enhance the university's research reputation. Again Levine's answers were solid. Not inspiring, but decent. Dominic was last up. His two questions couldn't be further apart. One was based on the candidate's presentation or past research, hence the need to be attentive throughout. The second was a pet subject of his. Dominic tapped his pen on the table and looked up at the candidate, 'So, a bit of a change of subject now, can you tell me how you would contribute to the equality goals of the department and to the university's key aim of attracting students from lower income backgrounds into higher education?'

There was a pause. Dr Levine swallowed before continuing. 'Well obviously, I would treat all students the same, regardless of their background.'

Dominic nodded, but didn't offer any other prompt. He let the silence hang for a moment, to see if the candidate would say more. Nothing was forthcoming. 'Anything more specific than that?' he prompted.

'Well, of course one has to be even-handed, but we can't lower standards, can we? Students still have to achieve the required standard. If you don't maintain that you end up pandering to them.'

Dominic forced his eyebrow not to rise. 'Pandering?'

The candidate glanced at him, apparently aware that he may not have made the smartest word selection. 'Well I don't mean pandering. Obviously. I just, well I'd treat all my students the same.' His voice petered out.

'All right.' Dominic placed his pen at the side of his papers. 'Was there anything you were wanting to ask us at this stage?'

Dr Levine asked a question about how the department saw the postholder's career progression. Dominic let Theo answer and only half listened to the reply.

'Okay.' Dominic gestured towards Mrs Addams. 'Do you have anything to add?'

She shook her head, and she addressed the candidate. 'You're all clear about the hours, salary etcetera?'

'I am.'

'Very good.' Mrs Addams got up and gestured Dr Levine towards the door. 'We'll be in touch. We're aiming to make a decision as soon as possible, but don't be concerned if you don't hear until next week.'

She returned to her seat. Dominic looked at his fellow interviewers. Professor Midsomer was beaming. 'Good candidate. Just the right sort.'

The right sort? That again. Dominic was the right sort for Emily. Levine was the right sort for the job. Dominic didn't reply for a second. 'I thought he struggled with the final question.'

Theo shrugged. 'Well, what else is a man supposed to say? Of course you treat them all the same.'

Again, Dominic let the comment pass. It was correct in a way, and he knew that Theo was a decent bloke and a very fair teacher. He'd supported Dominic's own career all the way, but the attitude rankled. The idea that there was a right sort, and the knowledge that if there was Dominic himself probably wasn't it struck an uncomfortable chord. He looked at the clock and back to his list of candidates.

'Time for a coffee before the next one?'

Chapter Fifty-Two

Helen

Helen was ridiculously early. Of course she was ridiculously early. Her interview was at 12 noon, and she'd been ready to leave the house at quarter past eight. Alex had made her sit down and refused to let her move until eleven, but she was still nearly half an hour early, so she was plonked on a chair in the corridor, trying to look cool and unconcerned while she waited. She rehearsed her presentation in her head. *British Abolitionism and the creation of a new masculinity.* It was Alex's idea to focus on masculinity, so she didn't come across as the token woman who could only do women. It was a good presentation. At least it would be if she managed to say all the words in the right order.

Helen checked her watch. 12.03p.m. Her stomach flipped. She could do the job. She knew she could do the job. She just didn't know if she could do the interview. Interviews were the first dates of the employment world. Helen preferred a strategy of hanging round for a decade or so and hoping the job made a move on her.

'You can come through now, Dr Hart.' It was Dominic, standing in the doorway to Professor Midsomer's office. He stepped towards her and let the door swing closed for a second.

'I didn't know you were on the panel.'

'Sorry! Neither did I.' He smiled. 'Obviously, I can't be biased, but you're going to be great. Good luck.'

He pushed the door open again and ushered her into the room. The computer was already set up, displaying Helen's presentation on a TV screen at one end of the room.

The interviewers had chairs around three sides of a small rectangular table, with an empty chair on the short side nearest the computer.

Professor Midsomer stood as they entered, and offered the formal introductions. 'Dr Hart, you already know Professor Collins. And this is our colleague Josephine Addams, from Human Resources.'

Mrs Addams half-stood and leant forward to shake hands.

'So we'll start with your presentation, and then there's a couple of questions from each of us, and obviously there'll be time for you to ask questions at the end.'

Helen nodded, moved over to the laptop and took a deep breath. She could do this. She was, after all, all cheerleader, and her own woman or something to that effect. 'All right. Well thank you for inviting me to interview. I'm Dr Helen Hart, and I'm going to talk for a few minutes about one of my research specialisms – abolitionism and masculinity – and hopefully give you some suggestions as to how my research fits into and enhances the wider work of the department.'

Dominic nodded along, and Helen clicked to slide two. The presentation went well. Helen remembered everything she'd intended to say, and remembered to talk about how her research would enhance the department, rather than only about her subject. She finished precisely on the allotted ten minutes and sat down ready for questions.

'Why do you want to work here, Dr Hart?'

Well, because she needed the sodding money. Helen resisted the urge to say the first thing that popped into her head. 'I've been part of this department since my undergraduate studies. There's a great research and teaching ethos here, which I'm already part of as a sessional lecturer, and I'd welcome the opportunity to contribute further and be a full member of the team.'

It was a dull answer, but hopefully one with nothing contentious in it. The personnel woman nodded, and opened her mouth to move on. Professor Midsomer held up a hand.

'Yes Dr Hart.' He was looking at the application form on the table in front of him. 'You have been with us a number of years. I wonder if you can put your finger on why your career hasn't progressed more quickly to date?'

Helen opened her mouth and closed it again. She could hear Alex's pep talk in her head. Don't panic. Don't rush. If you get nervous imagine them naked. She didn't try that. Imagining Dominic naked wouldn't help her interview performance. 'Well, obviously academic posts don't come up that often. I have applied once before, but I was very young then and possibly didn't have enough teaching experience. I do think that this is the right time for me to make this move though. Really, it's the here and now that I'm focusing on.'

'Not much good for a historian.' It sounded like it ought to be a joke, but Professor Midsomer didn't smile.

The personnel woman asked her second question. Helen managed to repeat the list of skills and attributes she'd rehearsed. Then it was back to Professor Midsomer. Could she give examples of her excellent teaching practice?

She could and she did. His second question was about enhancing the department's research reputation. It would be poor form to suggest that without Dominic the department wouldn't have a research reputation. She also refrained from pointing out that Professor Midsomer hadn't actually contributed any research for several years, but still got a name check on the PhD papers of students supervised by the teaching staff under him. Instead, she talked about her own research interests. This wasn't chit-chat. This was the stuff that Helen could talk about for hours. Men and women and how they interacted in different cultures and places and times. She was an expert, a purely theoretical expert unfortunately.

Dominic was up next. He asked one question about abolitionism and masculinity which Helen dealt with easily. If the whole interview were talking about history it would have been a walk in the park.

'And my last question, can you tell me how you would contribute to the equality goals of the department and to the university's key aim of attracting more lower income students?'

She took a breath. It was a question she could answer so many ways. It was probably best to plump for an option that didn't involve the phrase 'tweedy old gits.' But what was her answer? There was all the stuff she could say about government targets, and using the media to expand the reach of the university, and engaging more with the community, but they all sounded like platitudes. She took a breath. 'Actually, this is an area that does concern me. I sometimes worry that we're doing worse rather than better in higher education.'

Midsomer's eyebrows shifted upwards at that. She was sounding negative which was bad, but she'd toed the party line for nearly forty-five minutes. There were limits. 'I mean, when I think about my own childhood, my mum didn't go to university, but it was absolutely expected that I would. There was this aspiration all the time, the idea that your children should do better than you. I worry that we've lost that, that higher education is becoming a closed shop again. To be honest I'm not sure what we do about that. Perhaps expanding the school liaison programme, giving kids a chance to come and see what we do and get a taste of the place for real?' The positive suggestions were bland, but the sentiment was right, she thought.

Dominic smiled, which would have been reassuring if he

hadn't been the only member of the panel doing it. 'Great. And do you have any questions for us?'

She asked her pre-planned question about the anticipated balance between teaching and research, and Professor Midsomer gave a vague, pat sort of an answer, and that was that.

She walked down the corridor in a daze, and kept walking until she got to the hourly-paid lecturer's office. Alex was there, getting dagger looks from the two other inhabitants. Helen saw why. He was hogging the one good computer playing Words with Friends. He jumped up when she came in.

'How did it go?'

Helen glanced around the room. Dr Levine and Dr Harries, both awkwardly and uncharacteristically suited up. 'Oh fine. Good I think.'

Alex remained oblivious to the sartorial clues to what his colleagues were up to. 'I need details.'

Two other pairs of ears were almost visibly twitching.

'Come on then. You can buy me a coffee.'

Alex logged off the computer. They headed to the canteen, leaving Levine and Harries devoid of gossip and free to fight over the good PC.

'I can't shake the feeling that Midsomer doesn't like me.'

Alex shrugged. 'He's all right. Better than Professor Collins anyway.'

'Why are you down on Dominic?'

He shrugged. 'No reason.'

It was sweet of him to be protective but unnecessary. Best to nip it in the bud.

'You can't blame him for how I feel.'

'What?' Alex looked confused for a moment.

'The nearly moment was years ago, and seriously, it was just a moment. It's not his fault it's a moment I never got over.'

'What?' He was still looking blank. Then his expression shifted. 'Right. Yeah. I know.'

'So, if I'm over it, and he's over it, maybe you should get over it too?'

Alex stared at his drink for a minute. 'Sure.' He didn't sound convinced.

'Anyway, according to Emily, they're talking marriage and babies, so no more dwelling on what might have been.'

Alex's gaze shifted from his drink, to Helen and then over her shoulder.

'What are you two up to?' Emily approached them from behind Helen.

'Helen's just had her interview.'

They chatted for a moment or two about how it went.

'Actually there was something I wanted to talk to you about.' Alex was staring at Emily.

'What?'

He stopped. 'Er, the projector in lecture room four. It's not working.'

Helen furrowed her brow. 'Isn't that an issue for estates?'

Alex froze, half out of his seat wedged against the fixed plastic table. 'I thought Emily might be able to fix it.'

That didn't make any sense. 'Well, it was fine yesterday.'

Alex managed to stand up properly. 'And it's broken this morning.'

'How do you know? You weren't teaching this morning.'

There was a light sheen sweat on his forehead. 'I covered for someone.'

So that was why he was acting weird. He must have covered a lecture so one of her competitors could go for an interview. Helen shook her head. She wouldn't have minded. It was like his objection to Dominic all over again. She didn't need him to get all protective like this.

Chapter Fifty-Three

Emily

I follow him out of the canteen and along the corridor. I chatter about work as we walk, keeping everything light, fighting the urge to just reach over and touch him. 'I can fill in a work request for the projector, but it'll probably be ages before anything gets done.'

He twists his head back towards me. 'What?'

'The projector in room four?'

Alex doesn't answer. We turn towards the stairwell. It's quieter here. He reaches back, grabs my hand and pulls me through a door behind us. He slams it shut and flicks the lock across.

We're in the disabled toilet. Alex leans against the mirror and takes a deep breath. He's not between me or the door or anything, so I don't think it would count as a kidnapping, but I'm not at all sure what it is. 'What are you doing?'

'Sorry.' He looks around. 'Sorry. I needed to talk to you.'

'Well I have an office and a phone and email, any of which would have been more normal than this.'

'Sorry.'

'Again?'

He breaks into a half grin. 'Yeah.'

The grin is infectious. I have a strong feeling that I ought to be cross with him. I fold my arms across my body like a person who was cross might. 'What did you want to talk about?'

'I've got something for you.' He pulls a folded sheet of A4 out of the back pocket of his jeans, and holds it out to me.

I unfold the paper. It's a drawing, a pencil drawing of me. I stare at the picture. I don't even let people take my photo until I've checked my face and hair normally. In the drawing my hair is working its way free from a pony tail and hanging in wisps around my face. There's a smudge under one eye like my mascara has run, but the eyes themselves are incredible. It's just a few strokes with a pencil, but he's managed to give them feeling. 'Do I always look this sad?'

'Only when you don't think anybody's watching.' He glances at the floor. 'What would make you happy Emily?'

I don't answer.

'I don't think you should marry Dominic.'

All I can think about is the picture. He drew this for me. I drag my attention to what he's saying.

'I don't think Dominic will make you happy.'

Now I really am cross, and all the perfect drawings and sexy grins and flickering eyes won't change that. I hold the piece of paper in front of him, screw it up and drop it on the floor. 'What's that got to do with you?'

He watches the drawing fall. 'Maybe I'd like it to have a lot to do with me.'

'What do you mean?'

'What if I don't want to be the friend guy? What if I'd prefer to be the guy? Your guy.'

Something inside me jumps. I squash it down. Alex isn't marriage material. Alex is living in the moment and regretting it in the morning material. 'You can't be my boyfriend.'

'Why not?'

'Well you're not sensible. You don't have a proper place to live. You earn peanuts.'

'But you work full time.'

'That's different.'

'How?'

It sounds pathetic even in my head. 'I want someone to look after me.'

Alex almost laughs, and then shakes his head. 'You're a grown-up. You need to look after yourself.'

'But what would it be like?' I can't picture it. I can't picture our home. I can't picture our children. I can't picture the dinner parties with grown-up friends or the two cars on our driveway.

'It'd be however we wanted.'

'Where would we even live?'

'Wherever we want. Here. London. New York. Vegas.' He smiles for the first time. 'Vegas. I've always thought it would be kind of insanely brilliant to actually live in Vegas.'

'You're mad.'

'And I love you.'

Chapter Fifty-Four

Alex

As the words left his lips, Alex closed his eyes. Shit. It was true wasn't it? He loved her. He'd told himself he was doing Helen a favour. He'd thought it might be fun to have a little fling. He hadn't even made it as far as the fling, and now he was in love. He'd been wondering why he hesitated to make his move when she'd been at his house. He'd been wondering why he'd put off calling the speed dating women. He'd been wondering why he'd started staying in and watching TV rather than going out on the pull, and he hadn't had a clue until the words were out of his mouth. Alex was stupid. Stupid and in love.

Emily hadn't said anything, but she hadn't run away either. Alex guessed that meant the ball was still in his court. He took a breath. 'And I think you could love me. And I know you don't love Dominic.'

That must be true, mustn't it? She'd have walked out by now if she did.

'You don't know that. I'm very fond of Dominic.'

That confirmed it. 'I do know that. Nobody under eighty says "very fond" and nobody, of any age, says they're "very fond" of someone they want to shag senseless.'

'There's more to love than shagging each other senseless.'

Alex grinned. 'But it's a really really good start.' He hadn't won her over yet. He needed to do some 'in love' stuff. What did people in love do? 'I could be a boyfriend. I could get a better job. I could get a house. We could go shopping for curtains and look at wallpaper samples.'

Alex's ideas about long-term relationships were hazy, but he suspected they were heavy on DIY.

She shook her head. 'You're all about living in the moment.' But she sounded unsure, less angry than she had before.

'But what's a plan other than a series of moments?' He stepped towards her. 'And I'd do everything I could to make every single moment incredible.'

He left the gap between them. This had to be her decision. She had to take the final pace. She stepped towards him and lifted her face. He pushed his lips against hers, and felt her response. He'd expected her to be tentative, but as soon as their lips touched everything changed. Hands grasped at his belt. His were already tugging at her skirt, until it pulled up over her hips. She kicked her shoes into the corner and stood back from him, just long enough to drag her tights and knickers away and fling the ball into the corner, while he pulled a condom from his wallet and put it on. He pressed her backwards against the wall, and pulled one leg up against his hip, gripping her thigh. He pushed into her and felt her gasp against his neck. He thrust again, desperate to feel everything she could give him. Her fingers clung to his hair. Her breath pressed hot into his neck. He thrust again and again, quick and hard and urgent. They came close together, stickily, gleefully, ecstatically.

Alex paused for a second. He pulled his head back slightly and found her lips again, kissing her more slowly, trying to tell her all the things he wasn't sure how to put into words. Eventually he pulled back.

Their eyes met. She giggled, as she pulled her skirt down.

'Right.' She stopped with her head bent forwards against his chest. Her hair smelt like wildflowers. He kissed the top of her head.

'Yeah.'

Alex stepped back and hauled his jeans and boxers back on, allowing Emily to squeeze past him and retrieve her underwear.

'So what now?' Alex asked the question as casually as he could manage.

Emily leant back against the wall. 'I need to talk to Dom.'

'Yeah.'

She stepped towards the door, and then stopped. 'You won't tell anyone? About this?'

Alex shook his head. 'Not til you've talked to Dominic.'

'Good.' She looked around the room. 'Our little secret then.'

Alex nodded. 'You go first. I'll wait a minute before I come out.'

Emily raised an eyebrow. 'Not your first public toilet then?'

Not his first public toilet, but maybe his last. He gazed into Emily's face. So this was love. 'You could stay a bit longer?'

She looked around. 'Here?'

'No. Obviously. We could go somewhere.'

'I can't.' She looked down at the floor. 'I'm still with Dominic.'

'But just for the time being?'

She nodded, and then shook her head, and nodded again. 'Yeah. I've got to go.'

Chapter Fifty-Five

Emily

I walk back to my office, convinced that everyone can tell. Sienna from main reception says 'Hi,' as I walk past and I jump three feet out of my skin. When I get back to my own corridor, Matt from estates stops me and tries to make chit chat about the weather or the football or the price of petrol or something. I don't take a word of it in. I make my excuses, telling him I'm in a hurry.

'That's all right pet,' he grins. 'Be good! And if you can't be good be careful!'

Be careful? Oh god. Well at least he had a condom. I hear myself laughing as I think that. It could be worse. The laugh turns a bit hysterical. I run to my office, slam the door shut and sit down behind my desk. I pull my emergency chocolate bar from the back of the bottom drawer. This isn't the everyday chocolate bar that I buy from the vending machine every lunchtime and kid myself I'm not going to eat until about half past three when I give up and inhale the whole thing. This is my emergency big bar of chocolate that only gets cracked open in times of extreme need. This is a time of extreme need.

My hands are shaking as I unwrap the chocolate. This is what I do. I mess up. I break things. I push people away. Dom. He's so good, and so right for me, and Alex is all wrong. Helen says he has a different woman every weekend. I'm a notch on his bed post, without the dignity of having made it as far as the bed.

There's a knock at the door. 'Hold on a minute.' I stuff the chocolate back in my drawer, and check my face in the mirror on my desk. It's not too bad. I'm not actually crying, but I'm on the brink of it. I can force myself to be business-like. I can check things on the computer for people. I can be Work Emily. 'Come in.'

It's Dom. Everything stops. He takes the two paces from the door to the desk. I hold my breath. He's going to be able to tell. Or maybe someone saw me coming out of the toilet. Or maybe Alex has already told him. Or maybe I stink of guilt. He smiles. 'Just wanted to check you're still on for dinner tonight?'

I remind myself to breathe and blurt out an answer. 'Yes. Of course. Why wouldn't I be? I said it was fine. Why wouldn't it be fine?' I'm babbling. I must stop talking.

He laughs. 'Okay. Okay. I thought you might be doing wedding stuff.'

I shake my head.

'Good.'

'I'll meet you at the restaurant.'

Wait. No. I'm supposed to be meeting Helen later to go through the charade of sorting out costumes. I'm not going to have time to go home and then out again on the bus. 'Can you pick me up at home?

'Fine.' We arrange a time. He leans across the desk and kisses me quickly before he goes. I start to relax. This is fine. I've bought some time to think. That's all I need. I've got almost five hours before we go for dinner. That's plenty of time to decide what I'm doing with the rest of my life.

I pick up my bag and coat and catch the bus into town on autopilot. Five hours to think, and I spend the first twenty minutes in a daze. I go straight to the shop. The second I walk into the costume room I'm in love. I check with the girl before I start. 'I can try anything on?'

She nods. 'Is it just you?'

I tell her that Helen will be joining me.

'I'll send her up when she gets here.' She gestures to the Aladdin's cave of clothing rails. 'In the meantime, yeah, try anything.'

I can try anything on. For the next hour I can be anybody I like. Anyone other than myself. Sod making decisions about the future. I'm in a lovely dressing up box cocoon. I'm not Emily the scarlet woman. In here I'm an astronaut, or a genie, anybody but me.

Chapter Fifty-Six

Helen

Helen pushed open the door of the costume hire shop. It was every bit as horrendous as she'd imagined. Plastic swords, plastic wigs, plastic masks of politicians – mainly of really out of date politicians. Thatcher, Reagan. There was a George W. Bush and a Barack Obama, but no Tony Blair or David Cameron. Recent Prime Ministers must have boring faces.

A *Myth and History* costume party. The history bit sounded okay. Helen was wondering if she could go as a suffragette. She approached the girl behind the counter.

'I'm here to get a costume for a party tomorrow. I'm supposed to be meeting my friend here.'

The girl nodded. 'Miss Midsomer is already upstairs.' She pointed towards a stairway at the back of the shop. 'All the medieval and Tudor costumes are out on the rack but you can try on whatever you like.'

Helen headed up the stairs. As promised, Emily was already ensconced, standing with her back to the stairwell inspecting her outfit in the full-length mirror in front of her.

'What are you wearing?'

She spun around. 'It's called Sexy Pirate. What do you think?'

It was tiny. 'I'm not sure it's very practical for the high seas. Actually, I'm not sure piracy is a particularly sexy occupation. It's basically smuggling with interludes of kidnap and murder, and incredibly basic living conditions.'

Emily pouted. 'I like it.'

'I'm not sure Dominic'll like it.' Of course Dominic wouldn't like it. He'd prefer something with a bit of class, or wit to it. Helen took a breath. He was with Emily. It wasn't up to Helen to say what he might like. 'And maybe not for your dad's party?'

She shrugged, and started flicking through the clothes on the rails. There were actually some reasonably classy dresses once you worked your way past the sexy pirates and naughty nurses.

'What about this?' Emily held out what appeared to be a green suede bra and a pair of leather pants for her friend's inspection.

'No.'

'It's historic.'

'How?'

'It's called Sexy Outlaw.' Helen could picture Professor Midsomer's face. She could picture her own face.

'What are your dad and Tania wearing?' Helen decided she needed a handle on the general tone of the evening before she started offering further fashion advice.

'Henry the Eighth and Anne Boleyn.'

Helen laughed. 'Does she know what happened to Anne Boleyn?'

Emily shrugged like a girl who couldn't give a toss what happened to Anne Boleyn. 'It's only a costume.'

'You know the theme?'

'Yeah.'

'Well "historic" so I could go as a suffragette or Marie Curie?' Helen suspected she already knew the answer to that. It was going to be pretty history only, wasn't it?

'I think it's supposed to be more like Maid Marion and King Arthur and that.'

Helen shook her head. It wasn't even real history. Not even from one coherent myth construct. She went back to the rails. King Arthur she'd said, and here he was. King Arthur. Chainmail, crown, tabard, sword, the lot. Alex had already sorted his own outfit, but otherwise this would be an option, although it looked like it would be about four sizes too big for Alex. It wasn't Alex she was picturing in the outfit anyway. It was Dominic. It was always Dominic. In this image he was on horseback, riding across fields in full armour, flag flying, just in time to rescue the damsel in distress. Well not rescue obviously. And not damsel. Probably not even distress. Whatever the problem is Helen was sure she could manage fine with it, so he'd be riding to meet up with the independent woman in mild, but ultimately manageable, inconvenience.

She kept one hand on the King Arthur costume and flicked to the next costume on the rail. Guinevere. The dress was dark green velvet with a cream underskirt and gold stitching. Maybe she could get Alex to be King Arthur after all.

'Wow!' Emily grabbed the dress from Helen's hand. 'That's gorgeous.'

'It goes with this.'

She held the King Arthur suit up for her to inspect.

'Fantastic!' She grinned.

It didn't look like Helen would get a shot at the dress then. That was fine. She was happy to let Emily have it. She usually let Emily have what she wanted. Sometimes she wondered if it was her way of over compensating for all the bad thoughts she had about her friend. Helen waved the chainmail. 'I can see Dominic in this.'

Emily nodded but didn't answer. 'What about Alex?'

'What about him?'

'Nothing.' Emily's eyes dropped to the floor. 'Just wondered what he was going to wear.'

Helen shrugged. 'He's already ordered something. Actually, I'm supposed to pick it up.'

Helen ran downstairs to check Alex's order. It was labelled as 'Robin Hood style' and seemed to consist of tunic and tights combo, complete with bow and arrow and also sword. At least he'd be well prepared if things at the party kicked off.

She showed Emily the costume. 'I suppose I should look for something Maid Marian-ish then, if I'm supposed to be his date.'

Emily furrowed her brow. 'You're his date?'

Helen laughed. 'Only because neither of us could find a proper plus one.'

'So it's not like a *date* date?'

Helen shook her head. 'Nah. That would involve Alex committing to spending the whole evening with one woman.'

'And you don't think people can change?'

Another shake of the head. 'Not Alex.' Helen paused. 'Why are we talking about him anyway?'

Emily turned her back. 'I don't know. You started it.'

Had Helen started it? She couldn't remember. 'So Robin Hood and Maid Marian for me and Alex. King Arthur and Guinevere for you and Dominic then?'

Emily nodded. 'I guess so.'

'We'll have to hope there's no one dressed as Lancelot.'

'What do you mean?'

'Well Guinevere had an affair with …'

Emily turned around. 'What are you saying?'

'Nothing.' Helen peered at her friend. She was jumpy today. 'Are you okay?'

Emily nodded. 'Why wouldn't I be?'

'No reason.' Helen went back to looking through the racks.

'Helen, can you do me a favour?'

'Sure. What do you need?'

She smiled. 'It's nothing major. I need you to collect something for me tomorrow afternoon and bring it to the party.'

Chapter Fifty-Seven

Dominic

It was beginning to feel like a very long day. Dominic glanced at the clock and tried to refocus on the final candidate's explanation of why he'd like to work here. It was a waste of time. His presentation had been dreadful. There was already no way this guy was getting the job. Dominic knew it. Mrs Addams knew it. Theo knew it. Dominic suspected that even the candidate knew it. Unfortunately, there was no socially acceptable way of everyone simply acknowledging the fact and agreeing to call a halt to the whole thing, so they asked their questions, took cursory notes on the answers and watched the clock. When Theo finally stood up to show the interviewee out Dominic closed his eyes for a second and leaned his head back between his shoulder blades to try to ease the tiredness in his neck.

Theo came and sat back down. 'Well a decent crop I thought.'

Dominic nodded even though he didn't agree. They were an average crop. It was going to come down to Dr Levine or Helen. Everyone already knew that but they ploughed through the interminable scoring and discussion of each candidate before admitting that out loud.

By the time they officially agreed that it was between Dr Levine and Helen they were knackered. Dominic had scored Helen higher. Theo had scored Dr Levine higher, but not as high as Dominic scored Helen. Mrs Addams from Human Resources felt they were fairly evenly matched, and excused herself to get back to her office. Apparently, she thought the academics could deal with the contentious bit.

'Dr Levine's presentation wasn't as strong.'

'But his research record is more substantial.'

'Dr Hart was better on diversity.'

Theo rolled his eyes.

Dominic saw. 'What's that mean?'

'What does what mean?' Both men were tired, irritable, and ready to be somewhere else.

Dominic inhaled. 'You don't seem to place much importance on diversity and equality.'

Theo shrugged. 'It's a teaching and research job. We should be concentrating on that.'

'Fine.' Dominic spat the word out. 'Helen's a stronger teacher.'

'Dr Hart is a perfectly adequate teacher, but so is Dr Levine.' Theo stood up. 'Again, I can't help but wonder if your judgment is being affected by your personal relationships.'

'Is that why you gave her such a hard time?'

Theo didn't answer.

Dominic paused. 'They're both friends. And I'm starting to wonder why you're so hung up on my friendship with Helen?'

'I'm not,' Theo said grimacing at the phrase, '"hung-up" on your relationship with Dr Hart. I'm wondering whether you are.'

This again. Dominic didn't know what to say. There was no relationship. There never had been, at least not in the way Theo was implying. There'd been a moment, possibly, once, a very long time ago. Dominic stood up. 'I think perhaps we'd better discuss this later.'

Theo shook his head. 'We need to discuss it now.'

'Well if we add both our scores up, Helen wins. Nothing more to discuss.'

'I think we have to weight teaching and research above all this box ticking.'

Dominic reminded himself to hold his temper. He could imagine what Emily would say if he had to take time out from the wedding reception to argue with her Dad about academic appointment criteria. 'It's not box ticking. It's widening participation.'

Professor Midsomer closed his eyes. Just for a second Dominic could see the old man, usually obscured by Theo's vigour and constant activity. Maybe Dominic wasn't the only one who harboured thoughts of a different life. 'But teaching and research are the things. That's what we're actually here for.'

'Maybe we could make a final decision when you get back?' It seemed unfair to make the candidates wait, but they weren't getting anywhere. 'Sleep on it?' Dominic was aiming for a conciliatory tone. The words were right at least.

Theo nodded. 'As you wish.'

Dominic left without saying anything more. Why was he so angry? Yes. He was friends with Helen. Yes. He wanted her to get this job. Did the accusation of bias hurt because it was true? He tried to run the two interviews through in his head. However he thought about it, he did genuinely believe Helen was the better candidate. He was angry on her behalf as well. She had been overlooked, and she was a brilliant lecturer. He wanted to see her get a chance.

Chapter Fifty-Eight

Emily

'I'm not in for dinner.' I'm expecting Tania to have a go at me for not letting her know earlier. Right now I'd love her to have a go at me. I could take all the stuff that's rushing through my head and channel it all into taking her down.

'Fine.' She's sat in the conservatory with Dad with the laptop on her knee. I stick my head through the kitchen door before I go through to them. There's nothing even in the oven anyway. I make myself take four deep breaths before I go through. I'm not going to say anything to her today. I'm going to wait until I've got all the evidence. I'm not going to give her time to come up with a lie or an excuse. I go into the conservatory and sit on the armchair. 'I said I won't be in for dinner. Dom's taking me out.'

I don't dwell on that. Dom's taking me out and I'm going to tell him it's over. Probably. It has to be over, doesn't it? Otherwise what happened with Alex was definitely cheating. I'm not a cheater. I know what some people think of me. They think I'm spoilt. They think I'm self-involved. But I don't cheat. I keep trying not to think about the evening, trying not to picture Dom's face, or imagine what I'm actually going to say. It's just a vague distant thing in the future.

'That's fine.' Tania is all smiley. 'I haven't even started making anything.'

My dad looks at his watch. 'We could get takeaway. Or go out?'

Dad never suggests takeaway, or going out on a week night.

'Chinese? I'd love a Chinese.' Tania scurries off into the kitchen to find a menu.

I wait for her to get back. 'Full of MSG. That's like so bad for you. And you'd better not have fried rice. You've still got a wedding dress to get into.'

I hear myself doing this to her all the time. It's becoming a habit I can't break. She looks at me. 'The dress fits fine.'

She turns to my dad. 'Anyway, do you think we should tell Emily what we're discussing?'

He nods. My stomach tightens. I knew she was acting weird. Maybe she's pregnant. She can't be. She's too old, isn't she? I can picture it. Tania lolling around the place all day with a horrendous screaming brat latched to her boob.

My dad's talking. I try to tune in. '... been thinking about it for a while, but I'm wondering if it's the right time to retire.'

Retire? That means he'll be lolling around the house all day. Better than a baby at least. It won't happen though. I laugh. 'Oh Dad. You're never going to retire. You're a workaholic.'

He nods. 'That has certainly been true, but I'm getting older, Emmy, and it's all bureaucracy these days. A younger man's game I think.'

He sounds serious. That means I'll be working for someone else. I've always worked for my dad. Ever since I dropped out of university as a student after one term, and he got me the junior departmental assistant job, I've always worked for him. A new boss. I'm not sure I like that.

Dad keeps talking. 'And, once I've retired, we think that it's time for Tania and I to make a new life for the two of us.' He glances at her. 'So we're thinking of moving. To Northumbria maybe.'

Tania spins the laptop around so I can see. It's an estate agency site. Houses in the country. Cottages by the coast.

Outbuildings. Secluded gardens. Sea views. All that crap. Northumbria. It's where we used to go on holidays when I was little, after Mum... went away. 'You can't move to Northumbria.'

Tania responds. 'Why not?'

'Well, where will I live? I live here.'

My dad smiles. 'Well I don't think you'll be living here much longer anyway.'

'What do you mean?'

'Come on. I know things are getting serious with Professor Collins. You're not going to want to live with your dad once you're married, are you?'

'Well ...' And I can't finish the sentence, because that is the plan, isn't it? Marry Dom. Live with him. He can take care of me, and provide for me and for our children, and maybe I won't even have to worry about the new boss. Probably I could stop work altogether to look after our perfect babies and do yoga, like Tania, and meet people for lunch. Somewhere in the back of my head there's a voice, Alex's voice, telling me something different, but I decide to ignore it. I'm not like him or Helen. I'm not strong. I need looking after. Dom can do that. There's nothing wrong with letting him.

Chapter Fifty-Nine

Helen

Helen leant on the door frame at the entrance to Dominic's office. It was almost seven. Most of the offices were empty already. 'Still here?'

He jumped in his chair, and scooped something off the desk into his pocket. 'What are you doing back here? I thought you were with Em.'

She could lie. Pretend to have forgotten her keys or something. In truth she gravitated back here. Everything she loved was in this building. Her work, for one thing. She shrugged. 'Just finishing up. What've you got there?'

'Nothing.'

She wasn't sure what to say now. She couldn't ask him about the interview, and she didn't have a reason for coming to talk to him. She didn't really have a reason for being in this corridor. It wasn't on the way from her office to the way out. It was just that she walked this way every day, and usually Dominic had already gone or his door was shut because he was out teaching or in a tutorial, but she walked this way every day, because that was what she did.

'You interviewed well.'

'Thanks.' She forced herself not to ask.

'We've not made a final decision yet.'

'That's okay.' It was always the same. She didn't know what she thought would happen; that he'd ask her for a drink, that a drink would turn into dinner and that all of a sudden they'd be dating. Sometimes they did go for a drink, but a drink was simply a drink. His hand never accidentally on purpose brushed her leg. He didn't insist on buying her 'just one more' when it was time they ought to be going. They didn't have moments. They'd had one moment, and it was so long ago that Helen had started to wonder whether it was a moment at all, or whether she'd simply thought about it so hard that she'd imagined it into being something that it never was. 'I'd better get going.'

'Wait. Actually, have you got a minute?'

'Course.'

'Come in then.' He stood and shut the office door behind her. 'There was something I'd like to ask you.'

She sat on the chair next to his desk. 'Anything.'

Dominic rummaged in his pocket and pulled out a box. You know the sort of box. Small. Expensive looking.

'Oh.'

He flicked it open. 'What do you think of this? I ... I don't know ... I don't buy a lot of jewellery.'

'No.' It was beautiful. Helen had never dreamed of getting married. It wasn't one of her fantasies, but if she was ever going to get engaged, this would be the ring. A super slim band of gold, proper gold, not white gold or platinum like was trendy now, and a single large round opal. It was exquisitely restrained. 'It's perfect.'

'Do you think so? I'm terrified she won't like it.'

She? Right. Of course. Emily. 'I'm sure she'll love it.'

Helen stood up. 'I really do have to get going I'm afraid.' She pulled the door open and half-ran through it. She kept running along the corridor and into the ladies' toilet. It was empty. She locked herself in a cubicle and sat down on the lid. She knew this was coming. If it hadn't been Emily it would have been someone else. Helen sat very still. She remembered fainting once. She was fifteen and it was hot and she hadn't eaten enough, and she'd simply passed out. Right before it happened, everything around her went dark. The blackness had appeared in a ring all around the edges of her vision and then rushed inwards, until there was no light visible at all. That was what this was like, only this darkness had always been there at the edge of everything. She'd kept it at bay by keeping busy, making jokes, pretending it wasn't there at all, but now the blackness was all she could see. It was filling everything and she couldn't imagine it ever going away.

Chapter Sixty

Alex

Helen was sitting on the floor in the middle of the living room. Alex stood in the doorway. 'What's the matter?'

She held up her empty bottle for him to inspect.

'The vodka's broken.'

'What do you mean broken?'

She tipped the bottle upside down to show that no more would come out. 'See. Broken.'

'That was three quarters full. You didn't drink all that?'

Helen put the bottle down on the floor and clapped her hands together. 'Vodka all gone.' Her brow furrowed for a second. 'Need to get more.'

Alex watched her tip herself from sitting to all fours and then stop as she tried to work out what to do with her limbs next to get to vertical. Sympathy eventually overtook curiosity as to how she might manage it, and he put one arm around her back and helped her up and then over to the sofa.

'I think you might have had enough vodka.' He picked the bottle from the floor. 'Seriously you drank all that? I've never seen you have more than two glasses of wine before.'

Helen shrugged. 'Vodka doesn't count. Is like water. Just goes straight through.'

He sat next to her. 'Why did you drink all the vodka? What happened?'

'Nothing.'

It clearly wasn't nothing. His never-out-of-control, never-irresponsible landlady was hammered. Properly hammered. Truly gloriously hammered. She had achieved a level of inebriation of which even Alex himself would have felt rightfully proud. 'Did you not get the job?'

'Don't know yet.'

'Then what?'

A silent shrug.

'Tell me. We're mates. I want to help.'

'Dominic.'

'What about him?'

'He's going to marry her.'

'I don't think so.'

'He is. I saw the ring. S'lovely.'

Alex shook his head. 'That just means he's going to ask her. She might say no.'

'She won't say no. I don't want her to say no.'

'Why not?'

Helen took the vodka bottle off him and had a fruitless attempt to get another slug from it. 'It'd break his heart. Broken heart's all shitty.'

'But you could help him pick up the pieces.'

Helen shook her head. 'He loves Emily. No point.'

Alex paused. 'She won't say yes.' He was absolutely sure of that. No matter what she was thinking about him. No matter that she was ignoring his calls. Emily Midsomer was not a woman ready for marriage.

'How do you know?'

Alex paused again. 'I know.'

'How?'

'Because she's seeing someone else.'

'She's not. She'd have told me.'

Alex shook his head. 'No. She wouldn't. You'd have told Dominic.'

Helen frowned. 'So who's she seeing?'

'Me.'

Alex watched Helen's face. The wonder of alcohol meant

that her usually closed-book exterior was showing all of her mental working. She was puzzled and then momentarily amused, before she frowned again. 'But Emily's with Dominic. That's really ...' She tailed off.

'Really what?'

'Really ... bad.'

'But not if she's not supposed to be with him. I sort of did it for you.'

'Did what for me?'

'Shagged Emily.'

'Don't be ridiculous.'

Alex stopped. It was ridiculous. It was a perfectly decent rationalisation. Helen loved Dominic, so it was the act of a caring friend to break up Emily and Dominic. He reviewed the thought. Actually it was a completely terrible justification, and it was also a lie. Even if Emily wasn't actually engaged yet, she was in a serious relationship. A serious relationship with a senior work colleague. Thinking about it now, it did seem like the whole situation could be construed as breaking the age old good advice about not defecating in one's own dining area.

'I think I need a drink.' Alex got up and moved towards the kitchen.

'You can't. I drunked all the drink. All the drink.'

He laughed. 'I've got a secret stash I nicked from the minibar at the last wedding I went to.'

Helen shook her head and pointed at the plastic wastepaper bin in the corner. Alex peered. Six individual bottles sat amongst what looked like about two thirds of a box of tissues. 'Bloody hell. When you go for it, you really go for it.' He sat back down. 'Are you mad with me?'

'Too fuzzy-headed to be mad.' Helen leant forward as if she was going to try to stand up, and then slumped straight backwards again.

'Do you think you might be mad with me in the morning?'

'Don't know.' She stopped. 'Can't talk. Need to concentrate.'

'On what?'

'Not sicking.'

Alex jumped off the sofa and grabbed the bin. He held it in front of Helen. 'You sick all you need.'

'No.' Helen shook her head. 'I'm never sick. However drunk I get, never been sick.'

She closed her eyes. Alex watched her breathing in and out, clearly concentrating hard. Eventually she gave up and sat forward, bending her head over the bin as she retched.

Alex rubbed her back. 'First time for everything, ay?'

Chapter Sixty-One

Dominic

Dominic sat at the very pleasant table in the very pleasant restaurant and waited for his very pleasant girlfriend to come back from the, undoubtedly, very pleasant toilets. He ran through what he was going to say one more time in his head. Was this the right approach? It was what he'd planned all along, but now she was half expecting the question was it enough? Should he be doing some all-singing, all-dancing affair and posting it on YouTube? Should he have hidden the ring somewhere, in the wine maybe? It was too late now. He'd picked this restaurant and this night, and he'd asked her father like he was supposed to, and if he didn't do it soon then questions were going to be asked about what on earth he was playing at.

Emily came back to the table and took her seat opposite him.

'Emily.'

'Mmm?'

'Emily, you know that I'm very fond of you, don't you?'

'Very fond?' She sounded underwhelmed with the sentiment.

'What? Well ...' Dominic paused. He was so much his father's son. Warm words and effusive gestures were not in his repertoire. He was proposing though. Finding the right words mattered tonight. He tried to think of what he ought to be saying. 'Sorry.'

She shook her head slightly. 'It just sounds a bit formal.'

'Sorry.' This was going badly. Dominic took a breath. Say the right thing, for goodness sake. 'Of course, I'm more than fond of you. Emily, if you'll let me you know that I would never let you down, don't you?'

She nodded.

'I'll take care of you. I'll do whatever I can to look after you and make sure you have everything you need, and maybe one day, if we have children, well you know I would care for them too, don't you?'

Another silent nod.

He reached into his pocket and found the ring box. He flicked it open and held the open box out across the table.

She took a deep breath in.

'I was hoping that you would do me the honour of becoming my wife?'

Emily was still staring at the ring. She nodded quietly.

'Is that a yes?'

She nodded again.

Behind Dominic a small volley of applause broke out. He looked around. He hadn't realised that the adjacent tables were quite so aware of what was going on. He raised a hand in acknowledgement and tried to look nonchalant.

'Right.' Dominic lifted the ring out of the box and moved to slide it onto his new fiancée's finger. 'It fits.'

Emily was staring at her finger. 'It's not very sparkly.'

'You don't like it?'

She nodded and then shook her head and then stopped. 'It's very pretty.'

'I mean we can change it. You can choose something for yourself if you want. I don't mind.'

Emily stared at the ring. 'No. It's lovely. It'll be just right.'

His lips formed a smile. 'So that's a yes?

Emily gave a tiny nod. 'Yes.'

Part Three

Summer

Chapter Sixty-Two

Helen
Midsummer's Eve

There were noises. There were banging noises. Helen did not like the noises. She screwed her eyes up, pulled the duvet over her head and pretended the noises weren't happening.

'Helen. Helen.' It was Alex. Then the banging noise started again. It wasn't banging. It was the thing with the door. Knocking. There was knocking. Helen stuck her head out and tried to open her eyes.

'What?'

'Time to get up.'

No. No. At least she knew he was wrong about that. The one and only redeeming element of yesterday's horrendousness was that Helen knew she didn't have to get up today. She wasn't teaching. There were no departmental meetings. She had to collect something from the library for Emily but that wasn't until this afternoon, and then there was the party this evening. She shut the thought down as quickly as she could. The Midsummer Party, where Dominic and Emily would be together, all shiny and fresh and perky and newly-engaged. Helen took a deep breath and felt herself gag on it. She decided not to think about the party. It wasn't for hours yet.

'Go away.'

'You've got to get up. I've made coffee.'

Interesting. 'Proper coffee?'

There was a pause. 'Sure.'

'You're lying.' Helen put her head back under the duvet.

'I'm coming in.'

The door opened.

'Go away. Still sleeping.'

'Are you decent?'

'What?' She stuck her head out. Alex was standing in the corner of the room with a coffee mug in one hand and the other covering his eyes.

'Yes. I'm decent.' She looked down. She was more than decent. She was still fully dressed in yesterday's clothes. 'Why are you waking me up?'

'It's time.' He pointed at the clock. It was half past nine, which was late for Helen, but not the sort of time that justified a person's lodger forcing them from their beauty sleep.

'What for?'

'For Operation Win Back Your Man.'

'What?'

'I thought about it after you'd gone to bed last night. It's stupid. You should be with Dominic. You need to stop sitting around on your arse waiting for him to realise that. You need to make it happen.'

Helen sat up in bed and held out her hand. 'Coffee.' He passed the mug and she took a sip. 'This is instant.'

Alex shrugged. 'Not the point.'

Helen closed her eyes and leant back on the headboard sipping the terrible coffee. She didn't deserve proper coffee. She deserved to sit here, with small impish creatures banging hammers against the backs of her eyeballs, and have a good long think about what she'd done. She was a terrible person. She'd drunk everything there was to drink in the house, and been sick in the bin. She'd had to be dragged up the stairs to bed – literally dragged, having sat down halfway up and refused to move until Alex got hold of her under the arms and hauled. And she did all of that because someone who had absolutely no idea that she was in love with him decided to get engaged, which he was entirely entitled to do, and he was entirely entitled to expect her to be happy about, because so far as he was concerned they were just good friends. Helen was a terrible friend, she decided, a terrible friend who was absolutely, definitely, with 100% certainty never ever drinking alcohol again.

Something about what Alex was saying started to filter into her fuzzy aching brain. 'Operation what?'

'Win Back Your Man.' He said it with a weird American accent.

'Why are you saying it like that?'

'It's my Tammy Wynette voice.'

'That was stand by your man.'

'Same concept.' He sat on the end of the bed. 'The point is that you're going to get him back.'

'Dominic?'

'Exactly.'

'I can't get him back. I never had him. Anyway I'm getting over him.'

Alex raised an eyebrow. 'How's that going?'

'It's a work in progress.' Helen took a deep breath, and dredged her memories of the night before. One thing rippled to the surface. Alex was a terrible person too. 'I thought you said Emily was going to say no anyway.'

He nodded. 'She will.'

'You haven't heard from her?'

He shook his head. 'Think her phone must be off.'

'Why does Operation Win Back Your Man have to start so early?'

Alex looked at her. He was not making a happy face. 'Well you need to be looking fabulous tonight if you're going to lure him away from Emily.'

'I thought Emily was going to say no.'

Alex paused. 'Then you need to look fabulous tonight if you're going to lure him out of his post-dumping depression.'

'What's wrong with how I always look?'

'Nothing. It's fine. Well no. It's horrendously middle-aged. You have cardigans older than me.'

'That's an exaggeration.' Actually, she did have charity shop cardigans that might have been older than him. She tried a different defence. 'They're vintage.'

'They're ancient. And I thought maybe we could do hair and make-up. The whole deal.'

Helen wasn't really a hair and make-up sort of woman. She could imagine what Alex was picturing. He'd be working on the notion that if he dressed her up and made her perfect looking, Dominic would see her across the crowded party and their eyes would meet. Helen knew he shouldn't have been allowed to watch so many romantic comedies at a formative age. Romance movies were at the root of a lot of people's problems, Helen thought. It was no use going through life thinking that if you maintained a ditzy yet loveable persona then 'happy ever afters' would fall in your lap.

That wasn't the point. Her vodka-addled brain struggled for a moment to remember what the point was. Oh yes. Alex wanted to do her hair. She wasn't going to win an argument with him in his current mood. She could point out that he'd devised a whole plan, when a sensible and mature person would deal with the fact that they might not have got the girl, but he wouldn't listen. She was going to be primped and preened and dressed up like a Barbie doll whether she agreed or not.

'A bit of hair and make-up isn't going to take all day.'

Alex leant forward and patted her hand. 'You didn't see what you looked like last night. I sort of thought the first few hours would be jet washing the congealed sick off your face.'

She closed her eyes again. She really was a terrible person.

Chapter Sixty-Three

Emily

Arden Manor is beautiful. It's a rambling old stately home, with gardens and woodland all around it. I sip my champagne and take a half-hearted walk about the room. It's annoying to know that it's going to be so utterly tarnished by all the rabid Tania-ness that there's absolutely no way I'm going to be able to have my own wedding here. 'So is the building like Victorian or something?'

Dom is sitting in the lounge. He glances up from his copy of the *Guardian*. 'I think the oldest parts are medieval, but it's been added to.' He twists in his seat and peers through towards the function room, which armies of Mia's little worker bees are currently decorating with ivy and wildflowers. I shudder thinking of all the bugs and spiders there must be in amongst the foliage. 'I'd guess that was eighteenth century. It might have been rebuilt since then though.'

I sit down next to him, and get my phone out. They're late. It'll be Tania's fault. She'll be cleansing her aura or balancing her chakras or something before she leaves the house. Maybe it would be better to tell him next week anyway, once she's out of the picture.

'Do you think we should tell them after the wedding?'

Dom furrows his brow. 'I thought you'd want to tell everybody straight away.'

I nod. 'I do. I do. I just don't want to steal Dad and Tania's thunder.' That sounds reasonable doesn't it? Not stealing their thunder is a nice thing.

'But that's why we came early. So we could tell them before anyone else got here.'

Solid. Reliable. Secure. That's Dom. Also stubborn, hard to distract, dogged. He's right though. That is why we came early.

'Sweetheart.'

I stand up when Dad comes in and hug him, properly hug him. When he pulls away he goes straight to the other side of the table and sits down by Tania.

'I thought you'd be here ages ago.'

Tania shrugs. 'The party isn't for another two hours. We've got plenty of time.'

'We've been waiting for you.' To be fair, it's not exactly been onerous. I told a bored-looking girl that all my drinks would be on Daddy's bill and she brought us champagne, which Dom doesn't like anyway.

'I'll get some more glasses.' Dom goes to the bar, and the three of us sit for a moment. Tania leans closer towards my dad and wraps her fingers around his. I take a big swig of my champagne. It's a relief when Dom comes back and I can concentrate on the bustle of drinks being poured and handed out.

So here we are. Dom takes hold of my hand. 'Do you want to tell them what we're celebrating, or shall I?'

I don't want Tania to be here. It should just be my dad. Me and my dad. That's how it's always been and it's always worked absolutely fine. Everything's changing. Even if he doesn't marry Tania, that's only a temporary solution. There could be another Tania along at any moment. I need security, and that means Dom. I take a gulp of champagne. 'Well, we wanted to talk to you before the party, because we wanted to tell you that ...' Another, bigger gulp of champagne. '... We're engaged!'

Apparently this is wonderful news. Dad shakes Dom by the hand. That leaves me with Tania. 'Congratulations.'

She leans forward to hug me. I turn my head and keep

my arms down by my side, forcing her to lightly kiss my cheek and then back off. 'Thank you.'

'You must be very excited?'

'Of course.'

'And the ring?'

I hold my hand out for her. I can't help but keep thinking that it could be sparklier.

'Oh. It's beautiful. So elegant.' She steps back and addresses both of us. 'So when's the big day going to be?'

'No hurry,' I say.

'Soon.' Dom answers simultaneously. There's a moment of silence before we remember to laugh.

'I meant no hurry until after this wedding.' I carry on the laugh, but now everyone else has stopped, it's just me giggling manically. I stop. I suppose there's no reason to wait, is there? There's a voice in my head telling me I'm young, that I don't need to be settled down anytime soon. I don't want to listen to that voice. It sounds a lot like Alex. This is my choice. Me and Dom, and a nice home, a flat nearby for my dad, and four beautiful children. I'm going to fill my time with wedding plans, and supper with friends, and book groups, and mother and baby coffee mornings. If I fill all my time then there'll be no space for the darkness and the worry to get in, and I'll be tired, but good, happy tired so I sleep every night without fear.

We all sip our champagne, and I let the conversation carry on around me. That's it then. It's official. Telling people makes it real. I like that idea. It sort of implies that things you don't tell anyone about aren't real. Those things can fade away into nothingness if you never speak of them, if you never tell.

Chapter Sixty-Four

Helen

Helen had been brushed and teased and plumped up and squashed down, to the point where Alex finally deemed her party-ready. The medieval Maid Marian dress she was squeezed into was underpinned by some fairly serious boning and lacing. There were bits of Helen she hadn't previously known she had fighting for air out of the top of her corset. Alex had also done her hair, in a style selected by the method of Googling 'Medieval party hair' and then spending an hour watching YouTube clips of American teenagers demonstrating how to do post graduate level plaiting. She was sporting a hair do that her housemate promised said "Medieval maiden" but risked tipping over into "Princess Leia on a bad day". 'I feel silly.'

'You look great. Can we go in yet?'

Helen peered through the windscreen. They were parked outside Arden Manor. 'Not until I see someone else in costume.'

'Don't be daft.'

'What if we're the only ones?' This was why Helen didn't do fancy dress. It was stomach-churning. It reminded her of walking to school on non-uniform days looking out for other kids, terrified that she'd turn up and realise that she'd got the wrong day.

'We won't be the only ones. And anyway, we look cool.' Alex used the rear-view mirror to set his Robin Hood hat at a jaunty angle. 'Come on.'

The entrance hall was lovely but they were the only guests around. Helen kept her coat pulled tight around her, pending sightings of further costumes.

'Welcome to Arden Manor. My name is Nick. Are you attending the Midsomer-Highpole wedding?'

The young man looked familiar. 'Nick? You were on my first year module last year?'

The boy leant forward and dropped his voice to a whisper. 'I'm like working Doctor Hart. We're not supposed to like ...' He paused, searching for a word. 'Fraternise.'

'Sorry.' Helen stifled a giggle. 'Yes. We're here for the wedding.'

'Very good. Will you be staying with us overnight?'

'Yes.'

'Excellent.' He gestured behind him. 'My colleague ...' He tailed off and looked around for his colleague. 'Frankie!' he yelled. A young red-headed woman appeared, apparently from nowhere.

'What?'

'My colleague, Frankie, will find your keys. You are welcome to go up to your room, or make your way directly ...' On the word directly he pointed smartly towards some double doors to his left. '... into the Midsummer Ball.'

Helen leant forward. 'Are other people dressed up Nick?'

He furrowed his brow. 'The ball is in historical times. Guests are dressed historically.'

Helen couldn't stop herself pursing her lips. The boy was a history student. 'Which historical times Nick?'

He shrugged. 'Like olden days, but with fairies and that.'

'Thank you Nick.' Alex dragged her away. 'It's a party. You're not going to be examined on the authenticity of your costume.'

They collected their room keys – after a brief bit of haggling to explain that they'd definitely booked separate rooms. 'So check out the room?'

Alex screwed up his face. 'Party!' He handed their bags to the red-headed girl, and wrestled Helen out of her coat.

Nick's official pointing sent them towards a pair of heavy wooden doors, standing open. She ran her fingers over the grain. Alex pointed at the carving above the doors.

'The Green Man.'

Helen nodded.

'You know that term wasn't even coined until just before World War Two?'

She turned. Dominic was standing behind them. She scanned his face. Did he look happy or sad? Newly engaged or newly rejected? Maybe he hadn't proposed. Maybe he'd got cold feet.

Alex shook his head. 'Really? Green Man sounds like it should be proper old.'

'Proper old?' Dominic raised an eyebrow.

Helen was still staring at Dominic. She ought to greet him. She ought to ask how last night went, although the fact that he was here and not weeping into a pint somewhere a very long way away from Emily could probably be interpreted as a strong hint. What should she do about that? Whatever Alex thought there was no way Dominic was going to take one look at her heaving bosoms and fall into her arms. She'd been all set to let him marry Emily. She was going to be a good friend and buy a hat and everything, but now she knew what Emily had done. She knew what Alex had done. She was losing track of who she was supposed to be a good friend to at each given moment. Thinking about it was too much. She turned her attention through the doors and towards the party.

The room was huge and had been covered in ivy and wildflowers. At the far end the doors opened onto a garden, and revellers were spilling outside into the evening sun. The guests, Helen was relieved to see, had embraced the costume theme and the room thronged with medieval damsels sipping cocktails with elven lords, and fairies chatting happily to chainmailed knights at the buffet table.

'Shall we?' Alex pushed past Dominic and put his hand on her elbow. So, apparently that was the plan. They would be each other's moral support, plus one, and physical buffer zone to ensure the maintenance of a safe distance from any fellow party guests who might represent a source of potential emotional disquiet.

She took his arm. 'Let's.'

They stepped through the double doors and into the throng. A black-shirted girl appeared in front of them with a tray, and Alex grabbed two glass cups of suspiciously pink liquid. Helen put a hand on the girl's shoulder. 'What is it?'

'Summer fruit punch.'

'What's in it?'

'Well fruit.' She paused. 'Mostly.'

Alex pressed both cups into her hands and took two more. 'Excellent. Fruit is good for you.'

Helen took a sip of the punch. It tasted pink. 'I said I was never drinking again.'

Alex glanced back over his shoulder towards Dominic. 'Trust me. You can start that tomorrow.'

'Find the lady?'

'What?' There was a fairy, or possibly elf – Helen was not a fully paid-up expert on the distinctions – sitting at a small table, sliding three playing cards around and around in front of him.

'Find the lady and win a prize?'

'What sort of prize?'

He laughed. 'It doesn't matter. You're not going to win.'

He flipped over all three cards to show the Queen of Hearts sitting serenely in the middle, before turning them over again and starting to slide them, face down, across the table. Helen watched his hands, trying to keep an eye on the middle card. Round and round they went. Her eyes moved in time with his hands. It was almost hypnotic. Eventually he came to a stop.

'So find the lady.'

She still had a cup of punch in each hand, so no finger free to point. After a moment's fluster she downed the contents of one cup and set it on a passing waiter's tray. She pointed at the nearest card.

The elf flipped it over. Two of spades. He laughed. 'Bad luck. Try again?'

Helen shook her head. She knew when she was beaten and the spinning hands and the rapidly gulped punch were making her head whirl. Alex leant over her shoulder. 'I'll have a go.'

He set his cup down on the edge of the card table. Putting the cup on the table? Helen bristled. She hadn't thought of that.

The elf grinned. 'All right then. Here she is.' He flipped the remaining cards over to reveal the Queen. 'Keep your eyes on her.'

Watching the guy's hands was making Helen's head spin unpleasantly. She took a sip from her second punch cup and stepped away.

'Doctor Hart!' Professor Midsomer clasped her hand and shook it enthusiastically. Very enthusiastically. Helen wondered how much punch he'd had. 'So pleased you could make it.'

'It's a lovely party.' That's what Helen actually said when what she was thinking was, 'Why the hell haven't I heard about the job yet? You must have decided. You could have let me know and then I wouldn't have had to get dressed up in this ridiculous get-up and troop down to this, very lovely but hugely expensive, party at all.' But she didn't say that, which was, she thought, supremely professional and evidence of why he should have offered her the job already.

A woman she didn't recognise appeared at Professor Midsomer's shoulder. 'Theo!'

'Isabel!'

The pair exchanged cheek kisses. 'Have you met Doctor Hart?'

The woman turned. 'Dr Hart? Helen Hart? Would I have read a paper on female abolitionists?'

Helen nodded. 'Last year?'

'Fascinating. Although I wondered about your linking of abolition with prison reform.'

What had Alex's advice for the evening been? *It's a party, not a conference.* Apparently that meant that she was supposed to talk about what Alex termed 'fun things', which, she guessed, didn't include the frankly very obvious parallels between the abolitionist movement and early prison reformers. Maybe it was best to keep things general rather than getting drawn into an argument. 'You're interested in slavery? I mean abolition.'

The woman shrugged. 'Not specifically. It's not really my area, although there are cultures that still practise slavery, of course.'

Helen nodded. Alex would almost certainly not consider slavery a party-topic. 'I'm sorry. I didn't catch your name.'

The woman held out a slim, heavily-ringed hand. 'Isabel Sutton.'

Oh God. Isabel Sutton. Professor Isabel Sutton was head of the inter-disciplinary centre for gender studies in Manchester. She was practically famous. Not just an anthropologist, but an anthropologist who'd been on telly. BBC Four admittedly, but it was still telly. And radio too. Helen was at a party talking to an actual person who'd been on the Moral Maze. The light-headed feeling rushed back. She took another gulp of punch. If it were socially acceptable for professional academics to have posters of their crushes on their bedroom wall, Helen would have had Isabel Sutton. How could she have failed to recognise her? The fact that Professor Sutton was wearing a medieval serving wench outfit complete with cotton bonnet might not have helped.

And Helen had been trying to keep things light and not get into a lengthy academic monologue. She was Professor Isabel Sutton. She could take it. She probably thought Helen was an imbecile for not robustly defending her paper the moment she mentioned it. Helen opened her mouth.

'Well it was lovely to meet you.' Professor Sutton was moving away. 'I probably better get back to my partner.'

'Elizabeth Fry!' Helen blurted the name at Isabel's retreating back, but it was too late. She muttered it again for good measure. 'Elizabeth Fry.'

'I lost.' Alex appeared fresh from a failure to "find the lady". 'What about Elizabeth Fry?'

'She was a noted prison reformer with an interest in abolishing the slave trade.'

'Okay.' The tone of his voice implied that it was not okay, but that he didn't really want to enquire further.

Chapter Sixty-Five

Emily

'They're over there.' Dom points across the room to where Helen and Alex are standing. Alex. I feel sick.

'They're probably busy.'

Dom looks at me. 'It's a party. How would they be busy?'

I shrug. It was a stupid thing to say, but we can't go over there. In my imagination I think I thought I could somehow not see Alex all night.

'Come on.' Dom starts across the room.

I scramble to catch up. 'Do you want another drink?'

He shakes his head.

'I wonder what's outside.'

'What?'

'Tania wanted a trapeze.' I point towards the exit. He's staring at me. He can tell, can't he? My face must be burning red. My hands are sweating.

He shrugs. 'I thought you'd want to tell Helen.'

'I do.'

'Well now's as good a time as any.' He pauses. 'I guess she'll be your bridesmaid.'

Bridesmaid? Well it makes sense doesn't it? We're engaged, so of course we'd be thinking about our wedding. And weddings have bridesmaids, don't they? I nod. 'I guess so.'

'Come on then.'

He grabs my hand and I have no choice but to follow in his wake across the party, buffeting maidens and woodland folk out of the way as we go. Alex is still there. We can't tell them. I have to think of something. I have to do something.

Dom comes to a halt. 'Hello again.'

I stand next to him, keeping hold of his hand. My fiancé's hand. I'm aware that I'm looking at the floor. I need to stop that. I raise my eyes. There he is. Alex. Stupid, impulsive, skinny, unreliable Alex. Our eyes meet, and that feeling comes rushing back – the drowning feeling where I'm cut adrift with nothing to hold onto at all. I try to tell him something with my eyes, but I'm not sure what. Sorry? Don't say anything? I can explain? It's too much to put into a look, and I'm not sure it's all true anyway. I definitely am sorry, but I have no idea how I'd even start to explain. I break away and try to tune into Helen and Dom's conversation. It seems to be about Elizabeth Fry. I try to concentrate. Helen leans towards him. 'And have you seen some of the costumes?'

Dom laughs. 'I know.' He gestures at his own outfit and then Alex's. 'King Arthur and Robin Hood. I mean we're not even a consistent set of made up people.'

She laughs too. 'That's what I thought.'

I look around the room. I think people look nice.

'Anyway we have news.' Dom smiles in my direction. 'You might have already noticed, but ...' He tails off. 'Do you want to tell them?'

I shake my head, trying to keep smiling. I'm not sure I trust myself to speak.

I feel Dominic's grip on my hand tighten. 'Emily and I are engaged. We're going to get married.'

There's a second before anyone says anything. It must only be a second but it feels like more. I can't look at Alex, so I keep my eyes on Helen. Just for this one second her face seems to seize up. It's like she shuts down completely and then reboots into happy mode, but there's a gap. It's not a gap where she looks sad, or shocked, or angry, or excited. It's not a gap where she looks anything at all, but for a second she stopped, and then she remembered that she was happy and she carried on. I wonder if my face looks like that at the moment. I push the corners of my lips up higher and harder. I'm happy. So very happy.

'Congratulations!' Helen wraps her arms around Dom in slightly awkward hug and then comes and wraps her arms round me. 'Congratulations! You must be overjoyed.'

I nod, because what else am I going to do? As she releases me from the hug I allow myself a tiny glance at Alex. He's looking away. Please don't let him say anything. He has to understand. This is what I have to do. Dom can give me what I need.

Alex breaks into a grin. 'Another single guy bites the dust, then?' He shakes Dom's hand. 'I won't complain. That's one less shark in the water for the rest of us.'

Dom smiles but doesn't laugh. I'm not sure he would ever really have been considered a shark in the water.

Alex is still grinning. 'So we're celebrating? We should probably raise a glass then.'

'I don't want to drink too much.' Helen tries to excuse herself from the round.

'Don't be daft. I'll get some more punch. You heard the girl. It's mainly fruit.'

I suspect it's mainly fruit in the same way that vodka is mainly potato, but I don't say anything. I could use a drink. Alex flags down a passing waiter and starts handing cups of punch around. My fingertips brush his hand as I take a cup. If he notices he doesn't show it. He turns back towards us. 'To the happy couple.'

Helen nods. 'The happy couple.'

I chink my cup against Dom's and take a sip of punch.

Alex swigs most of his cup down in one go. 'Well we better not keep you. I'm sure you've got lots of people you want to share your news with.'

Helen nods. 'Yeah, and we've got to ...' She gestures towards the doors but doesn't finish the sentence.

'Wait.' I remember the other thing, the thing that this time yesterday was the most important thing in the world. I take a step after her and grab her arm to slow her down. 'Did you get the thing I asked you to collect?'

She stops and stares at me. 'What?'

'The thing from the library.'

'Right. It's in my bag. Do you need it now?'

Of course I need it now. It's vital to the plan. Then I remember that Helen has no idea about the plan. I force myself to smile. 'Please.'

She nods. 'I'll catch up with Alex and then I'll get it for you.'

'Thank you.' I try to keep my voice calm, but this is it. I've got the evidence. I've got Tania exactly where I want her. I scan the room. She's standing by the bar with her arm linked through Dad's. He's smiling, a big beaming smile. I remind myself that none of this is my fault. Tania's the one who's in the wrong. If he's upset it'll be her fault. I'm bringing the truth to light. I'm doing a good thing. I'm doing the right thing.

Chapter Sixty-Six

Alex

Helen caught up with Alex as he made it into the foyer. He let her take his arm. It was a gesture of support, without it being at all clear who was supporting who.

'Are you all right?'

Alex paused. It was what he'd been about to ask her. He nodded. 'You?'

'I think so.'

There was a 'quiet room' set up on the other side of the hallway, where party-weary guests could rest their feet and heads. The night was young, and enthusiasm for the revels was yet to fade, leaving the room deserted. Alex and Helen collapsed onto a sofa. Neither of them felt the need to fill the silence.

Alex closed his eyes for a moment. They were moist. He screwed his lids closed more tightly. If no tears got out, then he wasn't crying. It was a point of pride. Alex Lyle did not cry over girls. He was a shark. A lone hunter. He didn't do meeting parents, or making plans, or joint Christmas cards. He didn't do emotional involvement, or lazy lie-in, or third dates. Alex was self-sufficient. A connoisseur of all the delights of femininity, rather than a committed devotee of any one example of the form. Whatever he'd been thinking about Emily was an aberration. Alex absolutely did not do falling in love. He opened his eyes.

Helen was sat next to him, staring straight ahead. He remembered her performance with the vodka and the wastebin last night. 'Are you sure you're okay?'

She nodded. 'It is what it is, isn't it?'

'And what is it?'

She shrugged. 'I think it's like the stages of grief. The last ten years have been denial. Last night was the start of depression. I've got anger to get through and then acceptance and I'm sorted.'

That didn't sound right. 'I think anger comes before depression.'

'Maybe it's different if nobody's actually died.'

'And I think there are five stages of grief.'

Helen screwed up her face. 'Well what's the other one then?'

'I have no idea.'

She sighed. 'Maybe I can make a deal with the universe?'

'What?'

'Maybe if I really never drink again, or if I eat all my greens or something, he won't go through with it. Or maybe I need to actually do something, rather than being all nice about this, or maybe if I'm really strong and hold out a bit longer he'll change his mind?'

'That doesn't sound like doing anything.'

'Give us a coin.'

'What for?' Alex searched through the pockets of his Robin Hood hose. 'I don't have any change.'

'Never mind. It was stupid. I was going to toss a coin. If it was heads I was going to go and throw my body at him.'

'And if it was tails?'

'Probably just stick with the waiting.'

Alex laughed. 'It would have been tails.'

Maybe she was right though. Maybe they did need to do something. A thought popped into his head almost immediately. 'Wait there.'

He returned a few minutes later bearing two more cups of punch. He handed one to Helen.

'I'm not sure this is mainly fruit.'

'Screw it.' Alex downed his drink, and tried to formulate a plan inside his increasingly fuzzy punch-brain. 'Here's what we're going to do. We're going to get back on the horse.'

'What horse?'

'The *horse* horse. You know, you have to get straight back on it.'

'Right.' Helen didn't sound entirely convinced by his plan. Alex replayed the conversation in his head. That might be because he hadn't actually explained what the plan was.

'What we're going to do is, we're going to go back into that party and we are going to have an amazing night.'

Helen shook her head. 'How?'

'Well how do you normally have an amazing night?'

She shrugged. 'I like reviewing dissertation proposals.'

Alex closed his eyes. Sometimes his landlady had no idea at all. 'It's a party. Dissertation proposals aren't party-ish. Why did we come to this thing to start with?'

'Because of the job.'

That was right. That had been the whole point of this expedition; to allow Helen to dazzle and impress her prospective permanent employer. 'Right then. So you're going to get back in there and be all clever and that.'

'All clever and that?'

'Yeah.' Another thought struck him. 'Maybe have another punch. I think the punch definitely makes us sound cleverer.'

Helen smiled. 'I'm not sure that's right. Anyway I've already talked to Professor Midsomer. He didn't seem very interested in me.'

'That's not the point.' Suddenly Alex had a great sense of clarity. Helen was going to get her job. He was going to get back on his horse. Everything was going to be all right. 'You need to make him interested. Flirt with his friend or something.'

'What?'

'It never fails. Hot girl. Fat friend.'

'Alex!'

'Hot girls always have a fat friend. The hot girl won't look at you twice, so you chat up her fat friend. Suddenly she's not getting all the attention and she'll do anything she can to get the spotlight back on her.'

Helen was silent for a moment. 'Are you suggesting that I try to secure a serious academic position by making the Head of Department jealous?'

Put like that it did sound like a stupid plan.

'It's brilliant.' Helen jumped off the sofa.

'Where are you going?'

'To talk about Elizabeth Fry.' Alex watched her stomp out of the room, only slightly unsteadily. Right. That was one of them back in the game. Now it was his turn. He sat up straight and closed his eyes. Just a few metres away from him was a room full of party guests. Disgruntled nineteen year old nieces who would give anything not to have been cajoled into costume and dragged to Uncle Theo's stupid party. Divorcee friends of the bride drowning their jealousy in pints of punch. Waitresses. Waitresses were people too, Alex reminded himself. Never underestimate the level of boredom and desperation achieved by the staff at this sort of event. And all of them bound together under a banner of romance and love, and then fuelled with alcohol. A celibate monk would struggle to walk the length of that room without pulling. Alex tilted his head to one side and then the other, before rolling his shoulders and standing up. Game on.

Chapter Sixty-Seven

Dominic

Dominic stepped up to his fiancée, as she watched Helen run out of the party after her housemate. 'What were you talking about?'

Emily shook her head. 'Nothing.'

Dominic frowned. 'Are you sure? It sounded pretty intense.'

'It's private.'

Dominic furrowed his brow. They were engaged. It was new territory for him, but secrets on day one seemed like a bad sign. 'We're getting married. You know you can tell me.'

Emily looked away for a moment. Dominic stayed quiet. Sometimes you could let a silence do the work for you. It was a tactic he used in tutorials. Less confident teachers panicked if they asked a question and didn't get an answer right away. Dominic knew better. If you let the silence hang, after about seven or eight seconds the awkwardness would overwhelm at least one student and someone would come up with an answer. He watched Emily shuffle her feet, and waited.

'It's Tania,' she blurted.

'What about her?'

Emily took a step towards him so she could talk directly into his ear, the rabble of party noise blocking what she was saying to passers-by. 'You know I said she wasn't right for him? Right from the start?'

Dominic nodded.

'Well I found out what she's been hiding. I'm going to tell

my dad tonight, before he chucks the rest of his life away on her.'

Unease sent a shiver down Dominic's back. 'What's she been hiding?'

'Well ...'

Dominic stood back and held up a hand. 'Actually don't tell me. Isn't it up to her what she tells people?'

Emily folded her arms. 'Not something like this. It's really bad ...'

'I said don't tell me.'

'She's been to prison.'

Dominic closed his eyes. To be fair, that did sound quite bad, but the principle still held. A person could be born one thing and choose to be something else, or even be raised to be something else. He thought about his father sitting in his chair, muttering under his breath at the football on the telly and reading *The Sun* or *The Mail*. And now his son went to parties in manor houses with fancy caterers and funny pink drinks. 'And unless she's recently escaped and on-the-run, she's paid her debt to society, hasn't she?'

'It's all right for you. It's not your dad.'

'That's true, but think about that.' Dominic took his fiancée's hand. 'You're so close to your dad. That's incredible. I barely spoke to mine, except to get a new dose of guilt, and now it's too late to change it. Don't throw away your relationship with Theo by doing something that'll make him miserable.'

She wrapped her fingers around his. 'It's for his own good.' For the first time there was a hint of uncertainty in her voice.

'Will he see it that way? If you go to him and tell him whatever it is about Tania?' Dominic circled his thumb gently on the back of her hand. 'You've heard people say "Don't shoot the messenger"? Well you're the messenger. He might not thank you.'

She shook her head. 'He'll understand.'

Dominic pulled his hand away. 'Em, I'm not sure.'

She smoothed her dress down and wiped a hint of a tear from her face. 'It's not up to you.'

'True.'

'Good, because I've decided what I'm doing.'

'I don't think …' He stopped talking as his fiancée walked away across the room. Dominic felt a flicker of irritation. He hadn't been telling her what to do. He thought back over the conversation. Well, maybe he had been telling her what to do. He shook his head and set off after her.

'Professor Collins!'

He stopped abruptly at the voice. 'Nick?' His wayward student was standing in the middle of the room holding a tray of bright pink punch.

Nick grinned. 'I told you I got a job.'

'Yeah. So I see.'

'This is like a way cool party. Have you seen the magicians?'

Dominic nodded. He'd seen various fairies and elves performing tricks for the entertainment of the gathered guests.

Nick pointed towards a tall, dark-haired man, dressed in green and brown, his face painted like the bark of an aged tree. 'He's the best. He showed us this card trick before it all started that like blew my mind.'

Dominic watched the man for a second. He certainly seemed to have the group of guests standing round him rapt. Suddenly the man raised his voice. 'I need a volunteer!' He looked towards Dominic. 'You sir?'

Dominic shook his head and dropped his gaze to the floor. There was no way he was going to be a magician's stooge. Next to him, Nick had no such inhibitions. He flung his free arm into the air and thrust his tray towards Dominic with the other. 'Hold these.'

Nick bounded forward. The magician shrugged. 'Very well.'

Dominic took a step forward to watch the performance. The magician had his patter down. 'All right young man. What's your name?'

'Nick.'

'Excellent Nick. And can you confirm for the ladies and gentleman that we haven't met before today?'

Nick nodded.

'That's great. And have you ever been hypnotised before?'

Nick shook his head.

'Very good. Okay Nick. You're feeling very calm. I want you to close your eyes for a moment, and picture a wheel. Can you see the wheel in your mind Nick?'

Nick nodded.

'That's great. Very slowly I want you to make that wheel turn in your mind. Watch the wheel. Round and round it goes, slowly turning, and you're watching as it goes round and round and round. You're feeling calm. You're relaxed. The wheel goes round and round. And sleep.'

Nick remained standing, but his head dropped onto his chest. Dominic took a step closer.

The magician grinned at his growing audience. 'Time for a little bit of fun.' He turned to a woman in Tudor finery at the front of the small crowd. 'Pick an animal.'

She giggled. 'I don't know.'

'Any animal? It doesn't matter.'

The woman shrugged. 'A donkey.'

'Excellent.' The magician turned back towards Nick. 'Nick, in a moment I'm going to tell you to open your eyes, and when you do you will believe that you are a donkey.'

A volley of laughter greeted the idea. Someone off to the right shouted out, 'How's he going to serve our drinks?'

The magician smiled. 'Good point. Nick you will still be

a waiter, but you will also believe that you are a donkey. You will have a yearning for carrots and you will believe that your ears have grown long and furry.'

Another volley of laughter broke out at the image. Dominic shook his head. This was a distraction. He picked up a cup from the tray and downed it. He'd been running after Emily, but why? She'd stormed away from him. She was set on exposing some deep, dark secret of Tania's. That was the danger, wasn't it? If you set out in life with a part of yourself hidden away, there was always a risk you could be exposed.

A hand tapped on his shoulder. 'You didn't want to be a volunteer?'

The elf who was doing the hypnosis show grinned broadly at him, flashing glimpses of long pointed teeth.

Dominic shook his head. 'Not really my thing.'

'Fair enough.' The man was still smiling. 'People get nervous about hypnosis. There's no need. It only works if the volunteer's up for it.'

'Really?'

The elf nodded. 'I could demonstrate.'

'No thanks.'

'Humour me.' The elf tilted his head to one side. 'Go on. Just close your eyes.'

Dominic sighed. He supposed it couldn't hurt to play along. 'No turning me into farmyard animals though.'

'Trust me.' The elf smiled broadly. 'It's a wedding party. From now on tonight is all about love.'

'All right.'

'Now just close your eyes and picture a wheel.'

Chapter Sixty-Eight

Alex

Prime hunting ground. That was what this was. This was open savannah and he was the shark. That didn't quite sound right in Alex's head but the basic principle was sound. Room full of sweeties and he was the kid with a free pass to the shop.

He grabbed two cups of punch off a passing tray and surveyed his territory. Maidens and princesses as far as the eye could see. Many of them already being squired by men they arrived with, but that was one of the traditional downsides of wedding parties. Everyone dragged along to a plus-one, which made it tricky to work out who was happily married and who was being accompanied by a reluctant cousin they'd bribed into helping them avoid social embarrassment for a weekend.

His eyes settled on a group of women to the left of the door, gathered around the 'Find the lady' game. He wandered over. 'How are you getting on?'

The woman nearest him smiled. 'They keep losing. They won't believe me when I tell them it's a fix.'

Her friend squealed. 'It's not a fix. I'm going to get it this time.'

Alex watched the guy's hands for second. Round and round and round they went. He turned back to the girl who'd talked to him initially. Medium-height, curvy, long red hair hanging in curls down her back. Blue eyes, like Emily. He shut down the thought. Like Emily or not like Emily wasn't the point. He was indifferent to Emily.

'So you're not having a go?'

She shook her head. 'What's the point in playing if you know you're not going to win?'

'Not much I guess.' He held out his second cup of punch. 'For you.'

She raised an eyebrow. 'For me? Should I be flattered?'

He offered a smile, which he hoped was more sweet than lecherous. 'I noticed you when I was standing over there.'

He saw her look him over, her eyes pausing for a second on his face. That was fair enough. 'So you saw me for the first time from over there?'

Alex nodded.

'And you just had to come over and offer me some free punch?'

He laughed. 'So it's not the most extravagant gesture, but I did notice you. That's gotta count for something?'

'You would think, wouldn't you?'

Alex paused for a second. He was striking out. That seemed pretty clear. He wondered what he could work in the way of damage limitation. So she wasn't into him? That was her prerogative, but she was with a group of five mates. Maybe he could stay sufficiently in favour to ingratiate himself with the group. Keep her talking. That was the key thing. Keep her talking, rather than letting her fade back into her group of friends. 'So why doesn't it?'

'What?'

'Well noticing you doesn't seem to be getting me much credit. Why not?'

Her eyes settled on his face again. 'You really don't know, do you?'

Alex shook his head.

The girl leant towards him. 'You don't recognise me at all.'

He took another look. Hair. Face. Blue eyes like … well, blue eyes. 'Should I?'

'You slept with me three years ago.'

'Did I?'

The girl nodded. 'I'm Beatrix.'

Beatrix? Bea? Trix? The name didn't ring a bell. 'I'm sorry.'

She shrugged. 'Don't be. You were perfectly adequate.'

'What?' Alex was outraged. He was more than adequate in that department. His reviews to date had been exemplary.

Beatrix shook her head. 'You can't be offended. You don't even remember me.'

His heart had somewhat gone out of the pursuit, but old habits died hard. 'And you don't fancy, you know ... for old times sake?'

Another shake of the head. 'I've got a boyfriend, and also no. Just no.'

'Right.' Alex turned to slope away.

'Wait. Actually, there's something else.' Her voice was softer suddenly. She looked serious.

'What?'

'I didn't have your contact details you see, and you know, we didn't know each other that well, and I wasn't sure how you'd react, but ...'

Alex felt his stomach tighten. 'What?'

'It's just that after we ... you know ... well I was left with more than the memories, if you know what I mean.'

'Well you didn't catch anything from me!'

'What?' Her face crumpled in disdain. 'No! Not that.' She looked serious again. 'My son. Our son.'

The room spun around Alex. A son. An actual son. Three years ago. She'd said three years ago. That meant, what? A two year old son. Two and a bit years of a tiny person who was part of him being on the planet without him knowing. He had a son. 'Really?'

The woman's face dissolved into laughter. 'Of course not. We used a condom.'

Alex reeled again. 'What?'

'Sorry. I couldn't resist. I felt like you deserved it.' She grinned and held out a hand. 'Even?'

Alex shook her hand. 'I have to go.'

She nodded. 'Probably best.'

So no son. Well that was good, wasn't it? The thing Alex was feeling would almost certainly be relief. No commitments. Nothing anchoring him to anyone. Alex staggered to the side of the room and sat down. He didn't want a child. He was in no fit state to be a father. He had a job he detested that barely paid enough to make rent to a landlady who didn't charge him proper rent. A woman who wanted to stay for breakfast was on the outside edge of his ability to commit. He certainly couldn't be a father. A father was someone who stuck with things, someone who followed through. Alex had never stuck with anything.

All around the room people were making connections. They were here with their families, their lovers, their partners. Alex was alone. At the far side of the room, Helen and Emily were standing together. What a contrast that was. Emily was worse than he was. It wasn't that she couldn't stick with things; it was that she didn't know when to stick and when to let go, and yet he'd offered to stick with her. It was barely twenty-four hours ago that he'd told her he'd be hers if she'd have him. But she wouldn't have him, and that was that.

'Mate! Will you volunteer?' A tall, slender man dressed as some sort of creature of the forest, with a face painted like tree bark, clapped Alex on the shoulder.

'What?'

'I need a volunteer.'

Alex nodded. He didn't have anywhere else to be.

'Gather round ladies and gentleman. We have a new volunteer.'

A small crowd gathered around them. The costumes, the scent of wildflowers in the air, the punch in Alex's system – it was all swirling together to make him feel out of control. The tall man leant close to Alex's ear. 'Just listen to my voice.'

He did as he was told. He closed his eyes. He pictured the wheel. He watched it spin around and around, and then everything went quiet. The sounds of the party drifted into the distance. Everything around Alex was calm.

'All right mate.' The elven man clapped him on the shoulder. 'Thanks a lot.'

Was that it? He hadn't done anything. The man wandered away, and the crowd dispersed. Alex blinked a couple of times. What had he been thinking about? Of course. Getting back on the horse. Maybe he'd taken the wrong approach before. Obviously he needed to get over Emily, but maybe jumping back on the same old horse again wasn't the right way at all. Maybe it was time to do something different. Maybe it was time to make a commitment, but this time he'd do it differently. He'd find someone who deserved it, someone who could make a commitment in return. Helen and Emily standing together. He pulled his eyes away from Emily and onto Helen. Helen. Perfect, enchanting Helen. He would make her his.

He stopped. Maybe he'd just have another cup of punch first.

Chapter Sixty-Nine

Emily

'Are you having a nice evening?' Helen doesn't answer. It's noisy in the ballroom. Maybe she hasn't heard. 'Are you having a nice time?'

She shrugs. 'Fine.'

She doesn't really like parties. I bet she'd rather be at home marking essays than all corseted up and forced to come out and socialise. I wonder if I should tell her about Tania, but after Dom's reaction I'm not sure. I should have known he wouldn't understand. He's not close to his parents. Maybe he's right about telling my dad though. A thoughts strikes. Perhaps there's another option. I scan the room. Tania is still wrapped around my dad. If I'm going to do this another way, I need to get her on her own. That means waiting. I look at the clock. Quarter to nine. I can't wait too long.

'Did you get that stuff for me?'

She nods without looking at me. 'It's in my room. Someone must have taken my bags up.'

'I need it.'

She rifles through her bag and pulls out a room key. 'It's on top of my case. Help yourself.'

I take the key. 'Thanks.' She doesn't reply. 'Are you okay?' She's scanning the crowded room in front of her.

Helen glances at me and then looks away.

'Seriously, what's up?

'Nothing.' She sighs. 'I'm looking for someone.'

'Who?'

'Isabel Sutton. I need to tell her about Elizabeth Fry.'

'Off the five pound notes?'

'Yes.'

'Why?'

'To make your dad jealous.'

I probably ought to ask her to explain that. I don't. I've got other things on my mind. Too many other things. Tania's still standing with my dad, so that one will have to wait. I pick one of the others at random. 'There was something I wanted to ask you.'

'Mmm?'

'Will you be my bridesmaid?'

This is the bit where she's supposed to squeal and hug me. Helen isn't the squealing type but there should be hugging.

She folds her arms. She's been quiet for a long time. Too long. Of course. Alex didn't say anything to Dom, but he'll have told Helen, won't he? They're practically family. I freeze. So that's how he's going to find out. Alex told Helen. Helen's going to tell Dom, unless I can persuade her not to. 'You know, don't you?'

'Yes.'

I don't reply. I can't. My heart is rushing. I put my hand against the wall to stop the world moving around me. 'It was ...'

'It was what?'

Tears come quickly, running down my face. I take a big snotty gulp. 'It was stupid. Really stupid.'

'He's my friend too.'

I don't know for a second which 'he' she's talking about. It doesn't matter. Alex and Dom. By screwing Alex, I've screwed them both. 'It'll never happen again. It was a stupid mistake. It didn't mean anything.'

All the things I can think of to say make me sound like a politician who's been caught shagging his intern.

'Is any of that true?'

I nod. At least some of it is absolutely true. It will never *never* happen again. It was definitely a stupid mistake, and

245

I don't want it to have meant anything. I wipe my eyes on the weird dangly sleeve bit of my costume. 'Are you going to tell Dom?'

'I don't know.'

She can't. She shouldn't. Friends are supposed to come before any bloke. She should be on my side. 'I wanted to tell you.'

She shakes her head. 'I'm glad you didn't. I wish Alex hadn't.'

I remember her face when Dom told her we were engaged. 'Is that why you weren't happy about the engagement?'

She pauses. That momentary pause before she arranges her face is there again, but then she nods.

I can talk her round. I know I can. It'll be like the time I threw up on a bouncer and then persuaded him I was still sober enough to get into the club. 'It won't ever happen again. I think I got a bit freaked out about how quickly things were going with Dom. I got scared and I did something stupid. That's all.'

She's still not making eye contact, but she hasn't stormed off yet. 'Don't you think Dominic has a right to know?'

'Probably, but what would the point be? It was before we were engaged.' Admittedly only about five hours before we got engaged, but I'm not going to dwell on that. 'And it would hurt him. What's the point in hurting Dom so that we get something off our chests?'

'Don't say "we".'

'What?'

'You said "so that we get it off our chests." We're not a "we." You did this. I'm not part of it.'

'I know.' I don't know what else to say. 'Please don't tell Dom.'

She sighs. 'I'm still thinking about it.'

I open my mouth, but she puts her hand out.

'Don't. Don't say anymore.' She walks away to the other side of the room, and I'm alone.

Chapter Seventy

Alex

Helen. Helen. Alex rolled the name around inside his head. Good old Helen. Reliable Helen. Wonderful Helen. Bewitching Helen. He watched his landlady walk across the room, sipping her punch. Actually, surprisingly hot Helen. He watched her swallow and saw her chest rise and fall at the top of her corset. Her cleavage was amazing. This was it, wasn't it? On this night, with all this noise, and music, and people, and the scent of the flowers filling his nostrils – this was the story he would be telling his grandchildren fifty years hence. Maybe without the bit about her cleavage. The grandchildren might get weirded out by too much chat about Nana's boobs.

He would go to her, he decided. He would declare his undying love which had started ... Alex stopped and thought about it. He would go and declare his undying love which was definitely eternal and therefore must, he reasoned, have started ages ago. He took a step, and paused for a moment while the room wobbled around him. Not to worry. A bit of light instability in the furnishings wouldn't distract him from his quest. His quest to ... he paused and looked around. There she was again. Helen. His quest for Helen. Boobs and undying love and lovely lovely Helen. He made it over to her.

'Helen.'

She twisted to face him. 'Oh man, you're drunk, aren't you?'

'I'm intoxicated on love.'

She frowned. 'I thought we'd sworn off love?'

'No.' Alex was adamant. 'Can't swear off love. All you need is love.'

Helen shook her head. 'Come on. I'll take you to get some fresh air.'

He let her take his hand and lead the way out to the terrace and then onwards into the garden. She stopped by a bench overlooking a small lake. 'Sit down. See if you sober up.'

Alex slumped onto the seat. 'Sit by me. There's stuff I need to tell you.'

Helen sat at the far end of the bench. 'Like what?'

She rolled her shoulders to get comfortable sitting down, making her boobs do the amazing rising and falling thing again. Alex grinned.

'About love. About you and me and love and ...' He gazed out across the lake, down towards the woodland at the end of the park. 'About everything.'

'What about everything?'

'You and me.'

'What about us?'

'I think we should give it a go.'

Helen was sitting sideways on the bench, leaning on the back, half turned back towards the party. He got the impression she was only half listening. 'Okay.'

'Okay?'

She turned back to him. 'Sorry. What?'

'You and me. We're gonna give it a go?'

Helen's mouth dropped open. 'Give what a go?'

Alex paused. Right. He was going to have to propose this again, and he was going to do it properly. 'You look amazing tonight.'

'I should think so, after the amount of time you made me spend getting ready.' Helen peered at him. 'Are you feeling all right?'

'I feel incredible.' It was true. Helen's face swam in front of him. So pretty, and so kind. Kindness. That was what he needed. 'Kindness is brilliant.'

She laughed again. 'Yeah.'

'And you're kind. I love kindness. I love you.'

Helen patted his cheek. 'Of course you do.'

She wasn't taking him seriously, was she? Words weren't working. Alex needed to try the other thing. Not words. Actions. He steadied himself with one arm along the back of the bench and he leant in. His lips touched hers, and he felt her freeze for a moment. He pushed his mouth against hers, not too hard. He felt her lips part, just for a second, before hands pushed at his chest.

'What are you doing?'

'Kissing you.'

Helen jumped away from the bench. 'Well obviously. Why?'

Alex's brain wasn't functioning for a moment. He knew the answer to this question though. He was sure he did. In front of him Helen folded her arms across her corseted cleavage. He remembered. 'Because I love you. I'm eternally in love with you Helen.'

'Don't be ridiculous.'

'S'not ridiculous. It's romantic.'

'You're drunk and it is ridiculous.'

Alex started to stand up. Helen held out her hand. 'Stay there. I'm going back inside. I think you'd be best staying here til you've sobered up a bit.'

She set off across the lawn. Alex watched her retreating back. He would not be staying here. He would definitely be going after her, just as soon as the ground stopped rippling under his feet like it was. As soon as that happened, he would absolutely go after her. Alex slumped back onto the bench and laid down. He might have a little minute here first.

Chapter Seventy-One

Emily

Eventually Tania breaks away from Dad. I follow her out of the ballroom and into the foyer. I hang back as one of the guests greets her. It's all cheek-kisses and bonhomie. If only they knew the truth.

After a minute of chit-chat she makes her excuses and sets off up the stairs. I follow again, but don't catch up with her until we're out of sight and earshot of anyone else. If I'm going to keep my dad out of this, everything has to stay between me and her. I wait until she's at the door to her room. The bridal suite, for goodness sake.

'I need to talk to you.'

She jumps. 'Emily? I didn't see you.'

I walk towards her. It's like a scene from a film. I picture myself storming past her into the room and laying some truth on her. In reality, she doesn't move out of the doorway as I walk towards her, so we end up sort of bumping awkwardly against each other for a moment, and both apologising. I kick myself. I shouldn't be apologising. I'm here to get serious with her.

I jostle my way into the room.

'What did you want to talk about?'

She sits down on the bed. I decide to stay standing. It feels less friendly, more in control.

'I know, Tania.'

She looks confused. 'You know what?'

I take a deep breath. Now I'm here I find I don't want to think too hard about what I'm doing. It might, I realise, be viewed as being a tiny bit blackmailish. I take another breath. It's for the greater good. I'm getting my hands dirty so my dad doesn't get hurt. I'm his gatekeeper. It's like telling people who phone up for him that he's out, when really he's avoiding them. 'I know the truth about you Tania.' I swallow hard. 'Or should I say Tina?'

As soon as I say her name, her whole body stiffens, but she doesn't reply. That's fine. I've got plenty to say. 'I found out about you. I know what you did.'

'What do you want, Emily?'

'I want you to go. I don't care what you tell Dad. You don't have to tell him anything, but you are not marrying him tomorrow. You can disappear, or you can tell him that you need some space, or that it's all happening too quickly, or that you think you might have feelings for someone else, or you can tell him all those things, so long as you go.'

She lifts her head to look at me. 'Gosh. Haven't you thought of a lot of reasons not to get married.' She stands up. 'You know nothing Emily. You're jealous, and you're immature and I'd like you to get out of my room now please.'

That wasn't how she was supposed to respond. I'd have expected tears at getting caught out, or anger maybe. She's icy calm. I suppose that proves me right. She's clearly not that bothered at having to leave Dad. I stop at the door. 'Before the morning. I want you gone before morning.'

She looks at me and shakes her head. 'Emily, I'm going to go back to the party. If you're sensible you'll forget that this conversation ever happened.'

She's unbelievable. She's actually acting like I'm the one who's done something wrong. She stalks past me, and I follow her back along the corridor and down the stairs. 'I'm serious. If you don't go I'll tell Dad everything. I've got evidence. You won't be able to wriggle out of it.'

She glances over her shoulder at me, but doesn't respond,

and she doesn't look at me again until we reach the door to the ballroom. 'Emily, your dad's happy. Try to be happy for him.'

Who is she to be telling me how to behave? I know what she is. I know what she did. She's the devil. I watch her walk away. A few feet into the party she's waylaid by one of the performers who've been skulking around the place all evening. He grabs her hand and twirls her around to face the small audience of partygoers who have assembled around him. He leans towards her. He's talking quite softly, close to her ear. I see her close her eyes, and few moments later her head drops forward onto her chest. The guests closer to the action giggle and whisper to one another.

I walk away. One thing stays fizzing round and around in my head. A lot of reasons not to get married, she said. Every time the words come into my mind it feels like there's a rope tightening around my neck. I need a distraction. I grab myself a cup of punch and look around the room. I let the light and noise and colour wash over me. Whatever else she's done, Tania can certainly throw a party. It's like being in another world. I can't see Dom or Helen anywhere. I scan the room again. I can't see Alex either. That's good. I'm a medieval princess at a mask ball. Tonight, nothing is real. Nothing is quite what it seems.

Chapter Seventy-Two

Helen

Helen went straight back into the party. Maybe the noise would drown out the sound of the Helen inside her head yelling obscenities at the Helen out here in the world. She hadn't kissed Alex. He'd kissed her, which wasn't the same at all, and he had been very drunk. So long as Helen hadn't kissed him back, she decided, it barely counted as a kiss at all.

She'd promised herself that she wasn't going to drink too much at the party, but the punch was lovely. Punch wasn't really drinking, was it? People kept telling her it was mostly fruit. Helen let a nice young man hand her another cup.

'Having a good time?'

Dominic appeared at her elbow. He looked more than a little uncomfortable in his chainmail. He'd abandoned the helmet and there was a thin sheen of sweat sticking his hair to the side of his face. Helen shrugged. 'The room looks nice.'

He glanced around. 'And apart from the décor?'

She wasn't sure what to say. Her head was spinning with Alex and her, and Alex and Emily, and Emily begging her not to say anything. Helen opened her mouth and closed it again, which Dominic seemed to interpret as simple party-weariness. 'Do you want to get some air?'

She nodded and then remembered that Alex was probably still out there. 'Maybe out the other way?'

'The car park?'

'Mmmm.' She smiled brightly, as if going and loitering in the car park in the middle of a party wasn't odd behaviour. 'Emily not with you?'

She formed the words as lightly as she could. Emily was

her friend. She absolutely did not hope that she'd fallen down a well.

Dominic glanced around as he held the main door open. 'No. I don't know where she is actually.' His tone was grim.

Had he found out? Helen kept her voice casual. 'No problem is there?'

He didn't answer straight away. 'She's probably dancing or something.' He pulled a face that suggested he viewed dancing as a strange and alien activity, possibly worthy of academic interest from anthropologists but not something one would wish to engage in personally.

Outside there were three steps in front of the door, down to the gravelled car park. They sat down, next to one another, on a low wall at the top of the stairs.

'Sorry we've not made a decision about the job yet.'

'Don't worry about it.'

'Ugh.' He groaned deep in his throat.

'What?'

'You're too nice. You should be furious with us. You're clearly the best candidate. Theo should have offered you a permanent job years ago.' Dominic shook his head. 'No. Not even that. You should be teaching in a far better department than ours. I don't get why you haven't been snapped up by some other university. What about Exeter? Weren't they expanding?'

'I don't know.' Helen couldn't make eye contact. 'I like it here I guess.'

'You're insane.'

He might have been right, but Helen couldn't leave the university. That was where Dominic was, so that was where she had to be. She had tried to get over him, but other men bored her. She thought back to the speed dating. Eighteen men she'd met and not a single one had been worth contacting again. It wasn't a problem with the men. It was her. She'd much rather see Dominic every day, even knowing she'd never be with him. The thought popped up that she could tell him about Emily and Alex. Then maybe ... maybe once he'd got over that? She shook her head. She didn't even have the courage to hope. Everything she felt for him had been screwed up into a tiny parcel, but instead of throwing it away, she'd kept hold of it, tight and secure in the very centre of her soul, and now it was a part of who she was.

'Do you remember the first time we met?'

The tightly wrapped parcel unfurled a little. Helen nodded.

'What do you remember?'

'Third year lecture series. The last lecture on a Friday afternoon, so it was always half empty. "The witch, the wife, the madonna, the whore – Anne Boleyn and the place of women at the court of Henry the eighth."'

'Wow. I didn't realise it made such an impression.'

'I've still got the notes.' She stopped. 'I mean I've got all my old notes.'

'But do you remember us actually meeting?'

She nodded. She remembered. It was the most highly valued and frequently examined few minutes of her life. 'I didn't pluck up the courage to come and talk to you until the end of the fourth lecture.'

He shook his head 'Pluck up the courage?'

'You were scary. Really sort of intense.'

'It was my first term teaching. I was bricking it.'

'It didn't show. I came to ask you to explain the assignment question, but you spent so long explaining that the cleaner came and chucked us out of the room.'

Dominic laughed. 'And do you remember after the cleaner chucked us out?'

Of course she did. It was the thing she always tried to

think about just before she fell asleep, so that she might have a chance of dreaming a better ending. It had barely even been a moment. The two of them standing in an empty corridor. For a second, not even that, a fraction of a second, she'd thought he was leaning towards her. She'd thought he was going to … It was only a moment.

She shook her head. 'It was a long time ago.'

'Of course. It was silly anyway. I nearly asked you to go for a drink you know.'

'I was a student.'

'I know.' He swallowed. 'Anyway that wasn't the first time we met.'

'It was!' Of course it was. She'd spent the last ten years thinking about it. He couldn't tell her now that she'd been fixating on the wrong moment.

He shook his head. 'Do you remember the start of that term? They had a sort of social thing for third years, PhD students and staff. I think it was supposed to inspire you to think about applying for post-grad study.'

Helen remembered. 'Yes! I had a really good talk with Dr Schaeffer about the place of gender studies within the wider humanities.'

'You had two glasses of red wine, trapped the poor man in a corner and told him he was a puppet of the patriarchal establishment.'

'That is not how I remember it.'

'Well it's what happened. I was watching.'

'You were watching me?'

'You were magnificent, like a lioness in full flight.'

'Lionesses don't fly.'

'In full flight doesn't mean literal flight.'

'I think it does.' Why was she arguing with him about this? Why wasn't she letting him call her magnificent? 'You noticed me?'

'I couldn't look at anything else.' He laughed slightly. 'I was devastated when you turned out to be a student. My student.'

She didn't know what to say. He'd noticed her. He'd noticed her before she even noticed him. And they had had a moment. It wasn't in her head. It was real. It was fleeting, but it was real. But it was still a long time ago. 'Oh well. It all turned out for the best.'

'What?' He looked confused.

'Well, you're happy with Emily, aren't you?' She asked the question lightly, but Helen was making a bargain with herself in her head. If he said he was happy then she wouldn't tell him about Emily and Alex, but if there was even the slightest hint that he wasn't, then she had no choice, did she? Because if he was already having doubts, then it would definitely be better that he knew the truth. 'And I'm ... I'm fine doing my thing.'

'Of course.'

Of course. So that was that. She wouldn't say anything, like she'd never said anything before, and Emily would get her big white wedding, and Helen would be her bridesmaid and people would make jokes about 'always the bridesmaid', and Helen would laugh politely to start with, and then a bit later she'd tell them off for making lazy gendered assumptions, and then, later still, she'd sneak out of the reception and cry.

They ought to go back into the party. He ought to go back to his fiancée. Helen stood up. 'Well, we'd better get back in.'

His fingers wrapped around her wrist. 'Wait.'

She stopped but didn't turn around. His hand was on her arm. It was such a tiny thing, but it was filling her senses. Her heart jumped.

'What if it hadn't turned out all right?'

She turned around. She didn't dare say anything. It was happening again. It was a real moment, and it was happening now.

'What if I was wasn't happy with Emily? Not unhappy with Emily even, with everything?'

'What do you mean?'

He stood up, and this time she knew she wasn't imagining it. He bent his face towards hers, and then stopped. 'Is this what you want?'

She couldn't respond. She should say no. She should push him away. She'd pushed Alex away without any trouble. That was exactly what she should do now. She didn't. She lifted her face to meet his. She told herself that he was kissing her, that he started it, and he did, but she didn't stop him. Helen wrapped her arms around Dominic's neck, and let him pull her body against his. She opened her mouth a fraction, and let him slide his tongue between her lips. She embraced him wholeheartedly, like she did every night in her dreams. Everything in the world was this kiss. Earthquakes could have struck, volcanoes exploded, hurricanes whistled right through the building, Helen would not have noticed at all. She certainly wouldn't notice a handle turning, a door being pushed, and a person standing dead still in the doorway beside them.

Chapter Seventy-Three

Dominic

'What? What are you doing?'

Dominic pulled back from the kiss, and looked towards the voice in the doorway. Alex. Something sank in his stomach. He almost wished it had been Emily.

'What are you doing?' Alex lurched towards them, pulling the plastic sword from his scabbard as he did so. Helen jumped out of the way, and Dominic stumbled backwards the three steps onto the car park.

Alex staggered after him still brandishing his sword. 'Avast you dog!'

'What?'

'Avast!'

Dominic shook his head. 'I think you mean "En guarde!"'

Alex stopped still for a second. 'Whatever. You were snogging. And you can't snog Helen because ...'

Helen marched down the stairs. 'Why can't he snog Helen?' She leant in close to her housemate and whispered something before raising her voice. 'He can snog who he likes.'

Alex frowned. 'That's not it.' His gaze drifted south towards Helen's chest. He turned back to Dominic. 'You can't snog Helen because I'm in love with her.'

'You are?' Dominic was surprised.

Helen shook her head. 'He's not.'

'I am.' Alex took another step towards his rival. 'So ...' He stopped. 'What am I supposed to say?'

'En guarde.'

'Thank you. So en guarde!'

Dominic watched as Alex charged, unsteadily, towards him. Clearly, they couldn't have a swordfight. He stepped smartly to the side, let Alex charge past him, and turned to see the other man stop and stagger in confusion, before navigating his way round in a circle back towards his adversary.

Then he came again. Dominic watched his approach as if in slow motion. Alex charged, sword aloft and Dominic watched him. That was what he did, wasn't it? He watched life going on around him. He had a plan. He had a reputation. He had mountains of memories of times when he'd done the right thing, stood back, not made a fuss. Dominic realised that he was smiling. Why the hell shouldn't he fight? It was obviously what Alex wanted. He was wearing a knight's costume. There was a fair maiden who had been dishonoured. Technically she had, he mentally conceded, been dishonoured by him, but still, there was some honour involved. He pulled out his plastic sword, and swung it in Alex's direction, failing utterly to make contact. No matter. This was happening. He was having a fight in a car park. Even given that it was a swordfight in full medieval dress, it was still probably the most dangerous thing Dominic had ever done, and it was cool. He was thrusting and parrying, channelling the two hours of fencing he'd done, aged ten with a foam sword at a holiday camp with his Auntie Karen.

By comparison, Dominic felt, Alex lacked technique, but was making up for it with sheer vigour and enthusiasm for the quest.

'Have at ye!' Alex yelled, and the two men bowled around the car park, thrusting and slicing through the air with their toy blades.

Dominic could feel the air racing from his lungs. Oh god, he was out of shape. Next week, he decided, he was definitely going back to the gym. He held up a hand.

'What?'

'Hold on a minute.'

Alex paused. 'You can't stop in the middle of a fight.'

'Course you can. It's like half-time in the football.'

Dominic glanced at his opponent and noticed a certain redness in the face.

Alex nodded. 'All right, but just for a minute.'

Dominic leant on a Land Rover for a second, and watched Alex crouch down. Helen marched over to them. 'Have you finished?'

Both men shook their heads. 'It's just a break.'

Helen sighed. 'You're ridiculous. Both of you.'

Alex turned towards her. 'We're fighting for your honour.'

'My honour can look after itself.'

Alex shook his head. 'No. I love you.'

'No. You don't.'

'I do. And I have to defend your honour.'

'And what about you?'

Dominic looked up, and couldn't resist a smile at her furious face. He shrugged. 'I sort of got dragged in.'

'You're a highly educated professional. People like us do not get dragged in to brawls in car parks.'

He sighed. She was right. This was exactly the sort of thing people like grown up Dominic did not do. They didn't act on impulse. They didn't let things get out of control. He laughed. 'It's not a brawl. It's a sword fight.' He stood, pushing one leg forward and raising one arm behind him. He held his sword out straight towards Alex. 'En guarde!'

'Oh for goodness sake.' He heard Helen mutter as she stomped back a few paces across the gravel, but he didn't care. The fight was back on. He thrust towards Alex. Behind him Helen was shouting.

'You've got plastic swords. How are you even going to know when someone's won?'

That wasn't the point anymore. The fight was the point. His heart pounding was the point. The pulsing in his ears. The gasping and gulping for air. The burn in his arms. Being absolutely in this moment, not standing with one eye to the past and one planning for the future and completely missing the now. This moment. Right now. That was the point.

Helen was still talking behind him, but now there was more than one voice. Emily. Emily must have come outside. He ducked a thrust from Alex's sword, and tried to listen.

'They're fighting.'

'Yeah.'

'You told him, didn't you?' That was Emily. 'I can't believe you told Dom.'

He stopped. 'Told me what?'

Chapter Seventy-Four

Emily

One look at his face tells me that I'm wrong. My hand shoots up to my mouth, as if it's trying to push the words back in. Think. He doesn't know. He doesn't have to find out. Another thought rushes into my crowded brain. If he doesn't know … 'Why are you fighting?'

Dom stops. Behind him Alex is still pirouetting and thrusting his sword at the air, but Dom freezes. Something inside me freezes too. I turn towards Helen. 'Why are they fighting?'

She glances at the floor and shrugs. 'Boys, you know.'

I do know boys. I know that they very rarely get into sword fights. It's very much out of fashion when you think about it.

They all know something, don't they? They all know and I don't. I'm on my own. Helen's supposed to be my best friend. 'Tell me.'

Alex has finally caught up with the fact that nobody is on the other end of the fight anymore. 'I was defending my maiden,' he shouts.

'What?' That doesn't make any sense. If Dom doesn't know, then how could they be fighting over me?

'This oaf,' he waves his toy sword at Dom, 'had dishonoured my fair maiden.'

'What does he mean?'

Helen is still looking at the floor. Dom steps towards me, easing his sword back into its holder. 'He's drunk. He came at me.'

'No!' Alex shouts. 'I was defending my maiden.'

'From what?'

'From him.' He points again at Dom. 'He was kissing her.'

I don't understand, but I need Alex to shut up. At the moment he's talking nonsense, but he could let something slip. I try to keep my voice calm. 'Well he's allowed to kiss me. We're engaged.'

Alex shakes his head. 'Not you stupid.'

Dom jumps straight in. 'Don't call her stupid.'

That's sweet. He really is defending my honour. I quite like it. Dom is usually more of a tersely worded email sort of man, than the actual fighting duels kind. I quite like this side of him. Maybe this is going to be okay.

Alex hasn't finished though. 'Not her. He was kissing her.'

I follow his finger towards where he's pointing, even though I already know. It's not me. He's not pointing at me, so it must be her, mustn't it? She's the only other one here. She's the one who didn't look happy when her best friend told her she was engaged. She's the one that always sits by him in meetings. She's the one who I always asked what he'd like. Obviously, it's her.

Something guttural happens. I feel my muscles tensing and my body moving before my brain knows what's happening. I launch myself towards her. 'You were my best friend.'

I find myself with a handful of her hair, and I pull on it. I feel her grab my arm with one hand and push the other against my chest. I use my free hand to slam her arm away, and the weight of her body falls against me. I try to balance, but I can't and we both fall down onto the gravel. Pain surges through my shoulder as she falls on top of me, scraping my arm against the floor. She tries to push me away, but I react quicker and I roll, and we both roll, still clawing at one another's faces and arms. And then I feel another set of arms around my middle, pulling me away. I'm still shouting and grabbing at her hair, as Dom lifts me out of the fight. Alex runs to Helen's side and pulls her up from the floor. I can feel my chest rising and falling and hear my own breathing inside my ears.

'You bitch!' I shout again, using anything I can to force the fury out of my head and onto her.

She pulls herself towards me again. 'But you slept with Alex.'

Dom's arm is still wrapped around my middle. For a second everything is still and then I feel his grip relax and he steps backwards. His body unpresses from my back. The warmth of his breath leaves my neck. I hear his feet on the gravel. One step away. Two steps away. Three steps away.

'Is that true?' I turn around. His face doesn't give anything away. He asks again. 'Is that true?'

I look back towards Helen and Alex. They're standing a little way apart from one another, both staring at me. If I lie now their faces will give me away before they even have chance to speak. It's like I've being clinging onto this merry-go-round for the last twenty-four hours spinning faster and faster, and if I let go I'm going to be flung into the unknown. I don't have a choice. I nod.

Dom swallows hard. He walks another four paces away from me to the bottom of the steps and kicks his boot against the wall. Then he walks the four paces back. He doesn't touch me. He doesn't look at me. He raises his voice towards the others. 'Do you guys mind going back in? I need to have a talk with my fiancée.'

I glance up to see Helen nod. Alex picks up his sword from the ground. He takes a step towards us as if he wants to say something. I never find out what. Helen takes him by the arm and leads him up the stairs. It's less than ten seconds before they're gone, but each second lasts an eternity. Eventually, I hear the door close, and raise my eyes towards the man I'm supposed to be marrying. At least, whatever happens, I know it can't get any worse.

Dom looks straight at me. 'When?'

I was wrong. It can get worse.

'Do you really want to know the details?'

'When?'

I close my eyes. 'Yesterday.'

'For fuck's sake!' he yells.

'I'm sorry.'

'You're sorry? You're sorry that the day we got engaged you screwed someone else? Well that's all right then. I mean, I thought it was a big deal, but if you're sorry then I guess it's fine.'

I'm crying again. The whole thing is hopeless. 'I don't know what else to say.'

'When exactly?'

'What?'

'When exactly? Before or after you accepted my proposal.'

I shrug. 'Before.'

'And how many times?'

'Just once.'

'So what, you were getting it out of your system? Or was it the start of an affair?'

'No!'

'How do you know? If I hadn't found out, maybe it would have carried on.'

'I...' I pause. I don't know, do I? 'I didn't want to have an affair.'

'But you wanted to shag him?'

'No! Well, yes, but only for a second. It was a mistake.' I take a step towards him. 'Like you made with Helen?'

'That's not the same.'

Isn't it? Of course it is, unless that wasn't a one-off mistake. For the first time it strikes me that he might want to be with her. It makes sense. I'm broken. Everyone leaves me, and I can picture the two of them together, heads bent over a book or an article, deep in conversation. 'It was a one-off, wasn't it?'

He doesn't reply. I carry on. I have to be wrong. 'Anyone can make a one-off mistake. It would never happen again.'

'How can I believe that?'

I have to make him believe it. I've lost Helen. I've lost Alex. I might still be losing my dad to Tania. It's too much. I can't keep losing. 'I promise. It was before we got engaged, but we're engaged now. It's a fresh start. You and me. It's what you want, isn't it?' He doesn't reply, but he hasn't walked away yet. We had a whole future. He doesn't have a future with her. I need to find the words to make him believe in us. 'You've got your career, and your house, which I can make so lovely, and we were going to have children, and I'm going to stop work to look after them. It's all planned, isn't it? It was our plan.'

He sighs. 'I didn't plan the bit where you screwed someone else.'

I take another step forward and press my head against his chest. He doesn't stop me. 'I'll make it up to you. I'll never be that stupid again. We can make this work. We just have to do what we've planned.'

'And you love me?'

'I can't manage without you.'

He steps back. 'I need to think.'

'Don't go.'

He shakes his head and steps past me. 'I need some time.'

I can't let him walk away. Without Dom, there's just me and a great big unknown. I can't be just me.

'We've got to sort this out.' I grab at his hand, but he pulls it away. 'Don't leave me.'

'I need to think.' He starts along the side of the building and I follow. He stops. His voice is tired and low. 'On my own.'

I let him go. It doesn't seem like I have very much choice.

I go back inside. I'm almost surprised to find that the party's still going. It feels like everything should have stopped.

'Darling!'

Daddy bears down on me clutching two cups of punch. 'Have you seen Tania? I was bringing her a drink.'

I shake my head.

'Oh well.' He offers me the second cup. 'I'll get her another when she comes back.'

I take a sip of the fruity pinkness, and then a bigger sip, and then a gulp. I wonder how much it'll take to fill the gaping hole inside me. I lean my head on my dad's shoulder.

'Are you all right Emmy?'

'Yeah.' I don't want to tell him what happened, but I don't need to. He's always here for me, right from the very worst times when I was little. He's never left me or let me down. I remember when I was a little girl being in a grey cold room with plastic chairs and a scratched old table. I had a dolly that I was playing with but I remember that I was all on my own, and then my daddy came and he picked me up and he promised that he'd always be there to look after me, and he always was.

Chapter Seventy-Five

Dominic

Dominic walked the full circumference of the building and ended up back in the deserted car park. He realised that it had got dark while he was walking. It had been light when he left the car park, but now a dull grey dusk had fallen across the landscape. Even on the longest days of the year, eventually night would fall. The darkness was driving partygoers back indoors, but Dominic didn't follow them. Emily and Helen and Alex would be inside and there was talking, or more likely shouting, to be done. He couldn't face that yet. There had never been raised voices when he was growing up. Emotions had been things to be managed and controlled, not brought to the surface and acted upon. He heard stories from colleagues about huge fights breaking out over something that somebody's cousin had said about their auntie's ex-husband in 1984. It sounded like a different world.

He turned back around the building and walked back across the gardens towards a small copse of trees at the far end of the lawn. It would be away from people and noise. Maybe it would give him a chance to think. He stopped short of the trees. Not so far away from people it turned out. He paused and listened. There were two voices, one man and one woman. He could hear the woman giggling. 'I love your nice long furry ears.'

The male voice eey-ored in response. Dominic took half a step closer. The man's voice was familiar. 'You're like totally hot and that.'

Dominic shook his head. It sounded like Nick, his

student. He couldn't make out who the woman was. She giggled again. 'How did we get here?'

'Dunno really.'

Another female laugh. 'Oh well. I love everyone tonight. And I love the punch. But mainly, I love your furry ears.'

Dominic shook his head. Whoever it was, it didn't sound like a conversation he wanted to listen in to.

He didn't want to walk any further. He was sweating in his armour and the sword fight hadn't helped. In the absence of a better option he found his keys, and strode back to his car, parked at the front of the building. He sat in the driver's seat, and automatically put his key in the ignition. That was an option, he supposed. He could leave. He could go home. He could go anywhere. He could drive off into the darkness and leave everything that had happened here behind.

He didn't. She was inside, and however awkward things were they had to be resolved. His life broke down into moments, and he'd let too many pass by already. His whole future, everything he'd dreamt of, all the things he'd hardly dared to plan for, were in the building opposite him. He looked at his watch. It was late, and they all had the wedding in the morning. She'd probably already have gone to bed. Would she? Maybe she was lying awake, hoping that he'd come back. Dominic took a deep breath and took the keys out of the ignition.

Maybe she would still be waiting for him. There was only one way to find out.

Chapter Seventy-Six

Alex

'You need to go to your own room.' Alex was lying on Helen's bed with his hands clamped over his face. He'd come to help her get cleaned up after the fight, but he had to admit he hadn't been much help. Mainly he'd lain on the bed moaning to himself. He took one hand away from his eyes, and looked at his friend. She was standing at the end of the bed with a balled up piece of toilet roll pressed to her cheek.

Alex pulled himself up so he was resting on his elbows. 'I messed everything up.'

'She didn't argue.

'I had a sword fight.'

'Yup.'

'I told you I loved you.'

'Yup.'

'I slept with Emily.' That was the big one.

'Yup.'

'I tried to chat up someone I've already slept with.'

'What?'

'I didn't even recognise her.'

Helen laughed. Alex felt he ought to be angry about that, but couldn't raise the necessary self-esteem to care. Maybe he'd be better off focusing on somebody else's screw ups. 'You've messed everything up too.'

'That's not fair.' Helen sat down next to Alex's feet, and took the toilet roll away. At least her face seemed to have stopped oozing.

'You kissed me.'

Helen shook her head. 'You kissed me. And we are never speaking of that again anyway.'

'You kissed Dominic.'

Helen slumped backwards, adopting Alex's favoured lying down position.

'And then you had a proper fight with Emily. There was gouging. Actual gouging. I don't think I've ever seen a gouging before.'

'She started it.'

'Whatever. It wasn't a great moment for the sisterhood.'

Helen closed her eyes. 'About the being in love with me?'

Alex moaned. He'd been hoping that was covered by Helen's instruction never to speak of the kiss again.

'You're not are you?'

Alex sat up properly. 'No.'

'Right.' She sounded slightly deflated.

'Sorry.'

She shook her head. 'Don't be. Why did you say you were?'

'It's hard to explain. There was the girl I'd slept with before, and then Emily and then one of the magician guys, and then you were there, and you seemed all glowy and lovely and kind, and your chest was doing this incredible heaving thing. And I don't know. You seemed so different from all the others.'

'That's how you get laid so often.'

Alex peered over his shoulder at his prostrate landlady. 'What is?'

'You say stuff like that, not the chest bit, the other stuff. You make people feel special.'

Alex frowned. It was true, wasn't it? He'd always known he wasn't the best-looking, or the smartest, or the funniest guy in any room, but he made women feel like he was only interested in them, even if it was only for a few minutes.

Helen sat up. 'What magician guys?'

'What?'

'You said there was a magician guy.'

He shrugged. 'One of the performer people. The ones dressed as fairies.'

'What did he have to do with anything?'

'He was there. He sort of ...' Alex tailed off. The guy had been there, and then he wasn't there. Thinking about it he suddenly felt overwhelmingly sleepy. Alex tried to blink the feeling away. 'I can't remember.'

Helen stood up and took a look in the fridge in the corner of the room.

'Anything good?'

She shook her head. 'Water. Lemonade.'

Lemonade wasn't going to cut it. 'I bet they do room service.' Alex reached for the phone on the bedside table. He pressed a button and gave the room number. 'We're going to need some of that punch bringing up.'

Chapter Seventy-Seven

Emily

'She's probably gone to bed.'

'Maybe.'

My dad is still fretting over his precious Tania. Hopefully, she's hundreds of miles away by now, but I can't tell him that. I have to wait, and let things play out. Obviously, he's going to be a bit upset, but I'll be there for him. For now, I just have to stay calm. Everything is normal. I point at the clock in the lobby. 'Look it's after midnight. She probably couldn't find you to say good night. She's not going to want to stay up late the night before the wedding. She needs her beauty sleep.'

'You're probably right.' He squeezes my hand. 'Are you all right pumpkin? You're a bit quiet.'

I don't answer.

'Not trouble with Dominic?'

I don't know what to say. I can't tell him about Dom. I can't face him being disappointed with me. That's not going to happen. I'm going to fix this. 'No. I had a bit of a falling out with Helen. No big deal.' It's as good a thing to say as anything. They say all the best lies are based on the truth.

He gives me a quick hug around the shoulders. 'You'll sort it out. I know what you girls are like.'

I can imagine what Helen would say to a comment like that. I nod, and let him get off to bed. Maybe that is one thing I can fix. I could talk to Helen. She's my best friend, and I'm sure she can explain what happened with Dom. Maybe if I start by making that one thing better, everything else will follow. I straighten down my dress and head upstairs.

Helen's room is at the far end of one corridor, almost opposite my own. As I approach, there's already someone in the hallway. Dom. 'What are you doing here?'

He spins round. 'I was ...' He looks around. 'I'm not sure. You?'

I shrug. Dom's supposed to be sharing my room. Was he coming to see Helen or looking for me or just going to bed? My brain is whirring from all the questions. My brain can go jump. I'm exhausted trying to keep tabs on how I'm feeling.

'Hi.' Helen opens the door a crack, only enough to see Dom. I cough pointedly. 'Right.' She opens the door. 'I guess you'd better come in.'

Chapter Seventy-Eight

Helen
Midsummer's Day

'What the hell?'

That was weird. It was exactly what Helen was thinking, but it wasn't her voice. That made no sense. Her thoughts. Her bed. It ought to be her voice.

'Where am I?'

It happened again, but this time it wasn't the first voice or her voice. Helen needed to open her eyes, and she would open her eyes, just as soon as she'd worked out how to unstick her eyelids.

'What happened last night?' That voice she recognised. That was Alex. Alex was her housemate, so they must be at home. If they were at home, things couldn't be that bad. She opened one eye. They weren't at home.

Helen forced herself to open the second eye. She was in bed. Not her bed, but a bed. She risked a tentative peer under the duvet. Still clothed. Sort of. Her dress had gone AWOL, but it turned out that historic costumes featured a lot of undergarments. She was still wearing more clothes than she'd happily leave the house wearing. That was fine.

She assessed the rest of the situation. Alex was lying next to her. She got a flicker of a memory from last night, and shut it straight down. Propping herself up on her elbows, she surveyed the room. The movement sent a shooting pain through her skull. There was a chaise longue in front of the window. Emily was lying on it under a blanket. Dominic was sitting up on the floor between the bed and the chaise, rubbing his face. He must have been the first voice. Dominic was wearing a T-shirt and boxer shorts and there was chainmail and a sword piled up next to him. The sword – another flicker of memory.

'I feel like death.' That was Alex. Helen sat up, swallowing down a wave of nausea.

'Are you gonna be sick?'

'No. Just can't move yet.'

She turned attention to Dominic. 'Are you okay?'

'Where am I?'

She waved an arm. 'Room.'

'Whose room?'

That was a good question. Helen tried to do remembering. She'd come up to her room after ... for some reason her brain didn't want to dwell on what it was after, but she definitely came up to her room. Then Alex came too, and then they ordered punch. After that things were hazier. There was a table straight in front of her with an empty glass bowl on it. An empty punch bowl, she guessed. 'I think it's my room.'

Dominic groaned. 'Why are we all in your room?'

Helen suspected the answer to that question might take a bit of processing.

On the chaise longue, Emily kicked one leg and flung an arm across her body, before sitting bolt upright. It was the fastest anyone had moved so far this morning. Watching her made Helen feel more nauseous. Emily yelped. 'Where am I?'

Dominic reached up and took her hand. 'At the hotel. You're safe. It's just a dream.'

Emily nodded. She looked around the room for a second before managing to pull a watch from amongst the debris of clothing and blankets around her. 'TIME!'

'What?'

'The time! My dad's supposed to be getting married in fifty-eight minutes.'

Panic competed briefly with hangover inside Helen's head. Panic won. She shoved Alex's arm. 'Go get dressed. Washed and dressed.'

At the other side of the room, Dominic pulled his chainmail on over his T-shirt, and Emily crawled under the chaise longue. 'I can't find my shoe.'

She dragged the blanket off the floor and shook it, apparently hoping to magic footwear from its depths. 'Sod it. I'll come look for it later.'

'Wait.' That was Alex. 'Aren't we going to talk about last night?'

Helen glanced at the others. Emily was pouting heavily, looking away. Dominic stared straight back at her. He shook his head.

'No.' Helen swung her legs out of bed. 'No time. Wedding first. Talking later. Much, much later.'

'She's right.' Dominic nodded. 'Let's get the wedding out of the way.'

Emily followed him towards the door, holding her hand out to Dominic. Helen looked away.

That left Alex. Business-like was probably the best approach. 'Right. Back to your room. Washed and dressed. I'll meet you downstairs in twenty minutes.'

He was still sitting on the bed.

'Alex!'

Chapter Seventy-Nine

Alex

Alex held up his hand. 'In a minute.'

Helen sighed. 'You've got to go. I need to get dressed.'

Alex was still in bed, covered by the duvet. He ran a hand over his torso, and down to his hips. No top, but he was still wearing the weird tight things that went with his Robin Hood costume. That was something. 'I think we should talk about last night.'

'I don't.' Helen stood up. 'We have to get ready for the wedding. Maybe we could agree never to talk about last night.'

She dragged the duvet off him. 'Hey! I could have been naked under there.'

Helen screwed her eyes up, and wedged her fingers in her ears. 'Seriously, never even say that.'

Alex hauled himself out of bed and found the T-shirt that went under his costume on the floor. Could he walk back to his room in T-shirt and tights? Would that be better or worse than the full costume? 'Helen?' She was still ignoring him. He raised his voice 'Helen!'

She took one finger out of her ear. 'You're not going to talk about being naked anymore, are you?'

'No. Promise.' He waited for her to open her eyes and free up the other ear. 'What are we going to do though?'

'About what?'

He shrugged. 'About everything.'

Helen glanced at the clock. 'We're going to worry about it later.'

There was a lump forming in Alex's throat. There was one thing he did need to clear up right now. 'We're okay though, aren't we? I've not messed that up?'

Helen shook her head. 'Of course not. You're stuck with me. We're practically family.'

His stomach clenched. 'Don't say that. It makes last night even weirder.'

'It's true though isn't it?'

Alex screwed up his face.

'Well not exactly family, but there's no fire is there?'

'What do you mean?'

'There's no heat between us. I love you. It probably would be easier if there was something like that between us, but ...' She tailed off.

Alex nodded. 'No passion.'

'Not a jot. So shall we just agree? No talking about ...' She mouthed the words too horrendous to say out loud. '... *the kiss* ever again.'

That sounded like a decent plan. Alex stood up and held his hand out towards her. She shook it. 'Deal?'

'Deal.'

That was one thing solved, but flickers of the true horrendousness kept jumping into Alex's brain. Emily's engagement ring. Dominic and Helen. The sword fight. Oh god. The sword fight. 'What about everything else though?'

Helen shrugged. She looked defeated. 'I don't think we can fix everything else.'

Alex placed one hand on each of her shoulders. 'Then let's focus on what we can fix. You're right. Let's get clean and dressed and get this wedding over with. You've still got a job to get. We might be destined to leave here every bit as sad and lonely as when we arrived, so let's at least see if one of us can get some career progression out of the whole debacle.'

Helen nodded. 'It's a plan.'

Alex smiled. It wasn't really a plan, but it had made one of them smile, and right now it was the best he could come up with.

Chapter Eighty

Emily

I stagger across the hallway. Dom and I are sharing, so we're stuck going the same way. I don't know what to say to him. I don't even know if we're still engaged.

'You probably need to go and see to the bride?'

Why would I want to go and see the bride? It takes my brain a minute to catch up with what he's saying, but of course, I'm a bridesmaid, aren't I? I was probably supposed to be in her room primping and preening her about an hour ago. 'Right. Yes.' I turn back towards Tania's room.

'Don't you need your dress?'

Not really. Hopefully, when I get to Tania's room I'll discover that she's long gone and all I'll have to do is sensitively break the news to my dad, and then let the wedding planner sort out the practicalities, while I take him home. I want to grab Dom and shake him and demand that he talks to me, demand that we move out of this limbo and get back to the plan. I don't. I'm too scared of what he might say if I try. Instead, I follow him back to our room and collect the long lilac dress from the back of the wardrobe.

He stops me as I'm leaving. 'Be nice to Tania. Okay?'

I nod.

'It's a big day. She's probably nervous.' He closes his eyes, like he's exhausted with thinking about anything. 'Just don't make trouble.'

I leave the room with his instruction in my ears. It's not fair. I'm not the one making trouble. She's the one who's trouble. Tania's room is around a corner at the opposite end of the building to my own. I knock three times and wait.

Nobody answers. This is it. She's gone. I've done it. I knock again, just to make sure.

'Who is it?' Shit. She's still here. She sounds half asleep though, which is wrong for a woman who's scheduled to be walking down the aisle in forty-nine minutes.

'It's Emily.'

There's a silence for a moment. 'Can you come back in a bit Em?'

No. I cannot come back in a bit. We're working to a schedule. I knock again. 'Open the door Tania.'

I hear her walking towards the door, which opens a crack. She's wrapped in a hotel robe, and it looks like she went to sleep with last night's make-up still on. At least we weren't the only ones who fell victim to the curse of punch. 'Emily, could you come back in a bit?'

I lean towards her. 'Why are you still here? I told you to go.'

Her face hardens. 'Go away Em.'

Why should I be the one who goes away? She's not supposed to be here anymore. I thought we'd reached an understanding.

She's still standing holding the door open the tiniest crack. She glances behind her, back into the room. There's something in there she doesn't want me to see, isn't there? I ram my shoulder into the door and push past her. I stop at the foot of the bed. I know who Tania is. I know what she's done, and I'm still shocked. I point at the prostrate, naked figure. 'You slept with that?'

The figure sits up. 'Morning.'

'He's about twelve.'

He furrows his brow with the effort of thought. 'I'm like twenty.'

Tania hurries back into the room after me. 'You have to go. I'm getting married today.'

282

The boy in the bed frowns. 'Woah. I mean you're like hot and that, for an old woman, but this is getting heavy.'

'What?'

'I mean. I'm like not ready for marriage.'

Tania screeches. 'I'm not marrying you!'

'You're not marrying anyone,' I point out. 'Not after I've talked to Dad.'

She takes an immensely deep breath, and glares at me. 'You stay there. Do not move. Do not go anywhere.' Assertive Tania is new. I find myself doing as I'm told. She turns towards the bed boy. 'You go.'

He also does as instructed, gathering clothes from the floor and throwing them on haphazardly. He pauses in the doorway. 'Well thank you for a lovely, like, evening.'

Tania stands completely still, eyes fixed on the floor. 'What are you going to do?'

'I'm going to talk to my dad.'

'Wait. I can explain.'

I don't want to listen to her explanations. I know what she'll say anyway. It was a mistake. It was a one-time thing. It didn't mean anything. It will never happen again. Yeah. I know exactly what she'll say. I storm out and across the corridor to Dad's room. Tania is right behind me, still wittering on about me not needing to do this. I knock. Dad answers straight away.

'I need to talk to you.'

A flicker of confusion moves across his face. 'Of course.' He glances at her. 'I thought you two would be getting ready by now?' I realise that I'm still dressed as a dishevelled Guinevere.

I look at my dad. He's already started getting dressed for his wedding. He's in suit trousers, with shirt and tie, and waistcoat, which is still undone. His shoes are sitting neatly together next to the wall, and his morning suit jacket is hanging on the wardrobe door. He's got a little tuft of hair sticking up above one ear. Tania smooths it down. I hesitate for a second. Whatever I say it's going to hurt him so badly, in a weekend where I've already hurt too many people. This is different though. I can't let him marry her.

'Sit down.' I gesture for him to sit on the bed. I sit next to him. I take hold of his hand. The skin feels loose across his knuckles. I've never noticed that before. 'I've found some things out about Tania that I think you need to know.'

He glances at his fiancée.

'She's been lying to you about who she is. Tania Highpole isn't her real name. She's called Tina Polanski.' I take a breath. 'And she's a murderer.'

My dad closes his eyes for a second. When he speaks it's to Tania, not to me. 'Did you know about this?'

He hasn't understood. Of course she knew about this. She did it.

Tania nods. 'Only since last night.'

'Why didn't you tell me?'

She shrugs. 'Em can do no wrong in your eyes. I didn't want you to think badly of her.'

He furrows his brow. 'Why would I think badly?' He turns back to me. 'Emily, were you trying to stop the wedding?'

I'm confused. Why is nobody focusing on the real issue here? I point at Tania. 'Dad, she killed someone.'

He nods. 'I know.'

'She's a murderer.'

He shakes his head. Tania moves to sit at the other side of him. 'It was involuntary manslaughter. I went to prison for four years, and when I came out I changed my name and I moved away, and I kept moving. I ended up in Italy about eight months ago.'

No. This can't be that simply explained. 'You killed someone.'

'I'm not denying it.'

My dad takes her hand. 'You don't have to talk about this.'

'It's okay.' She looks at me. 'He was my boyfriend. The whole story is too long and too horrible, but he hurt me, badly for a long long time. I'd decided I was going to leave him.' She swallows. Her eyes are moist, but she's keeping her voice low and under control. 'But he came home early. I was already in the car, and he was hitting the bonnet, shouting at me to open the doors. He was saying he was going to kill me. I had to get away. I had to. I reversed enough to try to go round him, but he jumped in front of the car. I couldn't stop. I didn't stop.'

I fold my arms. Dad might be going for her sob-story, but I'm not. 'If you were a victim of domestic violence you'd have got away with it. They have like special police and stuff.'

I see her and Dad exchange a look. He puts his arm around her.

'The police didn't believe me. He was a very respectable man. I was not a reliable witness, they said.'

'No.' It can't be right. 'How can you be marrying her if you know what she did?'

Daddy shakes his head. 'Tania's going to be my wife. You wouldn't marry someone and keep a huge part of yourself secret like that.'

That's not right. You have to make yourself into the person they want to marry. Of course you don't tell them about the bits that don't fit.

Tania leans her head against my dad's shoulder. He looks at me. 'I'm disappointed. This is my wedding day.'

There's a knot in my stomach. How can I be in the wrong? I was trying to protect him. 'There's something else.'

Tania sits bolt upright.

'There's what she did last night.'

'No!' Tania screams at me. 'That was ... I don't know what happened. It would never happen again.'

I glance at my dad. Half-dressed with his sticky up hair. He looks old. He turns to Tania. 'What happened last night?'

Her voice drops to a whisper. 'It's not important.' I open my mouth to disagree, but she keeps talking. 'I can't marry you.'

'Oh. Right.' There's no shouting or swearing. 'I see.' The calm is worse than the shouting would have been. He sounds defeated. 'Can I ask why not?'

She doesn't answer

My dad carries on. 'It's all right. I mean I know already. I don't know why I thought you'd want to really. I'm an old ...' His voice trails away. 'Just old.'

I'm blinking back tears. I've done the right thing though. A little bit of hurt now, to avoid a lot of pain later. That's the best thing.

'No. You're lovely. I just ...'

'Don't want to marry me. I see. I understand.'

'It's not that I don't want to marry you.'

Dad stands up. 'I'm sorry Tania. I think you've made it quite clear that you don't. It's probably better if you go now. There are things that will need to be sorted out. Cancelled.'

Tania stands up and walks to the door. 'I'm sorry.'

This is it. I've done it. She's going. She stops in the doorway. 'No.'

What's happening? She was going. I'd fixed it. She comes back and kneels down in front of my dad. 'I probably should walk away, but out of everything that's wrong, you're the only thing that's right. If I walk away from you I'll be miserable. It won't solve anything. Emily will still hate me.'

My dad shakes his head. 'Emily doesn't hate you.'

Tania glances at me. I don't say anything. She carries on. 'Yes. She does, but that's not the point. The point is I love you, and I know you love me. Let's get married today.'

'No.'

It's not what I was expecting him to say. Tania lets out a huge screechy cry and sits back onto her heels sobbing. For the first time I feel awkward. I shouldn't be here, but I can't leave in case she manages to talk him around. 'Why not?'

My dad's still sitting on the bed. 'Because you were right to call it off.'

'You don't want to marry me?'

'Of course I do, but I don't make you happy, do I?'

'You do.'

He smiles. It's a tiny little smile with no joy in it. 'Really? Have you been happy since we started living together?'

'Of course.'

'Honestly?'

Tania shakes her head. 'I'm scared of the house.'

'What?'

'It's too perfect. I feel like I'm imposing on it by being there.'

It's the first thing she's said that I agree with. She is imposing. It's our home, not hers.

My dad doesn't seem to agree. 'But you've not imposed on it at all. All your things are still in storage. I expected the first time I left you there alone, I'd come home and find African statues in the living room, and crystals in the airing cupboard.'

'I didn't want to mess it up.'

'It's your home. I wanted it to be your home.'

Tania laughs a tiny uncertain little laugh. 'There's more. I didn't want a big wedding.'

'I thought all women wanted big weddings.'

'No. I tried to tell you.'

My dad closes his eyes. 'I thought you were trying to be kind, stop me spending too much money.'

'No. I wanted something small, intimate.'

'Is there anything else?'

She shakes her head. 'So what do you think? Is there hope for us?'

'No!' I interrupt their little heart-to-heart. There's still the naked boy in her bed. She can't pretend that doesn't matter. You can't sleep with someone the night before your wedding and pretend it's not important. A voice in my head points out that I slept with someone the day I got engaged, but that was different. It has to be different. 'She still hasn't told you what she did last night.'

Dad holds his hand up. 'Not now Emily. I haven't had my say yet.'

Tania stares up at him. 'What do you want to say?'

'I don't want to say anything. I want to shake you.'

'Why?'

'Because you've sleepwalked us both into this, into this wedding that you say you don't want. You sleepwalk around the house, not really touching anything. When I met you, you were so alive. You were into everything. It was invigorating.'

'I thought you thought I was silly.'

'I thought you were wonderful.'

Tania shakes her head. 'I've been trying so hard to be what I thought you wanted. You might not like me when I stop trying.'

'Why not?'

'I'm scatty. I'm disorganised. I'm a terrible cook. I'm never ready in time for anything.'

He laughs. 'I know all that. There's something else.'

'What?'

He stops looking at her. 'You are much younger than me.'

'Not that much …'

He doesn't let her placate him. 'Enough for people to comment.'

'I don't mind that.'

'Maybe I do. I don't want to hold you back. I'm not looking for a nurse. I want a wife.' He glances behind them at the bed. Oh my god. My stomach turns. I want to retreat into a happy place somewhere inside my head and pretend this bit of the conversation never happened. 'I want you to be …' His voice tails off in a cloud of Englishness. 'I want you to be satisfied.' A tiny bit of sick rises in my throat.

Tania giggles. 'I am. I was. I would be.' She glances at me, and her cheeks colour red. 'I'm sorry.' She kneels up and takes his hand. 'I love you.'

'I'm a fuddy-duddy old academic.'

'And I'm a new age scatterbrain. You don't get to choose who you love. Theo?'

'Yes.'

'Will you marry me today?'

I knew she'd talk him around. I grab his arm, and pull it away from her hand. 'You can't marry her. She slept—'

'Emily!' He shouts my name. I stop short. I don't remember my dad ever shouting at me. Even when I was a child and I'd been naughty he never raised his voice. He continues more quietly. 'Emily, I want you to think very carefully about what you're about to do. Whatever Tania's done is between me and her, and whether I want to know is up to me.'

'But—'

'No.' He lets me keep hold of his hand, but turns his face back towards her. 'Tania, is there anything else that you want to tell me?'

She closes her eyes. 'I did a stupid thing.'

I see his Adam's apple jump as he swallows. 'Is it a stupid thing that's in the past?'

She nods.

'And you can promise that?'

'Absolutely.'

He stares over her head for a second. 'Then I don't want to know.'

'What?' That's crazy. How can you be safe if you don't protect yourself? How can you make a plan if you don't have all the information? You can't trust somebody just because you want to.

He turns towards me and takes hold of both my hands. 'Emily, look at me.'

I look into his face.

'Emily, I'm getting married today. I want you to be there and I want you to be happy for me. So what I'd like you to do now is go back to your room get dressed, do your hair, and come and be a bridesmaid. All right?'

I don't know what to say. I nod.

'Good. And while you do that, me and Tania have about twenty minutes to try and make this wedding fit the bride's wishes a little bit more.'

She laughs. She's happy. I look into Dad's face again before I go. He looks happy too. I've lost him. He thinks that loving her is going to be enough, and neither of them will ever forgive me for trying to split them up.

Chapter Eighty-One

Dominic

The ballroom had been transformed overnight. The ivy and flowers hanging from the beams were gone, as were the magicians and acrobats. In their place was the stage set for the perfect modern, middle-brow, middle-class wedding. The chairs, arranged in rows of six on either side of a central aisle, were covered in white calico with lilac bows on the back. At the front of the room, the registrar was arranging papers on the smaller of two flower-laden tables, while the groom paced, and then sat down, and then stood up again.

The room was filling up with people. Cheerful people. Brightly-clothed people. Loud people. Dominic closed his eyes in defence against the light and noise and colour. He could do this. It was one day. Get through the day. Smile for Theo and Tania. Everything else could wait until tomorrow. He forced his eyes open, and looked around. Helen and Alex were sitting together about halfway down the length of the hall. There was an empty seat beside them. Dominic paused. He watched Alex's head loll slightly to one side, and come to a fleeting rest on Helen's shoulder. A firm elbow in the ribs made Alex jump awake. Dominic smiled.

He took a seat, on his own, at the back of the room. The last few guests shuffled in around him. The scene was set. Everything was in place. All they needed now was a bride.

Dominic glanced at his watch. Five minutes past. That probably didn't even class as being 'fashionably late' yet. He peered forward, through the forest of bodies, at Helen. What was she thinking about last night? The back of her head wasn't giving him many clues. Maybe what happened last night was just a moment, and one moment every decade did not make a relationship, however electric those moments were. He had a relationship with Emily. They had plans and a future. She'd already picked new tiles for his kitchen. That was a relationship.

The stranger next to him shuffled in her seat and knocked his arm. He winced as a shot of pain pulsed into his shoulder. Tentatively he rubbed the arm. Really sore. Bruised maybe. The woman next to him looked concerned. 'Are you all right?'

He nodded. 'It's a sword fighting injury. You know how it is.'

Whether she knew how it was or not, she didn't get chance to respond. The music stepped up a notch into something vaguely wedding marchy. In the front row the groom and best man stood, and the motion rippled backwards through the room. Dominic twisted his neck to see the bride who walked slowly a few paces down the aisle. He twisted back again. Emily was following her. It was an odd experience – having a practise run at watching the woman you were going to marry walk down the aisle. He tried to imagine the tingle of excitement and nerves and anticipation that he would be expected feel if that big day ever came.

'Wait.' Dominic turned back towards the voice. Tania had stopped halfway down the aisle. 'Wait a minute.'

Theo stepped out into the aisle. 'What's wrong?'

'Nothing. Everyone wait a minute.' The bride hoiked up her skirt and ran out of the back of the room. A murmur went up. Dominic watched the registrar lean towards Theo who shrugged. In front of him, he saw Helen crane her neck to see what was going on. Their eyes met.

'Sorry! Sorry!' Tania ran back down the length of the room, clutching something in her hand. She hurried past Theo at the front of the room and accosted the waiter who'd been dragooned into pressing 'Play' on the music at the appropriate time. After a few seconds of conversation, she made her way back to her starting point. 'Sorry!'

A new tune blasted out of the speakers.

The woman next to him raised her eyebrows. 'What's this?'

'Blondie.' Dominic laughed. 'I think it's Blondie.'

A laughing Tania made her second trip down the aisle, and proceedings finally got underway. There was a reassuring quality to the promises the couple offered to each other. There was something solid about the idea that you were absolutely committed to another person for ever. That was what Dominic was supposed to have chosen. It was what he'd always been destined to choose. He watched Emily standing to one side of the happy couple and tried to muster the butterflies again. They wouldn't come.

Chapter Eighty-Two

Alex

Weddings always featured an awful lot of standing around. After the service, there were drinks and nibbles while the photos were taken. Alex helped himself to a second flute of champagne, and flagged down a waitress with a tray of tiny pastries.

'What are they?'

'Red onion and goats' cheese tartlets.'

Alex winced. Obviously, he could see that they weren't a full English breakfast, but as an option to soak up his hangover, a gussied up mini-quiche wasn't going to make the grade. He shrugged. 'I'll take the lot.'

He took hold of one side of the tray, and waited for the waitress to let go. 'You can't take them all.'

'I can.' He tugged the tray out of the girl's grip. There was a possibility that he was behaving like a jerk. He flashed a smile. 'Were you one of the evil temptresses handing out punch last night?'

The girl giggled and gave a tiny nod.

'Then I'm sorry but this is payback. Must have hangover food.'

She smiled back at him. 'Well if it's a medical need?'

'It totally is.'

She was still smiling as she walked away. Alex grinned to himself. Back on the horse.

'How did you get a whole tray?' Helen appeared at his elbow, and nicked one of his tartlets.

'Natural charm.'

'I doubt it. You smell like death.'

'Technically I smell like deodorant, sweat, vomit and a battered ego.'

'What does battered ego smell like?'

Alex gestured at the air around him. 'Like this.' He looked around the room. 'Weddings are weird.'

'Because of the implied subsuming of the female into the male?'

'No.' Alex cast his eyes around the room. 'Because of all this. It's all pretence, isn't it? Pretending that you can promise someone forever. You don't know, do you? You don't know what's going to happen tonight, let alone next year or in ten years? How can you promise that you'll still love a person in ten years' time?'

Helen shrugged. 'You can't know that you won't.'

'But that's not what getting married says. You're not saying "There's a statistical possibility that I could still love you in the future." You're saying that you definitely will.'

'Maybe if you really love them, then it is forever.'

'Is that how you feel about Dominic?'

Helen doesn't answer for a second. 'Yeah, but ...'

'I thought, if you really loved them there were no buts.'

She shook her head. 'It's a different sort of but. But you're right.'

Alex was surprised. Although, he did say an awful lot of stuff, he must be right some of the time. 'I am?'

'I've got to stop putting my life on hold. A moment every ten years? It's stupid, isn't it? I can't pay my mortgage, and I've reached the point where I'm seriously considering taking out a hit on the woman from the tax credits helpline. It's not a way to live.'

'So what are you going to do?'

'I'm gonna change it.'

Chapter Eighty-Three

Helen

Helen walked away from Alex feeling all powerful and in control. She was the author of her own destiny. She had come up with a plan. There were four easy steps:

Step One: Find Isabel Sutton and wow her with academic brilliance so that Sutton instantly offered Helen a job.

Step Two: Quit current job and move to Manchester, which was in The North, and therefore cheaper so she would definitely be able to afford the sort of dream home where the shower ran at a consistent temperature.

Step Three: Have a glittering career.

Step Four: Get over Dominic.

Easy. The first kink in the plan came when she couldn't find Professor Sutton. This was the sort of thing that would discourage a person less in control of their destiny. There was no need for panic. The esteemed professor had been here the night before. She was at the ceremony half an hour ago. So, logically, she must be here somewhere. The toilet? She might have gone to the toilet. Helen headed down the corridor to the ladies' loo. There was no queue but both cubicles were occupied. Should she wait? She shouldn't wait. Waiting for someone outside the toilet would be stalker-ish. Or maybe not. It could be like Helen had just happened to run into her here. One of the cubicle doors was opening. It probably wouldn't be her, in which case Helen could go into the cubicle, wait for a minute, flush and come out again. Nobody would think she was weird.

'Doctor Hart.'

It was Professor Sutton. What to do? She couldn't go

into the cubicle now because the professor would get away again, but if she didn't she was just a woman who liked to hang around in public conveniences. Hold on. Professor Sutton didn't know that Helen hadn't just come out of the other cubicle. She could still pull this back. She turned to the wash basin and ran the tap. Washing her hands. That was totally a normal thing to do. Helen started to relax.

'Doctor Hart?' She said it louder this time.

Helen ran the conversation over again in her head. She'd forgotten to answer hadn't she? She'd been concentrating so hard on looking normal that she'd forgotten to answer the question. Helen tried to smile and brazen it out. She turned and gave a slight jump, implying, she hoped, that she simply hadn't seen the other woman standing next to her in the two foot square space. 'Professor Sutton.'

'Isabel, please. Lovely ceremony.'

Helen nodded. 'Once they'd sorted out the music.'

Isabel laughed. 'I much preferred her second choice.'

She'd finished washing her hands, and was moving to the hand dryer. It was one of those super modern ones that dries your hands and makes you a cup of tea in less than ten seconds without trashing the planet. It also made about the same amount of noise as a jump jet taking off in the next room. There was no way Helen could impress anyone over that.

Isabel pulled her hands out of the dryer. 'Well, I'll probably see you later.'

She was leaving. She rounded the corner out of the door. It was now or never. Helen ran the four paces to catch up with her wiping her hands on her skirt. 'Elizabeth Fry!'

Professor Sutton stopped. 'I'm sorry?'

Helen dragged her voice down to a normal pitch and tone, as if shouting the names of eighteenth century reformers at the backs of passing academics was normal behaviour. 'You were asking last night about the links between the abolitionist movement and prison reform.'

Sutton stopped. 'I don't think one individual is of anything more than symbolic value.'

She was arguing, which was worse than her falling at Helen's feet in awe of her intellectual prowess, but significantly better than running away from the crazy toilet lady, and argument Helen could do. 'Well no, but there are parallels in the use of language around slaves and prisoners – the infantalisation and the othering.'

She nodded. 'That seems valid.'

Next came the tricky bit and Helen had no idea how it normally worked. The whole old boy network thing was outside of her expertise. She imagined there was some sort of special handshake and then you would all go and play golf. 'Do you play golf?'

Isabel shook her head. 'No.'

'No. Me neither.'

She glanced back towards the toilets. 'Were you waiting for me in there?'

Helen closed her eyes. This was it, wasn't it? Failure of the plan at Step One. She was destined to spend the rest of her life earning a pittance and mooning over her best friend's husband. 'I'm sorry.'

'Why? You know I'm straight, don't you?'

'What?'

'Gender studies. Female academic. People get the wrong idea.'

'No! I wasn't. I'm not. I don't want to …' Helen's mouth was still going. She was reduced to a mere spectator waiting to see what it would say next. 'I mean not that you're not attractive. You're not my type. I'm sorry. I said that already, didn't I? Sorry.' Helen clamped her mouth shut.

'Stop apologising. I can't abide women who constantly apologise.'

Every fibre of Helen's being itched to say sorry. *Must fight urge to apologise.*

'So why were you waiting for me?'

Helen gave up. She already looked completely ridiculous. 'I wanted to ask you for a job.'

'And you thought the ladies' toilet was the best place?'

Helen shook her head. 'Look. I'm not very in practise at this "seizing the moment" thing.' Isabel looked amused. Amused was better than horrified.

'Why didn't you say you were looking for a job?'

'I don't know. It seemed a bit forward.'

'But you already know I'm interested in your work. I told you that last night.'

It was true. She did.

'So come on. You don't get anywhere in life by babbling like an idiot in a toilet, do you?'

Helen supposed not. 'Can I start again?'

'Go on.'

Helen held out her hand for shaking. 'Hi. I'm Doctor Helen Hart. I'm an historian. I wanted to say that I've read a huge amount of your work, and I think the department you run in Manchester sounds incredible.'

'And?'

'What?'

'Now tell me what you want. Don't be so bloody polite.'

'Well I want a job.'

She nodded. 'All right then. Now we can talk.'

So they did, and it transpired that Isabel genuinely was familiar with Helen's work, and also had a departmental vacancy to fill.

'You're kidding.'

Professor Sutton shook her head. 'The posts were advertised in January, but we didn't fill them all.'

'So you're actually offering me a job?'

'No. I'm offering you an interview, but your publication record is good, especially considering that you don't have a full-time university post at the moment. And I would like to be able to offer dissertation supervision in your area.' She smiled. 'And you're clearly very keen.'

'Sorry about the toilet thing.'

Isabel held up hand. 'Don't apologise. I'm surprised you didn't apply when we advertised the post.'

Helen paused. 'I wasn't looking to move out of the area then.'

'And now you are?'

She took a deep breath. 'Now I realise that I don't have a reason to stay.'

'Okay. Well I've got your contact details on this napkin.' She held up the paper serviette Helen had pressed into service in the absence of anything as professional as a business card or notepad. 'Someone will contact you on Monday to set up an interview. Enjoy the rest of the reception.'

Don't do the happy dance until she's out of sight. Don't do the happy dance until she's out of sight. Helen waited until Isabel rounded the corner, and did the happy dance on her own in the hallway outside the toilets.

She didn't have anyone to be happy with her. Apart from Alex, of course, who seemed to have recovered from being in love with her dishearteningly quickly. Not dishearteningly because she wanted him to be in love with her. It would just be nice to think that she had sufficient allure to hold someone's interest for more than three hours. She hadn't spoken to Emily or Dominic since they'd been dispatched from the bedroom of shame. One of those problems felt too massive to think about. Helen looked up. The other was standing at the end of the hall. Emily.

Chapter Eighty-Four

Dominic

'Congratulations.' Dominic shook his soon-to-be father-in-law by the hand. 'Where's Tania disappeared to?'

'I think her and Emily wanted to adjust their hair.' Theo paused. 'Actually, I think Emily wanted to adjust Tania's hair.'

He put a hand on the younger man's elbow and pulled him away from the crowd. 'I did want to talk to you on your own though.'

'Oh?'

'Nothing to be worried about. Just work.'

Dominic thought back to their argument on interview day. It seemed like a very long time ago. 'The interviews?'

'No. No. Although we do still have to make a decision I suppose. But no. Something else.'

'Something wrong?'

Theo shook his head. 'I wanted to tell you that I'm retiring. I've got to give notice, but I presume they'll want to have someone new in post for the new academic year.'

'Wow.'

'Wow?'

'I just ... I don't know. I guess I didn't think you were the retiring sort.'

Theo chuckled. 'I don't think I was, but a good job, it's not the same as a good life, is it?'

'I suppose not.'

'The plan is to sell the house and move to the coast somewhere. I fancy Northumberland and Tania grew up by the sea.'

Dominic managed to arrange his thoughts into a coherent sentence. 'Well good luck. I hope it all works out for you.'

'I was thinking that you ought to apply for the job.'

'Your job?' Dominic shook his head. He'd only been a full professor for a couple of years. 'They'll want someone older.'

His boss chuckled again. 'Well you're not exactly the boy wonder anymore. Fifteen years in the department. Excellent publications record. Why not you?'

Why not indeed? It would fit with the plan, give him a nice salary boost, which would help support Emily not working and caring for the ever-increasing number of children she seemed to be visualising. That was the image in his head. It was what he'd been working towards. It was what his parents had sacrificed so much of their own comfort to offer him, and it was right there for the taking. Dominic found himself laughing.

'I have to go.'

'What?'

'I'm sorry. Enjoy the rest of the day.' Thoughts were rushing through his head. 'I have to go.'

'What about the job?'

What about the job? It was what Dominic had always worked towards. It was the sensible thing to do. It was the precise opposite of what a man who had sword fights in car parks would do. Dominic shook his head. 'I don't think so.'

'What if Emily's looking for you?'

'Tell her ...' Dominic paused. What should Theo tell her? 'Tell her I'll talk to her when I get back.'

He ran out to the car park and jumped in his car. What was he doing? Doubts started to crowd his head. He turned the radio on and up to drown them out. Another of his dad's old sayings jumped into his head. *It's easier to ask forgiveness than permission.* So maybe that was what he should do.

Chapter Eighty-Five

Emily

I stop at the end of the corridor. Helen is jumping up and down like a crazy person at the other end. I wait for her to see me. 'Do you hate me now?'

'What?'

'For what I did with Alex.' I'd understand if she did. I probably deserve to be hated.

She shakes her head. 'Do you hate me?'

I don't answer.

'For kissing Dominic?'

I shouldn't. She kissed my boyfriend, which is wrong, but the moral high ground's been moving too rapidly lately for me to want to risk clinging to it too tightly. 'I don't know.'

There's something I have to ask. 'Are you in love with him?'

She looks straight at me. She nods.

I don't understand. They were friends for years before he was my boyfriend. 'Why didn't you do something about it earlier?'

'He was with you.'

'Before that?'

'He was my teacher.'

'Not for a whole decade.'

She looks up to the ceiling. 'I'm a coward. If I never told him I'd never get rejected.' Tears are starting to form in the corners of her eyes. 'Anyway, it doesn't matter now. He's your fiancé.'

'Is he? He's hardly spoken to me today. I can't even find him. I think he might have gone home.' I feel like I'm floating in the middle of an ocean. I need something solid to cling onto. Without thinking I put my hand out against the wall next to me, and find myself sliding onto the floor. It's good. Good solid floor. Solid wall against my back.

Helen sits down next to me. 'He probably needs time to process it all. I'm sure he'll come back, or you can see him tomorrow.'

I don't think so. 'I've ruined it. I'm going to be alone.'

She wraps her arms around my shoulders. 'No. You won't. You've got your dad and your friends. You've got me.'

'Dad says he's moving to Northumbria.'

'Really? Who's going to be head of department?'

I look up. I'm not sure that's really the main point. 'What?'

'Sorry. It doesn't matter. He'll still be your dad though, won't he? People don't have to live in your pocket to care about you.'

Tears are building up behind my eyes. I give up. I let them flow. 'I can't manage on my own.'

'Yeah. You can. You can manage fine.' She moves her arm and grips my shoulders. 'You're far more capable that you tell yourself.'

'No. I'm not.' I wipe my eyes. It's nice for her to say it though. 'We'd better go back to the reception.'

She drags herself up, and then offers a hand to help me. 'You're going to be fine. Whatever happens with Dominic, you'll be all right. I promise.'

I try to smile. She's being kind, but she can't promise that, can she? Sometimes things aren't okay. Sometimes people leave and they don't come back.

Chapter Eighty-Six

Dominic

It was after four by the time Dominic pulled his car up outside his mother's terrace, and rang the doorbell. He listened for the sound of footsteps within, and was rewarded with the shuffling of her slippers on the worn carpet.

'Dominic! What are you doing here? Come in. Come in. Is something wrong?'

He followed her into the living room and sat at one end of the sofa next to his mother. The house could be full to bursting and still no-one in the family would sit on the armchair that remained in prime position in the room. His father's chair. 'Nothing's wrong. I came to tell you something.'

'Cup of tea? I'll get you a cup of tea.'

He put his hand out to stop her getting up. 'I'm fine.'

'A cold drink? A sandwich? There's some ham.'

'Really, I'm fine.'

'A beer?'

'I've got to drive back.'

Her face dropped a little. 'You're going straight back. You'll not stay for your tea?'

'Sorry.'

His mother shook her head. 'Don't worry. I know you young ones. Always somewhere to be.'

'I need to tell you something.'

Eventually she fell silent. 'Well go on then. I'll not bite.'

'I'm going to resign from my job.'

'Don't be daft.'

'I'm not. I'm serious. I'm leaving my job.'

She frowned. 'You're in trouble, aren't you?'

'I'm not in trouble.'

'Are you getting the sack? Is it these cuts?'

Dominic shook his head. 'I'm not getting fired. I'm resigning.'

She looked horrified. 'Why on earth would you do that? Your father worked at one place his whole career. You don't want to be chopping and changing about.'

'I'm not Dad.' He took a deep breath. The next part was the part he hadn't dared say out loud before. 'I hate being an academic.'

'Don't be silly. You've always wanted to be a Professor. You said so right when you watched those films.'

'What films?'

'You know.' She stared hard at the television, as though her force of mind might make the film in question appear on the screen. 'With the man in the hat and the snakes.'

'Indiana Jones? My job is nothing like Indiana Jones.'

'Well not the snakes.' She harrumphed. 'You could get yourself a hat. You'd suit a hat. Men don't really wear hats anymore, do they?'

'Mum, I'm going to resign.'

Her saw her brow crinkle slightly. She shot a look at the empty chair across the room. 'Your father always loved that you worked at a real university.'

'I know.'

'He'd tell strangers in the pub about you.'

'I know. And I know you sacrificed a lot to get me there.'

She shook her head. 'Well I wasn't having you going to the comprehensive. Not with the kids from around here.'

He had a flash of her sitting here alone night after night, never going out for fear of the local kids. 'I thought I might do teacher training.'

'Aren't you already a teacher?'

'Proper teacher training. Think of it that I want to give other kids the sort of help you and Dad worked so hard to give me.'

She pursed her lips. It struck Dominic how unchanging her life must have been. She'd cared for her husband, and for her child. What was she to do with herself now?

'Well it's up to you I suppose.'

That was the best he was likely to get. Dominic leant forward and touched his mother's hand. It felt small. She pulled it away. 'So you've to get back, you say?'

He looked at the clock. 'Perhaps a cup of tea before I go?'

She nodded.

Chapter Eighty-Seven

Emily

'I know it's a bit of a break from tradition, but I wanted to say a few words.'

Typical. Obviously Tania wants to say a few words. Why would she miss an opportunity to gloat about her victory? They're married now. She's going to make him move away from me. I try not to glower.

She thanks everyone for coming. Same old. Same old. Of course they're not here for her. They're all Dad's friends. Will I make a speech at my wedding? I try to picture what my wedding will be like. I can't see it. Even after all the bridal magazines I've been through with Tania, I can't picture the wedding I want. That doesn't matter though. When Dom comes back we can plan it together. I've decided that Dom is going to come back. He's my only option now Tania's won. I twist my engagement ring on my finger. I'm still engaged. I'm still going to be Mrs Collins. Nothing has to have changed.

Apart from Dom, who else will be at my wedding? My dad to give me away, which I suppose means Tania will have to be there. And Helen as a bridesmaid. Helen who kissed Dominic last night. Maybe not. That doesn't matter. All that matters is that there can still be a wedding. And we can have a wedding list with lovely silver cutlery and matching china and a gravy boat on it. I can still be a proper wife with a proper home.

Tania is still going on. She's thanking the caterers, and the florist, and the person who did the napkins. Actually the napkins were cool. They were folded into swans. Maybe I could have swan napkins too.

'And that just leaves the two most important people here today.'

Can you believe that? She's actually going to thank herself.

'Theo and Emily.'

What?

'Emily.' She turns to face me. 'You might not know all of this, but I've never had much of a family. I grew up with my grandparents, and I've never married.' She giggles slightly at her faux pas. 'Until today, obviously.'

The guests titter politely. She continues. 'So I never thought I'd have a family at all. I know we've had our differences, and I don't know anything about being a mother, and you're all grown up and beautiful and clever and clearly you don't need anyone to start being your mother now.' She giggles again. 'So you don't need a mother, and I have no idea how to be one, but I hope that you will accept me as a part of your family, because I am so grateful, truly, to be part of yours.'

I can feel myself welling up. I'm not going to start liking Tania. She's taking Dad away from me. I try to remember what Helen said. They don't have to be living in my pocket to care for me. I'm properly blubbing now. Tania's still watching me. I try to give her a little nod and a smile. Maybe Tania can come to my wedding but she'll have to wear something really ugly, and she's not calling herself the mother of the bride.

She turns back to her notecards. 'And finally, Theo. My husband.' She giggles again. 'Sorry everyone, but if you thought the last bit was soppy this is where it gets really unforgiveable.' She turns to face my dad. 'Theo, from the moment you picked me up out of the gutter in Verona ...' She turns back to the guests. 'That's a long story. But from the moment you picked me out of the gutter to this moment right now, you have been my salvation. There are mountains of books about how to find love, about how to make yourself ready for love, about what you're doing wrong if you can't find love – I know, I've read them all – but here's what I've learnt since I met you. They are all bollocks. Nobody is ever ready for love. You can't plan the perfect relationship or put in the right work at the right time to find the right man. Love is something that drifts past you when you're sitting in the gutter. All you can ever hope to do is grab hold of it when it passes, and then keep hold wherever it takes you. I love you Theo, and I promise to keep loving you no matter where it takes us.' She puts her cards down on the table and reaches for her glass. 'To Theo!'

The guests raise their glasses to Dad, but I can't stop watching Tania. My dad stands and kisses her, softly and quickly. She's got everything she needs.

I can't concentrate through my dad's speech. I think it involves some sort of metaphor about marriage and the English Civil War. I don't really follow it, but I can't imagine that it was a good idea. My brain is racing though. Tania's right. You have to grab love when it finds you. You have to take hold and not let it go. It's the only way you can ever be safe from ending up alone.

The second the speeches are over I excuse myself from the top table and run into the lobby. I'm going to need a taxi or a lift or something. How does this work in films? In films there's a man in a uniform and he makes a taxi appear. There's no man, and my phone is in my room because bridesmaids' dresses don't come with pockets, and the weird little satin pouch thing that goes with it is full of Tania's stuff. Nobody tells you that about being a bridesmaid. It's mainly carrying stuff for the bride that she'll never need.

I will not be defeated by this problem. I set off to run up the curved staircase to find my phone. I will ring for a taxi.

That will involve a half hour wait for it to come, but it's better than nothing.

'Emily!'

I stop halfway up the stairs. Dom is standing in the lobby.

'Dom!'

I lean on the banister rail. It's almost like Juliet leaning on her balcony, only this story is going to have the proper fairy tale ending. This could be it. This could be my big romantic moment where I choose to follow Tania's advice and grab love as it passes.

'We ...'

'I ...'

We both speak at once, and then both stop at once, and then both start up again. I giggle, and point at him. 'You go.'

He sighs. 'I think we need to talk.'

Yes. We do. And probably not by shouting at each other up the stairs. 'Do you want to come up, or shall I come down?'

He pauses. 'It's quiet outside. We could walk.'

I run back down the stairs, and follow him out towards the car park. The heat outside hits me like a wall. It's hot and close, the sort of weather that usually comes much later in the summer, and makes people mutter about humidity and gathering storms. We make our way past the gaggle of smokers by the door and onto the lawn.

'So do you want to go first or shall I?'

I ought to go first. If this is my moment to grab hold of love, I should go first and jump in with both feet. I shrug. 'After you.'

He closes his eyes and stands still for a moment. 'I don't know where to start. I mean there's all the stuff from last night, but I don't even know whether it's worth getting into that.'

Why wouldn't it be worth getting into that?

Dom starts walking again, slowly across the lawn. 'I think we have to start being honest about who we are.'

'I know who you are.'

He shakes his head. 'I think you know who I planned to be. I think you know who I've been trying to be.'

That doesn't make sense. Dom is exactly who I think he is. He's solid. He's reliable. He's the quick drying woodseal of potential partners. You know exactly what you're going to get. 'Of course I know you. We're engaged.'

Dom swallows. 'I think the jury's still out about that.'

Right. Yes. Of course. 'But that's what we need to talk about ...'

He stops and turns to face me. 'Stop. You need to listen to me.'

I shake my head. 'Don't be silly, Dom. I know who you are. You're a history professor. You live on Southside in a Victorian house. You went to an all boys' school.'

He puts his hand up. 'That's not who I am. For starters, I hate being called Dom. It makes me sound like I should be starring in fifty shades of whatever.'

I can feel myself pouting. 'It's cool. It makes you sound young and dynamic.'

'But I'm not young and dynamic.' He pauses. 'Sorry. That wasn't what I wanted to tell you. I'm going to resign from the university.'

'What?'

'I don't enjoy it. I'm going to leave.'

Leave? He can't leave. 'So you'll be unemployed?'

'Hopefully not for too long. I'm thinking of retraining.'

'So you'll be a student?' I can't be engaged to a student. Students don't live in nice houses. Students eat pot noodles. I don't want to eat pot noodles.

'Hopefully, and then I want to be a proper teacher.'

'But you're already a teacher.'

'Hardly. I want to work with kids when they're still young enough for it to feel like I'm making a difference. Maybe even primary school?'

'But that's a girl's job.' I can't help but imagine what Helen would say to that. 'What do primary school teachers earn?'

'I'm not sure. Enough I think. Less than I do at the moment probably, at least to start with.' He narrows his eyes. 'Is that all you're worried about?'

We had a plan. Dom was going to work at the university. He'd probably have ended up as Head of Department. I'd give up work to look after our children, or maybe a little bit before, maybe as soon as we were married. We were going to have a nice house and nice children and nice lives. 'I don't see how this fits into the plan.'

'That's the point. It doesn't really, does it? I might not get a job as a teacher. I might not get a place to train near here. I might have to sell my house and rent something smaller. It's all unknowns. I might decide against teaching altogether. I know I can't carry on like I am at the moment. It might change in a few months but today, right now, I can't promise you any sort of plan.'

This is worse than knowing he kissed Helen. That was a moment of madness. This is throwing away everything we'd agreed. I don't know what to say.

'I feel like we both came into this with an idea of the lives we ought to have. I wonder whether we wanted that dream or whether we wanted each other. So I guess it's up to you. Do you want me for me?'

I came out here to talk him into sticking with us. I came out here to grab hold of something and never let go, but now I'm not sure what that something was. 'It's hard.'

He shakes his head. 'No Em. It's easy. Do we love each

other? That's the thing we've never actually talked about. We had all these plans, but that's not love, is it?' He sighs. 'So it's a yes or a no. Do you love me Em?'

I try to take a long hard look at him. Dom. Sorry. Dominic. Just him. No promises. No plans. How can I love him? I don't even know him. 'No.'

Dominic nods, and then we both stand in silence for a moment. He kicks his toe into the turf and lets out a little whistling noise. 'Well this is a awkward.'

'Do you want the ring back?'

'No. It's fine. Keep it. I mean, unless you want to give it back. What do you normally do?'

What does he mean 'normally'? 'What? In my vast experience of breaking off engagements?'

'No! I don't mean "you." I meant one. One's a useful word, isn't it? People should say one more.' He looks at me. 'Sorry.'

I'm not cross. Probably I should be. 'Are you upset?'

'Honestly? A bit, but mainly I'm excited.'

'Why?'

'Because there's always been this plan for me, since I was five years old, and now there's nothing. I can do whatever I want.'

'That's terrifying.'

'And also brilliant. What will you do now?'

'I have no idea.' And I don't. Dad's going to sell the house. I'm not getting married. I'm going to have a new boss at work, so everything's changing there. And I tried to grab love like Tania said, but it hasn't helped. 'This is weird, isn't it?'

'How?'

I'm not sure. I'd have expected breaking off an engagement to be more dramatic. 'It feels like there ought to be weeping and wailing.'

He nods. 'Well maybe that's a sign.'

'What do you mean?'

'Maybe we both deserve something more. Something where we don't have to think about whether it's love. Something where we just know. A bit more passion.'

I'm not sure about that either. Passion is dangerous. Passion isn't going to look after me. 'I'd better get back inside. Are you coming?'

He shakes his head. 'Maybe I should go.'

'No. I mean you were invited, and it's still Dad's wedding. Stay.'

'Are you sure?'

I nod. I mean, why not? It's not like it can make the day any worse.

Chapter Eighty-Eight

Emily

I excuse myself as soon as we're back inside. Even though we seem to be attempting the amicable break-up thing, the idea of a whole evening making small talk is too much. The party has broken up a bit, but I can't see Dad or Tania anywhere. I decide to go for a walk for real, to see if I can clear my head. It's still hot outside. Normally I like hot weather. It makes me feel bright and hopeful. Today might as well be covered in black cloud. Everything I've done was pointless. Dad married Tania anyway. Dom left me anyway. I walk around the corner of the building and stop. Dad and Tania are squeezed together on a bench, snogging like loved-up teenagers. 'Oh sorry.'

Tania pulls back giggling. She smiles at me. 'Are you enjoying the day?'

I nod, because I don't really know what to say. Tania's still, smiling at me and she was so nice in her speech. I wonder why.

'Are you sure?'

'I'm fine.' I blink hard to try to stop the crying from starting. 'I'm going back inside.' I'll go back to my room, have a good cry there, and then I'll make a new plan.

'Wait.' Tania catches up with me in the doorway. 'You're not fine. What's wrong?'

'Dom. Me and Dom.' I shake my head. 'We can talk about it tomorrow. I don't want to spoil your day.'

'Don't be silly.' Tania drags me back to the bench. I let her sit me down between her and Dad. 'What happened?'

'We split up.'

Dad starts to get up. 'That man. I'll see that he's sorry for this.'

Tania puts her arm out. 'Sit down Theo.'

He sits down.

'What happened?'

I shrug. 'We split up. It's okay. Really. I just ... I'm just feeling a little bit alone.'

Tania puts her hand on top of mine. 'Because of Dominic, or because of all this as well?' She waves her free hand in a gesture that takes in her dress, and the wedding venue, and my dad.

I nod.

'And the fact that we're moving as well?'

'Yeah.'

Dad leans forward. 'Wherever we go there'll be a place for you to come and stay. Whenever you want.'

I glance at Tania. She nods. Maybe I could go with them after all. Maybe I could keep living with Dad. Maybe I don't have to be alone.

He wraps his arm around my shoulder. 'But ...' his voice is cracking as he talks. 'But I think that being on your own for a little bit might not be so bad.'

I shake my head.

'You're young. You've never lived anywhere but at home with me, and you were going to go straight to being somebody's wife.'

The tears start up again, and now I can't stop them. They're shaking my whole body. 'I'm always going to be alone, aren't I?'

'What?'

I turn to my dad. 'You're going. Dom left. Mum left me.'

He closes his eyes. 'Is this about your mum?'

My head drops forwards. I can't answer. 'Everyone leaves me.'

'Theo.' Tania hisses the word at him. I don't look up, but I sense that there are some looks being exchanged above my head.

I hear my dad sigh. 'How much do you remember about your mum, Emmy?'

I don't say anything. It's not something we talk about. It's not something we ever talked about.

My dad continues. 'You were so little, and after a few weeks you stopped asking after her, and then when you got bigger you always just said that she left. Is that what you remember?'

I screw my eyes up tight. I don't want to think about it.

I feel a hand rubbing my back. It's Tania. 'How long is it since she?'

'Twenty years.' I murmur. 'Twenty years ago. I was strapped into the back of Mummy's car ready for the drive home from school. Mummy looked tired, maybe, or maybe I just think that now.' I don't want to think about this, but now I've started it won't stop. The words come rushing out. 'And I remember noticing that she had driven a different way from normal. We went the wrong way out of school.' Again it's all half memories. I look at my dad. 'Is that right?'

He nods.

'She drove onto the bridge over the river, the new bridge out towards the motorway, and she stopped the car. Mummy walked to the edge of the bridge, climbed onto the barrier and flew. That's what I remember. I remember seeing Mummy trying to fly.'

I hear my dad gasp. 'You never talked about it. I took you to a counsellor. Do you remember that?'

I shake my head.

'You wouldn't talk about it. In the end we thought you didn't remember, or didn't understand.'

I'm back in that car, with the sirens and the police lady,

and then the trip to the police station to wait for Daddy. I remember when he arrived. He picked me up and squeezed me and told me he'd never leave me alone again. 'You lied.'

'What?'

'You said you'd never leave me alone.'

'When?'

'At the police station.'

He shakes his head. 'Sweetheart, I'm sorry.'

It's like I've picked the top off a scab, and now it won't stop bleeding. I want to push the memory back into its box, but I can't. 'And she lied too, didn't she? She was my mum. Mums are supposed to be there. They're supposed to look after you.'

'Your mum was very ill, Em. She was ill before we had you. I think loving you was probably the only thing that stopped her doing it sooner.'

'But she didn't love me enough, did she?'

'Your mum was very poorly.'

I shake my head. I don't want to hear what he's going to say. I get that she must have been depressed. Part of me even gets that it wasn't her fault, but she still did it. I was five years old, and it wasn't my fault either. 'She should have loved me enough.'

Dad squeezes my shoulders. 'She did love you.' He takes a deep breath. 'I'm sorry.'

I sit up. He looks so small and so scared.

'She didn't give up on you sweetheart. She gave up on herself.'

'Everyone leaves me.'

He looks over the top of my head to Tania. She takes hold of my hand. 'We're not leaving you. You're always going to be part of this family, but your dad has to let you grow up. You're not that little girl any more, are you?'

I lean against him. 'I can't manage on my own.'

'Of course you can.' My dad still has his arm wrapped around my shoulders. 'I remember you on the day it happened. When I got to the police station I expected you to be hysterical, but you were sitting in a corner drinking squash and playing with a doll they'd found for you. You were completely self-sufficient.'

Tania squeezes my hand. 'Sometimes you have to change how you think about yourself. You don't have to be the little girl whose mummy left her. You can be the woman who survived all that and grew up stronger. Think about it. You've survived the worst thing already. Whatever happens next you'll survive that too.'

I let her join in the hug. It's the first time we've done that. Maybe she's right. I can think about myself differently, and think about my world differently. It's not just me and Dad clinging together anymore; it can be looser, easier with space for people to come into my life, and space, as well, for them to go.

My dad rubs my back as I let Tania hug me. 'I'm not sure if this is the right time, but you'll have some money too. I won't let you struggle.'

I shake my head into Tania's shoulder. 'I thought I was supposed to be learning to stand on my own two feet.'

'You're entitled to it. I used your mum's life insurance to pay off the mortgage so you'd have somewhere secure to live, but now, well, she'd have expected some of that to come to you eventually.'

I shake my head. For some reason not taking his money suddenly seems important.

'It wouldn't be lots, but maybe enough for a deposit on a house.'

I shake my head again. 'Maybe you could keep hold of it for me.'

He nods.

Tania bats him with her hand. 'She's twenty-five. She doesn't need a house now anyway. She should be buying silly things, shoes or a racing greyhound or a beach hut or something. There's plenty of time for being a grown-up once you've finished enjoying being young.'

My dad laughs. 'Really? So when are you going to start?'

'What do you mean? I'm still very young.'

And I laugh too. It feels weird to be laughing with Tania, but it looks like she might be sticking around after all.

Chapter Eighty-Nine

Helen

The evening festivities tonight were in a more traditional wedding reception vein than the previous night's dreamy woodland folk and fairy themed spectacular. There was a DJ, proudly and repeatedly declaring his intention to play all the biggest hits from the 1960s right up to today. If the claim was true it was going to be a staggeringly long party.

Dominic was standing in the doorway, and Helen realised that she hadn't seen him since the ceremony, and in her excitement about the possible new jobs she hadn't missed him. At least, she'd missed him less. She raised an arm in greeting.

He waved back and wandered over. 'So, disco?'

Helen nodded.

'I hate discos.'

She nodded again. 'Me too. The only kind of dancing I can do is slow-dancing.'

The current song appeared to be based around the singer finding that his valued pet dogs had escaped and needing to query who might have let them out. It was an odd premise, but it gave Helen confidence that there was very little risk of a slow-dance in the immediate future. 'I didn't see you at the meal?'

Dominic shook his head. 'I had to pop out.'

'Really?'

'Just to see my mum.'

'That's a four hour round trip.'

'Nearer four and a half.'

'Is she okay?'

'She's fine. I ...' he laughed. 'It's going to sound mad.'

Helen waited.

'I needed to tell her I was quitting my job.'

Helen's throat clenched and the lightness in her chest evaporated. It was as if the perfectly lovely sedate little merry-go-round car she was riding on had become detached and slammed headlong into a wall. 'You're quitting the university?'

He nodded. 'I'm going to apply for teacher training.'

'Where?' She told herself to be calm. He could go where he liked. She was planning on leaving anyway. Whether he stayed here or not made no difference.

'It's late to apply, so wherever there's a space probably. I'm going to try to get somewhere in the North-west though.' He paused. 'Seeing Mum today. She's getting old, and she's alone.'

'Wow.' Helen didn't quite know what to say. They were talking, which she had decided to view as progress, but neither of them were mentioning the events of the night before. 'So, er ... how does Emily feel about moving?'

He looked straight at her. Stupid blue eyes. 'Emily won't be coming.'

Oh.

Across the room the DJ raised his microphone to his lips. 'Ladies and Gentlemen, please welcome to the floor, for their very first dance as man and wife, Mr and Mrs Midsomer.'

There was so much about the moment that Helen would normally mock, and Dominic was generally an excellent mocking partner. The whole notion of the *first* dance was laughable, as if this was a society where nice married couples spent the majority of their nicely married time waltzing. And then there was the fact that he said 'man and wife' rather than 'husband and wife.' Helen could have written a short essay on that element alone. Today she didn't say anything. Her brain had disengaged from her mouth and her senses. All she could do was watch as Professor Midsomer and Tania shuffled and twirled around the floor.

'Ladies and gentlemen, the bride and groom would like to invite you to join them on the dance floor.'

The DJ managed to entice two or three couples onto the floor. Dominic's arm moved at Helen's side. His fingers brushed against hers, and then wrapped around her hand. 'Shall we?'

She nodded and let him lead her onto the edge of the floor. She put one hand on his shoulder and his arm curled around her waist. Neither of them were great dancers but they held and swayed against one another in some sort of rhythm, and the music was soft enough that Helen could hear his breathing against her hair.

She leant her head against his shoulder, facing in towards his neck. 'So ... Emily?'

'We broke up.'

'I'm sorry.'

'There's no need. It wasn't right, was it?'

She didn't reply. They were probably a bit far down the line for her to be worrying about loyalty to Emily.

'Maybe we should talk about that kiss.'

'Probably.' There was so much she should say. She wanted to explain that he needn't think he could just jump from Emily to her, and she wondered whether she should also tell him the whole truth, that she'd loved him from afar for years, and that only that morning she'd decided to stop loving him. Obviously she hadn't actually achieved that yet but she had definite good intentions in that area, and in addition to that, even if she did keep loving him she wasn't at all sure how comfortable she was with the paradigm of the traditional relationship in which women are often seen as adjuncts to a male partner's needs and career.

'Actually no.' Dominic interrupted her mental argument.

'What?'

'I know us. I know what we're like when we analyse things and discuss them. We'll end up with lists of pros and cons, and we'll never actually do anything.'

'Well analysing the situation is good academic practice.'

'But this isn't an academic problem.' He laughed. 'I really fancy you. I've really fancied you for a very long time. I think last night you kissed me like someone who probably feels the same. And now we're both single. Stupid people could work this out.'

'What?'

And he moved his head ever so slightly, so she wasn't facing his neck anymore, but his lips, and then he brought his lips to meet hers.

She pulled back. 'I don't think ...'

'Don't think. I'm sick of thinking about this. Let's do whatever it is that we want right now in this moment.'

She stepped forward and raised her chin. Their lips met, firm and warm and right, and this time she didn't pull away.

Chapter Ninety

Alex

Alex nursed his pint on the edge of the dance floor watching his housemate and Professor Collins. A movement in the corner of his eye caught his attention. Emily walking out of the ballroom. He downed the dregs of his drink and set off after her. It was time to get serious. Time to stop messing around and grow up. He'd watched Helen wait and wait and break her heart before the moment she was clinging onto came to anything. He wasn't going to be the same. And granted a desperate shag in a disabled toilet didn't have quite the romantic wistful quality of a fleeting moment that never quite was many years past, but, on the other hand, it had shagging, so it was better really. Moments with shagging in them were always better.

'Emily!'

She stopped a few feet in front of him and turned around, her arms folded across her chest. 'Hi.'

He watched her shuffle from one foot to the other, keeping her eyes fixed on the ground.

'Hi.'

So now he'd run after her, he must need to say something. He wasn't sure what. Actually he was sure what; he just wasn't sure where to start. 'You saw Helen and Dom?'

She nodded.

'And how are you?'

She shrugged. 'Me and Dom split up.'

'I guessed from the ...' Alex pointed back towards the party. '... from all the tongues and everything.'

She nodded. 'Yeah. I guess he's moved on. Well I'd better get going.'

'Going where?'

She stopped. 'I have no idea.'

'Then stay.'

'Here? In the lobby?'

Alex looked around. It was as good a place as any. 'I wanted to talk to you.'

She shook her head. 'I'm talked out.'

'Then listen. I'll talk.'

'Go on.'

'I can change. I can be the man you need. I'll get a proper job. I'll get a house and we can have a nice safe car with the child seats in the back. I can be that guy.'

She laughed. She actually laughed at him. 'No. You can't.'

Alex's stomach clenched. This was his moment. He had to make her believe this. 'I can. I can change. I can grow up. I think I'm in love with you.'

'Because we had sex once?'

'No!' That was ridiculous. Alex had had sex with lots of women once. It had never had this effect on him before. 'I can't stop thinking about you.'

'Apart from last night when you were thinking about Helen?'

'That was the punch.'

Emily shook her head. 'Course it was.'

There was something in her face he hadn't seen before. A steeliness perhaps. 'So what are you going to do now?'

'I don't know. I might look for a flat or a new job or go back to college. I might buy a salmon farm off the coast of Scotland. I might buy a one way ticket to Thailand and go travelling.'

'Like backpacking?' Alex laughed. The image of Emily

backpacking was crystallized in his head. 'You know backpacking is sort of slumming it, don't you?'

She stuck out her chin. 'Don't you think I can manage?'

'I'm sure you can manage. I'm just surprised you think you can.'

'Maybe I'm learning to stand on my own two feet.'

Alex's heart fell. 'So you don't need me to take care of you?'

She closed her eyes. 'It's tempting, but I'm trying to do something different. It might be a horrible mistake.'

'But at least it's a different mistake. Right?'

'Yeah.' She took a final step towards him and kissed his cheek. 'Goodbye Alex.'

Chapter Ninety-One

Emily

I start to walk away. It's the right thing to do. He's cute, and he's funny, but he's not the man for me. Even as I think it a little voice nags in my head. He wasn't the man for you, but you're changing. Who knows who the man for New Emily might be?

'No.'

I stop and turn back towards him. The grin he always has is playing at his lips. He catches my eye, and I feel my lips curling into a smile. 'What?'

'Let's not say goodbye. Let's say until we meet again.'

I shrug. I mean that's fair enough. I probably shouldn't rule anything out completely on day one of my new life.

'So, what about this? Six months from today.'

'What about it?'

'Meet me.'

I don't understand. 'What are you talking about?'

'Six months from now.' He looks at his watch. 'Eight p.m. I will be back here waiting for you.'

'Why?'

'Because you need to prove that you can cope on your own, but once you've proved that, you'll have the choice, won't you? You'll be able to choose whether you want to carry on your journey on your own or ...'

'Or with you?'

'Exactly.'

It's a crazy idea. 'I don't know where I'll be in six months.'

He takes a step towards me. 'That's fine. I'll be here. Everything else is up to you.'

He's mad. 'So you're planning six months ahead. Are you sure?'

'Yeah.'

'I thought you didn't like to plan beyond your next meal.'

He takes one step towards me. 'I'm making an exception for you.'

It would be so easy to do this now. I could kiss him, and take everything he was offering. I could accept that he could be the guy who makes plans, and settles down. He says he wants to be that guy. Do I want to be that girl? I remember the date. Midsummer's Day. 'Six months today will be Christmas Eve.'

Alex grins. 'I'll bring some mistletoe then.'

'Okay.' And this time I do walk away, because if I stay I'll change my mind.

Part Four

Winter

Chapter Ninety-Two

Helen
Christmas Eve

Helen swore to herself as she wiggled the useless key Dominic had got cut for her in the temperamental lock of his flat door. She slung her bag on the sofa and went straight to the kitchen. As expected Dominic was at his laptop on the breakfast bar with a pile of textbooks on the floor at his feet.

'It's Christmas eve. Stop working.'

He grinned. 'Just got to finish this lesson plan.'

'You're writing plans for next term's teaching practice?'

'No. This is the last one for last term's teaching practice. It's a lot easier to know what's in the lesson after you've taught it.'

She walked around the table and wrapped her arms around his neck. 'I don't think that's how it's supposed to work.'

'Okay. Okay. I'm stopping.' He clicked save and shut down the computer. 'I'm officially off for Christmas then. We have about fifteen hours together before we have to go to my mother's.'

Helen raised her fist in a gesture of faux celebration.

'Are you sure you don't mind going to Mum's?'

'It's fine. I think she's warming up a bit. I'm sure she smiled while we were there last time.'

'I think that was wind.' Dominic swung his legs round so she could perch on his lap. 'I heard you swearing at the door.'

'It's a stupid lock.'

'You have to sort of lift and wiggle the key a bit.'

'If you moved in with me …'

He closed his eyes. 'We agreed that it was too soon to live together. We agreed that having separate places was sensible.'

It was true. They had. 'And how many nights have we actually spent apart since we agreed that?'

He glanced at the floor. 'Two.'

'Yeah. And that was because I went to stay with my baby niece while my sister was in hospital, wasn't it?'

He nodded. Sensible was proving expensive. 'I've got two more months on the tenancy.'

'And after that?'

He smiled. 'I don't know. I'm not sure I want to live in sin.'

'I live in Didsbury. It's a very nice class of sin.' Helen laughed again. 'Anyway, sin's all you're being offered. Make the best of it.'

He wrapped his arms around her. 'Sin sounds good.'

'Excellent.' She leant in and kissed him for a long time. When she pulled back she glanced at the clock. 'Hey. It's ten to eight.'

Dominic frowned. 'So?'

Helen rolled her eyes. 'Alex and Emily's big date.' Alex had banged on about their promise to meet up again in six months' time every time she'd spoken to him since Theo and Tania's wedding, until their last conversation a couple of weeks ago. Then he'd been strangely muted on the subject. Nerves, or cold feet? It had been impossible to tell. 'Do you think they'll both turn up?'

Dominic sighed. 'I don't know.'

Helen reached into her pocket and pulled out a fiver, which she placed on the table. 'Five pounds says they're both there.'

Dominic shook his head. 'I'll take that.'

Helen bit her bottom lip. 'Does it bother you?'

'What?'

'The idea of Emily with somebody else.'

He laughed. 'No. It's just weird thinking back to where I might have ended up. Married to Emily. Still in the same job. Perfect house. Perfect job.'

'And instead you're here?' Helen looked around his rather brown and dated kitchen.

Dominic was only looking at her. 'Exactly where I'm supposed to be.'

Chapter Ninety-Three

Emily

I glance at the clock on the dashboard. 7.55p.m. I'm only doing this out of curiosity. I don't care whether he's there or not. Of course he won't be there. It was a stupid joke six months ago. He won't be there. I'm simply curious to check. And if he's not, I'll just drive on to Birmingham and catch the last flight up to Newcastle, and spend Christmas with Dad, and Tania and the bump. Six months ago I had a fiancé and I was planning a brood of my own. Now I'm freaking out about being a big sister for the first time.

I pull onto the long gravel entrance road, and drive up to the manor. The building's in darkness apart from the lamps either side of the door. I guess people don't book big country weddings this close to Christmas. I get out of the car and sit on the low wall next to the entrance. I'm still early. The fact that he's not here now doesn't mean anything. I flick through the messages on my phone. There are two from work, even though it's three hours past finishing time on Christmas Eve. The new head of history takes workaholic to a whole new level. At least he took my instruction to contact me instead of his departmental assistant seriously. I don't want my replacement scared off in her first month.

This place is completely different in winter. The trees that were full of life in June are bare and grey now. I remember the noise and the magic and the costumes. It feels like a dream, something fleeting that disappears when you wake up. Only not all dreams are fleeting, and not all nightmares end when you open your eyes. Some of them have to be examined until they lose their sting, but they do lose their sting eventually. I count back in my head. Three and a half weeks since my last nightmare. Even longer since my last panic attack. Three weeks since my last counselling session. I wouldn't say I was fixed, but I'm a lot less broken than before.

I take another look at my watch. 8.13p.m. He's not coming, is he? The realisation hurts more than I expect it to. It's such a tiny little moment, in a year of huge changes. I've been engaged, cheated on my fiancé, broken off an engagement, changed jobs and moved house. My eyes start to sting and water. I try to swallow back the tears, but it's already too late. This tiny little insignificant moment is going to be one that stays with me. I find my legs carrying me to the top of the steps. I press one hand against the wooden door. It's locked. Of course it's locked. It was through that door, maybe ten feet from where I'm standing now, that he promised to be here. I lean my head against the wood and let the tears fall. It's crazy. He was one stupid mistake. Only he wasn't a mistake, was he? He was the moment that changed everything. He was the one who believed I could be something more than someone's daughter and someone's wife. He just didn't believe it enough to remember.

I force a deep gulp of air into my lungs and wipe my gloved hand across my eyes. There's a noise behind me on the gravel. 'Em?'

I turn around. 'You came.'

Alex looks up at me with those stupid dark eyes. 'Of course.'

I can feel a smile fighting against the tears. I force myself not to remember that I'm entitled to be cross with him. My lips purse. 'You're late.'

Chapter Ninety-Four

Alex

She was right. He was late, and he'd been running. He took a deep breath. What was it about this car park that seemed to compel him to do physical exercise? Six months ago he'd almost given himself a heart attack trying to run Dominic Collins through. 'My car broke down.' He pointed back towards the road. 'Had to walk. And then I was late. Had to run.'

Emily laughed. 'You broke down?'

Alex scuffed his toe against the floor. 'I ran out of petrol.'

'But you're here.'

He nodded. 'But I'm here.' A thought struck him. 'How did you get here?'

Emily pointed towards the silver hatchback at the end of the car park.

'You passed your test?'

'Yep.'

He raised his hands in a tiny round of applause. 'Miss Independent.'

'That's the idea.'

They fell into silence. Emily was still standing at the top of the stairs. Alex was eight feet away on the gravel. This wasn't how he'd pictured the scene. He'd imagined there would be romance and spontaneous leaping into one another's arms. He'd also imagined that he'd manage to get here without ending up with burning lungs and a scarlet face from the unscheduled run up the driveway.

'So what are you up to these days?'

'Sorry?' Alex was surprised by the segue into chit-chat.

'I've not seen you at the university. Did you finish your PhD?'

Alex shrugged. Finished was probably too strong a word. 'I stopped. I'm drawing now.'

Emily beamed. 'As a job? That's fantastic.'

'Illustrations. I'm doing a children's book about medieval peasants. It's all fighting and pooing in woods.'

She smiled. 'I'm pleased. You're a fantastic artist.'

'Thank you.' Alex found himself tongue-tied. He was proud of his new career but still nervous of telling people, as if they might spot him as an interloper in amongst the proper artists. 'So how about you? Still at the university?'

She nodded. 'I got promoted.'

'Really?' Alex heard the disbelief in his voice. 'I mean, not that I'm surprised.'

She held up a hand. 'It's okay. I didn't know I was good at my job until dad left. I never really had to try before. Anyway Faculty Manager now.'

Alex nodded. So it sounded like they'd both moved on. What if she'd moved on too far? What if the reason she was still at the top of those stairs was that she'd come here out of politeness to let him down gently? He'd spent the last six months working towards this moment, alternately telling himself he was crazy and pushing himself to be a better man. A man a girl like Emily might want to be with. Six months. One new career. One new home, admittedly still a room in a shared flat, but the new career was in its fledgling stages, and he was up to date with his rent and on top of his share of the cleaning rota. Zero one night stands. He'd almost had one a few weeks after the last time he'd been here with Emily. He'd met a girl. He'd talked to the girl. He'd got as far climbing into a taxi with her, and then he'd felt grubby. He'd stopped the cab, given the driver twice the fare he needed to get the girl home, and walked. And that had been that. He raised his gaze towards the woman at the top of the steps. 'So …'

She smiled. 'So …'

Alex paused. What would be the right thing to say? He didn't want to dress things up. He didn't want to lie. Something honest. Something simple. 'Come here.'

Emily took the three steps back down to the car park. 'I'm glad you came.'

Two paces forward to meet her. 'I'm glad you came.'

She tipped her chin up towards him and leant forward slightly. This was more like what Alex had been picturing. He bent his lips towards hers, and stopped. He stepped backwards. 'Wait.'

'What?' Her face started to crumple.

'No. Just wait.' Alex took a deep breath. He was being crazy again. He was also trying to be a better man. 'I lied to you.'

'When?'

'Six months ago.' The words were seared in his memory. 'I told you I could be the guy with the nice safe car, and the family house and the child seats.' Alex shook his head. 'I'm not that guy. I can't promise you those things. At least not yet. One day, but not yet.'

Emily stepped back. 'So what can you promise?'

That was the big question. Alex closed his eyes for a second. He needed to be honest. Above anything else, he wanted to tell her the truth. Maybe he could start there. He opened his eyes. 'I'll always tell you the truth, even if it's not what you want to hear. I will love …' He listened to himself use the word. It was true. He'd fallen in love with her months ago. 'I will love you even when you annoy me, and even when we fall out. I can promise you that we'll have so much fun together, and I can promise you that I will be there when you need me.'

She stepped back towards him. He held out a hand. 'I will probably be late. I might be broke. I will definitely be disorganised, and I can't promise that I'll be able to fix the things that make you sad, but when you need me I will be there. So is that enough? Am I enough?'

Emily paused. 'I don't need anyone to save me.'

He nodded. He knew that. He'd known that before she did. 'So?'

'You love me?'

He nodded.

She took a deep breath. 'I think I love you too.' She smiled, her beautiful radiant smile. 'Did you bring the mistletoe?'

Alex patted his jacket pockets. He groaned. 'It's in the car.'

Emily laughed. She bent down, flicked open her bag, and pulled out a sprig covered in soft green leaves and white berries.

Alex folded his arms. 'You thought I'd forget.'

'You did forget. I, on the other hand, am very organised.'

'So you saved me?'

She nodded. 'Absolutely.'

He reached forward, took the mistletoe from her hand and held it above her head.

About the Author

Alison May was born and raised in North Yorkshire, but now lives in Worcester with one husband, no kids and no pets. There were goldfish once. That ended badly.

Alison has studied History and Creative Writing, and has worked as a waitress, a shop assistant, a learning adviser, an advice centre manager, and a freelance trainer, before settling on 'making up stories' as an entirely acceptable grown-up career plan.

Alison is a member of the Romantic Novelists' Association. She writes contemporary romantic comedies.

You'll find Alison on Twitter, Facebook and Goodreads. Visit www.alison-may.co.uk for details.

More Choc Lit

From Alison May

Sweet Nothing

Book 1 in the 21st Century Bard series

Is something always better than nothing?

Ben Messina is a certified maths genius and romance sceptic. He and Trix met at university and have been quarrelling and quibbling ever since, not least because of Ben's decision to abandon their relationship in favour of ... more maths! Can Trix forget past hurt and help Ben see a life beyond numbers, or is their long history in danger of ending in nothing?

Charming and sensitive, Claudio Messina is as different from his brother as it is possible to be and Trix's best friend, Henrietta, cannot believe her luck when the Italian model of her dreams chooses her. But will Claudio and Henrietta's pursuit for perfection end in a disaster that will see both of them starting from zero once again?

This is a fresh and funny retelling of Shakespeare's Much Ado About Nothing, set in the present day.

Visit www.choc-lit.com for more details, or simply scan barcode using your mobile phone QR reader.

Holly's Christmas Kiss

Book 1 – Christmas Kisses

Happy Holidays? Not for Michelle ...

Holly Michelle Jolly hates Christmas and she has a good reason to. Apart from her ridiculously festive name which made her the brunt of jokes at school, tragic and unfortunate events have a habit of happening to her around the holiday season. And this year is no different.

After the flight to her once-in-a-lifetime holiday destination is cancelled, Michelle faces the prospect of a cold and lonely Christmas. That is, until she meets Sean Munro. Sean loves Christmas, and he wants to share the magic with Michelle.

With Sean's help, can Michelle experience her first happy Christmas, or will their meeting just result in another year of memories that she'd rather forget?

Visit www.choc-lit.com for more details, or simply scan barcode using your mobile phone QR reader.

Cora's Christmas Kiss

Book 2 – Christmas Kisses

Can you expect a perfect Christmas after the year from hell?

Cora and Liam have both experienced horrible years that have led them to the same unlikely place – spending December working in the Grotto at Golding's department store.

Under the cover of a Father Christmas fat suit and an extremely unflattering reindeer costume, they find comfort in sharing their tales of woe during their bleak staffroom lunch breaks.

But is their new-found friendship just for Christmas? Or have they created something deeper, something that could carry them through to a hopeful new year?

Another heart-warming Christmas novella from Alison May! Keep your eyes peeled for characters you may recognise from Alison's previous novella, Holly's Christmas Kiss.

Visit www.choc-lit.com for more details, or simply scan barcode using your mobile phone QR reader.

Jessica's Christmas Kiss

Book 3 – Christmas Kisses

Real Christmas miracles only ever happen in the movies – don't they?

When Jessica was fifteen, she shared the perfect kiss with a mystery boy at a Christmas party. It might have only lasted a moment, and the boy might have disappeared shortly afterwards but, to Jessica, it was just a little bit magic.

Fourteen years later, and Jessica is faced with a less than magical Christmas after uncovering her husband's secret affair. And, whilst she wouldn't admit it, she sometimes finds herself thinking about that perfect Christmas kiss, back when her life still seemed full of hope and possibility.

But she never would have guessed that the boy she kissed in the kitchen all those years ago might still think about her too …

Visit www.choc-lit.com for more details, or simply scan barcode using your mobile phone QR reader.

Introducing Choc Lit

We're an independent publisher creating
a delicious selection of fiction.
Where heroes are like chocolate – irresistible!
Quality stories with a romance at the heart.

See our selection here:
www.choc-lit.com

We'd love to hear how you enjoyed *Midsummer Dreams*.
Please leave a review where you purchased the novel
or visit: **www.choc-lit.com** and give your feedback.

Choc Lit novels are selected by genuine readers like yourself.
We only publish stories our Choc Lit Tasting Panel want to
see in print. Our reviews and awards speak for themselves.

Could you be a Star Selector and join our Tasting Panel?
Would you like to play a role in choosing which novels we
decide to publish? Do you enjoy reading romance novels?
Then you could be perfect for our Choc Lit Tasting Panel.

Visit here for more details...
www.choc-lit.com/join-the-choc-lit-tasting-panel

Keep in touch:
Sign up for our monthly newsletter Choc Lit Spread for
all the latest news and offers: www.spread.choc-lit.com.
Follow us on Twitter: @ChocLituk and Facebook: Choc Lit.

Or simply scan barcode using your mobile phone QR reader:

Choc Lit
Spread

Twitter

Facebook